A Photocopy Finish

"I had to take care of some department business. This department business involved you, Abby."

"I paid those speeding tickets," I wailed. "All five of them."

My betrothed bent his long, lean body and retrieved a crumpled sheet of paper from the front seat of his car.

"This just came in from Elkin, up in Surrey County. You recognize it?"

I stared at the paper. It was a facsimile of my engagement announcement in the *Charlotte Observer*, complete with a picture of me.

"Oh, gross! Look at those bags under my eyes. A family of twelve could pack for a three week vacation in those."

"Abby! This was found in the wallet of a crash victim along I-77. It was folded around an ad for some silver. You just bid on some silver, didn't you?"

My knees felt weak.

SO FAUX,
SO GOOD

A DEN OF ANTIQUITY MYSTERY

TAMAR MYERS

AVON BOOKS
An Imprint of HarperCollinsPublishers

This is a work of fiction. Names, characters, places, and incidents are products of the author's imagination or are used fictitiously and are not to be construed as real. Any resemblance to actual events, locales, organizations, or persons, living or dead, is entirely coincidental.

AVON BOOKS
An Imprint of HarperCollinsPublishers
10 East 53rd Street
New York, New York 10022-5299

First Avon Books paperback printing: June 1998

For the love of my life,
Jeffrey C. Myers

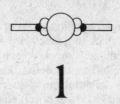

1

Billy Ray Teschel became a buzzard buffet along I-77 on a Monday afternoon at precisely 4:01 Eastern Standard Time. Eyewitnesses say his car careered down that steep incline between Elkin, North Carolina and Hillsville, Virginia, ricocheting first off the guardrail and then the opposite embankment. When it hit the guardrail the second time, the Honda Accord opened up like a pull-top can and parts of Billy Ray were strewn along the highway like a trail of Vienna sausages.

Since I had yet to even hear of the man, and had no idea how he would affect my life, I had no compunction about hosting a party at that exact moment in my shop, the Den of Antiquity, in Charlotte, North Carolina. It was a victory celebration. I, Abigail Timberlake, had just that morning come into possession of an exquisite antique English tea service. It had been a fast and furious auction at Purnell Purvis's Auction Barn in nearby Pineville, but I had been uncharacteristically reckless with my resources. Everyone gasped at my final bid, but it was the winner. At the party a few diehards were still gasping.

"You paid twenty thousand for that?" Wynnell Crawford asked for nearly the twenty thousandth time.

"You were at the auction, dear," I said, my patience wearing thin.

Wynnell is a fellow antiques dealer and my dearest friend, but she is stuck in a time warp when it comes to money. She is genuinely shocked each time we go out for coffee and the bill tops a dollar. The woman makes her own clothes—frightful creations all—because she refuses to pay even Goodwill prices. But trust me, Wynnell is well heeled, and in no need of your pity. Her otherwise tight fist opens up considerably when it comes to marking up her merchandise.

"Twenty thousand is more than I paid for my first house," Wynnell said, shaking her head in disbelief.

"That was in 1956, dear. Besides, I already have a customer lined up who will pay thirty."

"*Thousand*?" Wynnell's hedgerow eyebrows were arched in mock surprise. It was all an act. She would gladly sell it for forty grand if it were hers.

A sudden whiff of deodorant working overtime reminded me of the fact that we were not alone. Half the antique dealers on Selwyn Avenue had shown up for the impromptu bash—we are a close-knit community, after all. But that is not to say that we all like each other equally. Frankly, if it wasn't for his charming English accent, I wouldn't be able to stand Major Calloway, our local antique arms expert.

"Don't tell me it's that couple up in Belmont again," the major said. "That man who calls himself a captain?"

I smiled pleasantly. "That's confidential, dear. And anyway, who are you to question Captain Keffert's rank?"

The major claims to have served in the British army in Punjab, back in the days of the raj, and even dresses in uniforms of that period. Nobody in Charlotte believes him. Unless the man has had a total makeover by Cher's plastic surgeon, he isn't a day older than sixty, and even that would mean he was only an infant when he was assigned to his first posting on the Indian subcontinent.

"I'll have you know I was commissioned by the viceroy himself," he snapped.

"Captain Keffert was commissioned by Captain Crunch," I snapped back.

"Very funny," he growled.

"Our Abby's a hoot," Wynnell said kindly, although I really didn't need her to come to my defense.

"Yeah? Well, she doesn't let anyone else get a crack at the good stuff when it shows up at Purvis's Auction Barn. Just because she has big bucks, she thinks she's hot stuff."

I couldn't believe my ears. The man was actually bitter at having lost his bid for the silver. It didn't make a lick of sense because the major doesn't stock merchandise even remotely resembling English tea sets.

"I don't think I'm hot stuff," I hissed, "and my bucks are none of your business!"

The major turned sourly away and I glared dutifully at his back. Meanwhile more of my true friends circled round me like a string of prairie schooners.

"Congratulations, Abby!" Peggy Redfern squealed and wrapped me in her arms.

I gently pushed her away. Peggy attended the Tammy Faye school of makeup, and I was wearing a white linen jacket.

"Thanks," I said. "You were bidding pretty fast and furious against me there for a while. What happened?"

Bright blue eyelids fluttered as she shrugged. "I guess it's that 'cash and carry' rule mean old Purnell Purvis insists on. With those renovations I did to my shop last month, that much cash is a little hard to come by."

I nodded. The truth is, that woman is always hard up for cash thanks to her penchant for buying expensive presents for handsome young men. Rumor has it that Peggy has more notches in her bedpost than cable has channels.

A faint cough behind me was the signal that Gretchen Miller was gearing up to speak. I turned and smiled at her. She is the current president of the Selwyn Avenue Antique Dealers Association and a woman of few words.

Precisely because she is such a taciturn woman, I treasure each of her words as if they were pearls.

"You did well, Abby."

"Thank you, dear," I said. "I know you wanted the tea set. Better luck next time."

Gretchen raised and lowered her oversized tortoise-rimmed glasses in acknowledgment. Apparently four pearls were all she was willing to dispense that day.

"Hey, doll," a tall handsome man said, "I want you to know I covet your set."

I arched my back and poked Rob Goldman in the stomach. With my *finger*.

"They can be yours for the right price, dear."

"Hey, watch it there," Bob Steuben boomed. He is Rob's life partner, as well as business partner, and has a jealous streak as wide as the swath Sherman's troops cut through Georgia.

"I got a good deal, didn't I?" I asked exultantly.

Rob nodded. He is *the* expert on our street. On everything. His shop, the Finer Things, is quite possibly the most upscale antique shop in the metropolitan area.

"That's a genuine William Cripps creation, all right. Circa 1760. I'm not really fond of rococo, but the workmanship on this tea set is something else. It's definitely one of a kind."

I beamed.

"A toast is in order," Bob said, uncorking the first bottle of champagne.

My coworkers gathered around, their plastic goblets at the ready. Confidentially, it was Wynnell who supplied the faux glasses, but I supplied the champagne and had spared no expense. In fact, each of those three bottles of bubbly bore a double-digit price tag.

"To Abby!" Bob boomed, when we were all served.

"To Abby!"

My guests' cheers warmed the cockles of my heart. It had been a difficult year, but at last things were looking up. And I don't mean just in business matters, either.

In two months and three days I was going to marry the handsomest man in the Carolinas.

"To me!" I said foolishly.

I should have remembered my Sunday school lessons. Even in the Episcopal Church we learn that pride precedes a fall. Just about the time I was toasting myself, a rescue worker walking along I-77 discovered Billy Ray Teschel's wallet. In that moment, the course of my life changed dramatically.

2

I was born Abigail Louise Wiggins forty-eight years ago, but for over half of those years I have used the surname Timberlake. I got it from my ex-husband, Buford. His name and his seed were the only good things I got from him.

On my forty-fifth birthday Buford dumped me for a bimbo named Tweetie who was half my age. That would have been a good time for me to dump Buford's name. However, we had two children who shared that name, and I had just purchased—call it a birthday present to myself—a set of expensive, monogrammed towels made from the finest Egyptian cotton. Name changes could wait.

Susan and Charlie are both in college now, and so do not live with me. Well, if the truth be known, Buford got custody of both children and our dog, Scruffles. It's not that he was the better parent, I assure you. Buford just happens to be a crack divorce lawyer, and is plugged into the system more ways than there are to fix beans. I should have known something was fishy when I walked into the courtroom that first day of the proceedings and found Buford and the judge slapping each other's backs and laughing like schoolboys sharing a dirty joke. But I surely didn't expect to be left penniless and childless in one fell swoop.

At any rate, I live alone with my cat, Dmitri, in Charlotte, North Carolina. Call me old-fashioned, but I will not allow my fiancé, Greg Washburn, to move in with me until after the wedding. Not that it's your business, but I won't sleep with him until then either. One has to draw the line somewhere, especially when one expects one's children to toe it.

The Den of Antiquity is my life. Not only does my antique shop supply me with a livelihood, but through my business dealings have come some of my closest friends. Like Wynnell Crawford, for instance. And C. J.

Therefore I was not surprised to find C. J. waiting for me outside my shop Tuesday morning, the day after my impromptu bash. I was not entirely pleased, either. C. J. may be a friend of mine, but she has the annoying habit of telling interminable, depressing stories. If she made prison-visiting one of her ministries, capital punishment would be moot.

I had no time to die of boredom just then, but I couldn't very well be rude. "Hey, how's it going?" I asked and turned to unlock the door.

"Didn't you miss me yesterday, Abby?"

"Excuse me?"

The second the key turned, C. J. pushed right inside in front of me. "I wasn't at your shindig yesterday, or didn't you even notice?"

I smiled. C. J., whose real name is Jane Cox, is only twenty-four. Tell me, how many normal twenty-four-year-olds know, much less use, the word *shindig*?

"Of course I noticed," I said, "and I did miss you. Where were you?"

"I guess we Coxes are easily overlooked," she said, ignoring my question. "Did I ever tell you what happened to my Great Aunt Jane from Shelby?"

I glanced at the ship's clock behind my counter. "I don't believe you have, dear, but can we save it for another time?"

Alas, there is no stopping her once she's on a roll. "This is the same aunt I was named after, of course.

My grandmother's sister. Anyway, last year she took the bus into Charlotte and visited one of those new mega-bookstores we have here. When the store closed they made an announcement, but Aunt Jane is deafer than a white cat wearing earmuffs. Next thing she knew, she was locked in.''

"Bless her heart," I said, hoping to preempt the tale.

"Oh, she made out just fine. Aunt Jane likes a hard bed, so sleeping on the floor was no problem. And this store had a coffee bar that sold cookies and little cakes. When Aunt Jane got hungry, she just fixed herself a snack.

"Truth is, Aunt Jane had such a good time, that when the store opened the next morning, she hid behind the magazine rack until there were enough customers for her to blend in. She lived in that store, Abby, for two solid weeks."

"Get out of town!" I said.

"Scouts honor. Just like I said, she was just plain overlooked. Even Uncle Elroy back in Shelby didn't notice she was gone. At least not until the end of the first week when he sobered up enough to give her another beating.''

I shook my head in sympathy.

"Aunt Jane might well have spent the rest of her days happily reading, if it weren't for that all-night inventory the store took. One of the clerks finally found her, curled up asleep in the bathroom on a bed of paper towels. It was the only place she could think of to hide. Anyway, they didn't press charges or anything, but they did make her pay for a pound of coffee, and six dozen cookies. Then they drove her home."

"The poor dear."

"Oh, by then it was all right. Uncle Elroy had choked to death on a hamster bone, but that's another story."

"Spare me," I begged. "Besides, you still haven't told me where you were."

"I was at home. Doing my laundry. I wasn't here

because you didn't *invite* me!'' she wailed.

I was taken aback. Those were real tears in her eyes.

"Bless your heart,'' I said and gave her a quick hug. "These postauction parties are always spontaneous. Anyone can come—no one is *invited*. Didn't you know that?''

She blinked back the tears. "No.''

C. J. is the newest vendor on our street. Apparently the gathering at my shop was the first impromptu bash since she joined our ranks.

"I promise to invite you next time I hostess a gathering, official or otherwise,'' I said solemnly.

"You swear?''

"Cross my heart and hope to die, stick a needle in my eye.''

"Oh, don't do that, Abby. My cousin Maynard back in Shelby—''

I showed her politely, but firmly, to the door.

When I called the Kefferts to check on a convenient time to deliver the tea set, I got their answering machine. It took me a minute to figure out that the voice on the machine was Captain Keffert pretending to be a butler, and that it was not, in fact, a real butler. In the spirit of the game I pretended to be a maid, calling about an interview. Of course I left my name and phone number.

Just as I was hanging up the phone my mother struggled through the door, laden down by an enormous tote bag. It looked like an army duffel bag, but it was orange instead of green. At five foot one, Mama towers over me, but this bag was even too much for her to handle.

Mama lives just twenty-five miles away in Rock Hill, South Carolina, but she usually knows better than to show up at the shop uninvited. She may have given birth to me, but customers always come first. Something extraordinary—possibly even tragic—must have happened.

I am thoroughly ashamed to say that my first thought

was that dear, sweet Mama had gone totally off her rocker, killed someone, and then brought the body to me so that I could dispose of it. While I won't go so far as to say that my mother is a couple of sandwiches short of a picnic, she does at times run shy in the slaw department.

"Mama!" I cried. "What have you done?"

"I brought your wedding presents," Mama panted.

"You what? But Mama, my wedding is two months away!"

"Better early than late," Mama said.

I trotted over to help her. "What do you have in here? A washing machine?"

"All right, it's not just wedding presents. I have some of my clothes along as well."

I patted her arm appreciatively. "We're not the same size, Mama. I'm only four-nine and—well—not quite as developed you-know-where."

"Leave my bottom out of this," Mama snapped. "Anyway, I'm not giving you my clothes. I'm taking them with me."

"Where?"

"To the convent, of course. They won't issue me a habit right away."

"What *are* you talking about, Mama?"

"The Episcopal Convent of the Good Hope in Dayton, Ohio. Didn't I tell you? I'm going to be a nun."

I sat down heavily on a Bedemeir chair I keep by the front door. Mama's picnic basket was lighter than ever.

"A nun?" I asked, stunned.

Mama nodded and sat down on an ornately carved bishop's throne. She was, perhaps, getting ahead of herself.

"Ever since your daddy died I've been asking God what I should do with my life. Then I sort of set God a deadline. Well, wouldn't you know the next time I turned on the TV there was Julie Andrews singing her head off on a mountaintop in Austria."

I breathed a sigh of relief. "Ah, so you were just kidding before. You're really going on a tour to Europe."

Mama gave me a sympathetic look. "This isn't the Dark Ages, dear. I'm sure they wouldn't mind if you called in an emergency. You know where I am if you need me."

"You're serious?"

"As serious as a librarian with hemorrhoids, dear. My flight leaves in just under three hours."

"But seeing Julie Andrews on the tube is not a revelation from God," I wailed. "You need to ask for a backup sign."

"The sisters wear blue habits," Mama said happily. "I look good in blue, don't I?"

I thought fast. "What about your house?"

"I've already listed it with Coldwell Banker. I'm selling it as is. Fully furnished. Which reminds me, didn't you say you wanted that sideboard I got from Grandma?"

I nodded.

"Well, take it now then. Take anything you want."

"Your car?"

"Sorry, Abby, I already gave that away. My friend Miriam in Charlotte is going to pick it up at the airport after I leave."

"Your pearls?" I asked, hoping against hope.

Mama's last gift from Daddy was a string of eight-millimeter pearls that she never takes off. I fully expected to bury her in them someday. The truth be known, it isn't sentimentality over Daddy that makes her pearls de rigueur, but her firmly held belief that American culture stopped advancing on January first, 1960. Mama dresses like June Cleaver, with a tightly cinched waist, and full-circle skirt floating on layers of starched crinolines. While the convent might possibly permit Mama to take the odd phone call, they most assuredly frowned on postulants in pouffed petticoats pridefully parading their pearls.

Mama blanched and her hands flew reflexively up to her neckline. "I hadn't thought of my pearls. Well, I—uh—"

"I could keep them for you, Mama."

"Not for a moment, dear," she said without a moment's hesitation. "I gave you a coral necklace once, and you destroyed it within the hour."

"I was five!"

"Never mind. I'll figure out something. Maybe I'll wear them under my habit. Do you want to see your presents, or not?"

"Of course, but—"

"Please don't give me a hard time and just open them, Abby. I want to see the expression on your face. Convents may be more liberal these days, but I doubt if they'll let me out for the wedding. I won't have taken my final vows yet."

Ever the dutiful daughter, I placated Mama and unwrapped the first present. Even on her worst days, the gift-wrap lady at Belk can't touch one of Mama's creations, but this time Mama had really done herself proud. I felt sinful just untying the elaborate bow.

Finally, with the paper neatly folded, I tackled the plain brown box. It was heavy. Perhaps it was a vase she made in ceramics class. Lord have mercy if it was another cookie jar. A single woman living alone does not need cookie jars shaped like Snow White *and* all seven dwarves. As it was, Happy and Doc remained empty, while Bashful sat half full of stale snickerdoodles.

"Open it," Mama ordered. She was about to burst with excitement.

I opened the box. If there had to be a dwarf inside, at least let it be Grumpy. I could relate to him.

Mama does not cut corners when it comes to packaging. I had to dig through several inches of Styrofoam peanuts, and I touched my gift before I actually saw it. The cold feel of metal sent a shiver of pleasure up my spine. Mama knew nothing about metalworking. What I was about to receive was clearly store-bought.

"Oh, it's lovely," I squealed as I pulled my gift from its box.

"Do you really like it?" Mama asked, her face glowing.

I answered her by fainting.

3

It wasn't a dead faint, mind you, but more of a swoon. Luckily my bottom connected to the Bedemeir, so I didn't hit the floor. I was even able to lay my present down rather gently. But I felt sufficiently lightheaded so that my eyes rolled back and my mouth hung open like a nightjar in mosquito season. Or so Mama says.

"Abby, what is it?" she demanded. "Do you have the flu?"

I struggled back into full consciousness. "No, ma'am," I slurred.

"Oh my Lord!" It was Mama's turn to faint, but she often misses her cues. "You're pregnant, aren't you?"

"Mama!"

"Don't you Mama me. You're the one who's going to hear the patter of little feet. You know I never interfere in your life, Abby, but how's it going to look for me, an Episcopal nun, to have a daughter pregnant out of wedlock?"

I tuned her out and picked up the gift. It was a silver teapot, identical to the one I purchased at auction the day before.

"I-it's a t-teapot," I stammered.

"Of course, dear. But if I'd known what I know now, I'd have given you some saving bonds for little Mozella to use when she goes to college. Tuition costs are going

14

to be out of sight by then, or haven't you thought of that?''

I ignored her accusing tone. "I'm not pregnant, Mama."

"You sure?"

"I'm absolutely positive."

Mama sighed. "I suppose it was too much to ask for a little Mozella. I would have named you that, you know, but your father wanted you named Abigail, after his mama. Then when you had a daughter I got my hopes up, but you named her Susan—Susan Timberlake—what kind of a name is that?"

With shaking fingers I turned the teapot over to examine the bottom. "Where did you get this?"

"What a rude question, Abby. And you haven't opened the other presents yet."

I opened the remaining presents. There were two more, a silver cream pitcher and a silver sugar bowl. Like the teapot, they were William Cripps originals. *One of a kind*.

But of course that was impossible. There can't be *two* one-of-a-kind tea sets. The one I purchased was locked safely in the trunk of my car, awaiting delivery to the Kefferts as soon as I closed my shop for the day. The instant Mama left I would compare the two sets side by side, but I would be willing to bet my shop that the sets were identical. Trust me, I had all but taken my first set to bed with me the night before. I knew what it looked like.

"Mama, you have to tell me where you got these."

Mama's face looked like a jarred soufflé. "You haven't even thanked me."

I got up and gave my mother a tight squeeze. "I am absolutely stunned," I said. "I simply can't believe my eyes."

"Believe them," Mama said. She looked at me expectantly.

"Oh thank you, thank you, thank you!"

Mama gave me a skeptical look.

"I mean it, Mama. I'm overwhelmed."

"I knew you'd appreciate it. I hope what's-his-name does too."

"Don't be silly Mama, you know his name is Greg. And I'm sure he'll be stunned too."

"Just don't tell your brother Toy. He'll have conniptions if you do. He still thinks I like him best."

I wanted to ask her if it was true, but I had more pressing business. "Mama, did you buy this in Charlotte?"

Mama gasped. "Oh, heavens, no. You have to go to Atlanta to get something that nice. I found this last week when I went to visit your Aunt Marilyn."

"Where in Atlanta?"

"On some place on Peachtree. But this was the only one they had, Abby"—her face clouded—"you're not think of selling this in your shop?"

"Of course not. I just thought it would be fun to trace its history. I mean, it is a genuine William Cripps, isn't it?"

Mama giggled happily. "It better be for what it cost. It's a good thing that where I'm going I won't need any money."

I swallowed hard, willing the most impolite of all southern words to come out. "Just out of curiosity, how much did you pay for this?"

"Abby!"

"I just want to know how much you care, Mama. Do you care five hundred dollars' worth?"

To my surprise Mama laughed. "Try five thousand dollars' worth."

"Five thousand?"

"You've been a good daughter, Abby. You bought me a donut cushion when I had that hemorrhoid operation back in '86, and last year you told me how to make my ficus plant stop dropping its leaves."

My face stung with shame. A four-dollar pillow and a tip from *Indoor Gardener* were the sum of my altruism? I deserved to be in the pickle in which I found myself. A good daughter would help her mother with the yearly garage sales, have her over for dinner at least once a week, and perhaps gently tell her that the Macarena was no longer "in."

"Did you keep the receipt?" I asked humbly.

"Why, Abby, where are your manners? One should wait at least until after the wedding to return gifts. Besides, I didn't get it in a shop."

"What?"

Mama's sigh would have blown out a candle at twenty paces. "Oh Abby, you always make things so difficult. I knew you wouldn't approve, so I fudged a bit when I told you I bought it in a shop on Peachtree. The truth is I bought it through an ad in the Atlanta *Constitution*."

"What?"

"Well, the paper wasn't selling it, of course. I found it in an ad in the classifieds—you know, when I was there visiting your Aunt Marilyn last month. We had to drive to someone's house to pick it up."

The door opened and two middle-aged women walked in. They were obviously quite well-to-do, a judgment based not on their clothes, but on the amount of plastic surgery they'd undergone. The skin on their faces was so tight that each bone created its own plane. They looked like puppets. I waited until they had passed us before continuing.

"Do you remember where?"

"I remember we had to drive halfway to Marietta. Oh, and there were pine trees in the yard."

That was like telling me there was sand on the beach. I'm not sure if it's true, but I read someplace that there is a Georgia state law requiring all homeowners to be in possession of at least one pine.

"Well, you got a name," I said. "It's a start."

Mama's pearls made a nervous lap around her throat. "Of course I didn't get his name, dear. I never exchange names with strange men in Atlanta."

"Do you think Aunt Marilyn might know where he lives?"

Mama rolled her eyes. "Lord, Abby, where is your memory? Your Aunt Marilyn couldn't find her way around the block if she had a string tied to her car. That woman is geographically challenged."

Truer words were never spoken. I had to run with what she'd given me.

"You said it was a man, Mama. Was he black, white, fat, thin?"

"It was a man, but I can't remember what he looked like. Just sort of regular, I guess."

"Regular?" I wailed. "He wasn't a grade of gas, Mama. You have to remember *something*."

Mama shrugged. "I think he was white."

"I'm calling Aunt Marilyn," I said irritably. "She might not be able to find her way out of a paper bag, but she never forgets a man. She'll at least have a decent description."

Mama sighed. "Suit yourself, but your Aunt Marilyn didn't see him. She broke a nail getting into the car, and she refused to get out when we got to his house. She wasn't about to let a strange man see her without a fully manicured set. And anyway, what difference would it make if she had seen him? Abigail Louise, you tell me this minute—do you, or do you not, like my gift?"

I picked up the silver sugar bowl. It was exquisite, fake or real. The most miserable dinner party could be salvaged by bringing out this tea service at the conclusion.

"It's the most beautiful present I've ever gotten," I said quite honestly.

Mama beamed. "Use it in good health, dear. Now I've got to scoot, or I'll miss my plane to Dayton."

A good daughter would have found a way to stop her mother from charging off into a nunnery. A good daughter would have at least asked her mother if she had remembered to forward her mail and cancel the paper. But oh no, all I could think about was getting the William Cripps tea set out of the trunk and comparing it with the one I had just received.

After I compared the two sets I sat down on the Bedemeir again. This time I cried.

The woman who took my call at the Atlanta *Constitution* was very helpful. She took my name and number and within ten minutes she called back with the phone number from the ad.

"We're not responsible for the veracity of the ads," she said warily.

I complimented her on her vocabulary, hung up, and dialed the number. After the third ring a machine informed me that the number I had reached was no longer in service.

There was only one thing to do next. It was imperative that I close my shop and immediately seek an expert's advice. Preferably Rob's. Unfortunately, the puppet ladies were still on the premises. I found them earnestly inspecting a nineteenth-century spinning wheel from the mountains of North Carolina.

"Good morning ladies," I said. For my children's sake, in the months leading up to my divorce, I learned how to fake civility.

The taller of the puppets turned to me. "Does that thing really work?" she asked, without moving her lips.

"Actually it does, ma'am, and I'd be happy to show you how sometime."

"Show us now," her short companion said.

"Well, I'd like to, but you see, something's come up and I have to close the shop for a while."

They both stared at me, then I saw the smaller one's

lips move, although I could have sworn it was the taller woman's voice I heard.

"That's no way to do business, if you ask me. For all you know I desperately want to buy two of those."

"Then you'd have a problem, ma'am. Because I just have the one." I wisely refrained from telling her that I knew where she could buy two one-of-a kind William Cripps tea sets.

"Come on, Althea," one of them said, "let's take our business elsewhere. There are better shops near South-park Mall."

I would have followed them out the door, locking it behind me, except the phone rang. On the off-chance it was Mama calling from the airport to tell me she'd had a change of mind, I answered.

It was Mama, but she hadn't changed her mind. I gave it one last try.

"But I'm a spring," Mama said stubbornly. "Their habits are exactly my shade of blue. Give it up, Abby, it was meant to be."

"You'll be sharing a bathroom with fifty-eight women," I wailed. "Think of the lines."

"I didn't call so that you could badger me, dear. I called because I remembered something about my visit to Atlanta."

I sucked my breath in sharply. "Yes?"

"I remember that there was a car in the driveway with a Pennsylvania license plate," Mama said triumphantly.

"Right. You don't have a name or an address, and can't even begin to describe the guy, but you paid attention to a license plate? Give me a break, Mama."

"Don't you be a little Miss Smartypants, Abby. I remember the license plate because it said 'You have a friend in Pennsylvania' on top, and the letters on the tag were 'DV.' "

"*What*?"

"And I do have a friend in Pennsylvania, and her initials are 'DV,' so that's why I remembered it. Your godmother—Diana Venters—was one of my roommates at Winthrop. She lives in Philadelphia now. I've told you about her, I'm sure.''

That was certainly possible, but since Mama had more roommates than Elizabeth Taylor, I couldn't be expected to keep track of them.

''The name doesn't ring a bell,'' I said, ''but I'll take your word for it. Were there any numbers on the tag?''

''Of course,'' Mama said, ''but I can't be expected to remember everything. Hey, but speaking of bells—'' she burst into a rousing rendition of ''The Hills Are Alive'' from the musical, *The Sound of Music*.

The fact that I was alone in my shop, separated from her by several miles, didn't lessen my desire to find a hole in the floor into which I could crawl. Mama doesn't actually sing, she brays. True, she is a member of the choir at the Episcopal Church of Our Savior in Rock Hill, but she is what the less charitable refer to as a ''mercy member.''

Not only did David Lowry, our parish musician, take mercy on her when she asked to join the choir, but ever since then folks say ''mercy me'' every time Mama opens her mouth to sing. Poor Mama has no idea she is tone-deaf, and since she enjoys singing so much, no one has yet had the courage to say something to her face. My face, yes, but not hers.

''Have a safe trip, Mama!'' I shouted before hanging up.

There were tears in my eyes. No doubt about it, I was going to miss the best friend I ever had.

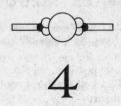

4

I have a boyfriend—okay, a *man*friend, but you know what I mean. Greg Washburn is a criminal inspector with the Charlotte/Mecklenburg Police Department. He is tall, dark, and handsome, with straight white teeth and Wedgwood-blue eyes. Females of all ages drool over him, and I'm sure a few men do as well. I suppose I should count myself incredibly blessed, because Greg and I are engaged to be married. The truth is, I am having second thoughts about going through with the nuptials. Dating a cliché is one thing, but spending the rest of one's life hitched to a stereotype is sobering, and I've been having a lot of sober thoughts lately. I called reluctantly.

"Hey, Abby," he said, his voice brimming with clueless enthusiasm. "I was hoping you'd call. That movie you wanted to see is playing at the Pavilion in Pineville. You want to go tonight?"

"Which movie?" I asked cautiously. After all, the Pavilion has twenty-two theaters.

"Damn, I knew I'd forget the exact title, but it has the word 'heart' in it. You know, the one where the ads show a businessman carrying his dying father around with him to board meetings."

You see what I mean? The man was too good to be true. If we saw a movie like that, he'd cry into my popcorn and rinse off the salt.

"Sorry dear, but I just remembered that I promised C. J. I'd stop by and help her streak her hair. But you can answer a question for me, if you would."

"Anything, babe."

"Is it hard to trace a license plate?"

"That all depends. Whatcha got?"

"It's a Pennsylvania plate. It has the letters 'DV' on it."

There was an expectant silence.

"It was spotted in the Atlanta area last week."

"That's it?"

"All I know is what I just said, and that it was seen at night in a yard full of pine trees."

Greg had the decency to stop laughing after a few minutes. "We don't have border police along the Mason-Dixon line, Abby. Yankees aren't required to register with the authorities—well, maybe in Georgia they are. Tell you what, I'll give them a call and see."

"Very funny!"

"Abby, what's this all about?" he asked, the sarcasm completely gone.

The fact that Mr. Perfect could tell that I was angry made me even angrier. "It's about my mother," I snapped. "I'm afraid she may have been taken advantage of by an ad she saw in the paper. She was sold a fake bill of goods to the tune of five thousand dollars. That's grand larceny, isn't it?"

"If intent to defraud can be proved," Greg said quietly. "Tell me about it."

I told him everything I knew, including the fact that Mama was off to Ohio, eager to become a nun. "You don't think they'll really take her?" I wailed.

Greg sighed. "My cousin Sammy started out as a Southern Baptist and ended up as the chief rabbi of Finland. So, anything is possible, Abby. Still, I have a hard time seeing Mozella Wiggins as a nun. Did you tell her that you think the tea set she gave us is a fake?"

"No, I didn't want to hurt her. Besides, I don't know

which one is the copy—it, or the one I bought at auction. Maybe they both are," I said, wiping away a tear which wasn't supposed to be there. "Two fake tea sets and a mother who's run off to find herself. How much more can I take?"

There was a long silence. I could almost hear the cogs in Greg's brain turning, as if he needed a little oil. The man is bright, but not brilliant, if you know what I mean. Thinking fast on his feet has never been his forte.

"I'm afraid I can't help you with authenticating the tea sets, Abby, but I might be able to help you with your mother."

"Oh?"

"Her flight doesn't leave for forty-five minutes. I might be able to catch her. If so, I'll tell her that I need her help in apprehending this forger."

"But then she'd have to know her present was a fake," I wailed. "It will break her heart."

"Would you rather break her heart or be out twenty thousand dollars?"

"You are so rude," I said, and then hung up so he could get to the airport in time.

I didn't just sit and twiddle my thumbs while Greg talked Mama out of donning a lifetime habit. I put both sets of silver into the trunk of my car for safekeeping, hopped into my brand-new, arrest-me-red Grand Am, and barreled on down to the town of Pineville, just south of Charlotte. Actually, the traffic was pretty heavy, so I crawled, instead of barreled. Not too long ago Pineville was a geographically distinct community, surrounded by cotton fields, but today it has blended so well with the burbs that it's hard to tell where it begins and Charlotte leaves off. But they are handsome burbs, with eat-your-heart-out houses, so I didn't mind the crawling so much.

Purnell Purvis's Antique Auction Barn on U.S. 21 in Pineville is the mecca for antique dealers across the Carolinas. Purvis has a penchant for sniffing out estates before the heirs have a chance to schedule a public sale. Instead of chasing ambulances, Purvis chases hearses. We dealers have our chance when Purvis holds his weekly "dealers only" sales. Although the man is a valuable asset to the business, he isn't the easiest person with whom to get along.

"Surely you can make an exception this one time," I pled. "This time there really are mitigating circumstances."

Purvis hitched his pants up, but since his belt was too small to fit over his considerable girth, it was a wasted effort. This seemed to annoy him further.

"You said the same thing when you bought that Chippendale chair last month. Like I told you then, little lady, if the vendor doesn't want to reveal his identity, my hands are tied."

"What if there's been a crime?" It was all I could do to refrain from calling him "big gentleman."

Purvis gave up the struggle to keep his pants aloft and motioned for me to sit. His office is a mere cubicle, undoubtedly smaller than Mama's prospective room at the convent, but it is sumptuously furnished. The chair offered was an early Empire gilt-wood chair, which Purvis claims is a genuine Marcion.

"I don't deal in stolen goods," he growled.

"I'm not accusing you of fencing, dear." I swallowed. "Is it possible one of your vendors deals in replicas?"

If a bear could glare, it could pass for Purvis. "Are you suggesting that I'm in cahoots with a forger?"

I shook my head vigorously. "Oh, no, not at all. I'm suggesting that someone might have *knowingly* sold you a forgery, and then you *unwittingly* sold it to me."

It was a hot May day but the cubicle was air-conditioned. Surely an innocent man wouldn't have beads of sweat appearing on his forehead with the regularity of microwave popcorn.

"Tell me who this person is," I coaxed, "and I promise to keep your name out of this if I can.''

Purvis has a penchant for Pernod as well, and he interrupted his glare just long enough to extract a gold flask from the drawer of his Wooten desk.

"What the hell are you talking about, Mrs. Timberlake?"

"That's Ms.," I said, "but call me Abby, for crying out loud. We've known each other for years."

He waved aside my gracious offer with the back of a hairy hand. "I said, what the hell are you talking about?"

"The silver, damn it! That silver tea set I bought yesterday. You know, the one *you* said was a genuine William Cripps creation? Circa 1760? Well, the not so funny thing is, another set has shown up. One that's identical. I can't tell which one is the original, and which is the copy. That makes me wonder how many others there are. For all I know there are dozens, and the one you sold me was made last week in a basement in New Jersey."

He rolled his eyes. It is a gesture I hate just as much when it comes from unrelated adults, as when it comes from my own two kids.

"*Or*," I drawled, "maybe it was made right here. Do you have a basement, Mr. Purvis?"

I was hoping that he would flinch. I surely didn't expect his meaty fist to come down on the Wooten that hard.

"You have one hell of a nerve, little missy. That damn silver was authenticated by Mr. Expert himself. Rob Goldman."

I squiggled my left ear with the tip of my little finger. It has been known to give out on me, so to speak, in times of extreme stress.

"What did you say?"

"I had your friend Rob Goldman check out the set as soon as I got it in. He declared it a masterpiece. Those were his exact words—'a masterpiece.' ''

"Uh—"

"So you can stick your accusations in your ear, girlie." He tried to stand up, but his belt buckle caught on a drawer pull of the desk, and he fell back into his chair with a plop.

I managed to suppress a satisfied smile. "I wasn't accusing you of anything, dear. Like I said before, I think someone pulled the wool over your eyes. Over Rob's too. I want to know who it is. Who sold you the silver tea set?"

Purvis sighed so hard I was enveloped by Pernod fumes. "I bought it through an ad in the *Charlotte Observer*."

"You didn't! I never saw that ad."

It may come as no surprise to you, but grizzlies can smirk. "It was a one-day ad. Saturday's paper two weeks ago. I was the first one to respond. I drove straight on over there and snapped that thing up like a cooter catching flies. Like they say, the early dog gets the worm."

I hadn't the time nor energy to correct him. "Purnell, you have to tell me who this person is. It's your civic duty. You owe it to me, as a colleague."

Purvis took a swig directly from the gold flask, once again proving my claim that money and class are not to be equated. In all fairness, however, he did wipe his mouth rather daintily on the sleeve of his pink silk shirt.

"I don't owe you anything, girlie, and you can't prove a crime has been committed. You said yourself you can't tell the original from the copy." He took a second swig, but neglected to wipe his mouth. When he spoke, the air was atomized with Pernod. "Now, I'm telling you this for the last time. I don't guarantee my merchandise but the tea set you bought here at auction is the real McCoy. You got that, missy? Is that clear enough for you?"

I stood up. "Got it, buster. It's as clear as Carolina clay."

I managed to slam the door behind me, but believe

me, it's hard to stomp off in a righteous snit when you're only four feet nine and weigh less than a hundred pounds. Still, I gave it the old college try, even though it nearly gave me shin splints and caused my bunions to ache for a week.

I'm sure Rob Goldman was glad to see me—it's just that he expected me to be hard at work in my own shop. Therefore he was understandably concerned to discover me lurking about in his shop, the Finer Things.

"Abby, what are you doing here? That ex of yours hasn't been hassling you again, has he?"

"Buford?" It was a silly thing for me to say, since I only have one ex, but the concern on Rob's face had thrown me off course.

"Just say the word, Abby, and I'll punch his lights out for you."

"Thanks, but no thanks," I said, and patted his arm affectionately. "I have no doubt that you could ring Buford's chimes with one hand tied behind your back, but you'd spend the rest of your life paying for it. Playing Satan is only a part-time job for him. In real life he's a lawyer, remember? Besides, this isn't about Buford."

Rob glanced at Bob, who was watching us from behind the register, before taking a prudent step backwards.

"Then what's this about?"

I couldn't help but smile. Bob's jealousy is understandable, only in that Rob is drop-dead gorgeous. Tall, fifty, with a full head of hair that is graying only at the temples, the man is a younger version of James Garner. But I've known Rob long enough to know that his arms, as well as his charms, are Teflon-coated when it comes to women.

"It's about you, Rob," I said, forcing a serious tone. "Why didn't you tell me that Purvis sought your professional opinion before he offered my tea set as a genuine William Cripps?"

Rob blinked. "Oh, that. Well, it didn't even seem worth mentioning. Purvis often asks me to validate his purchases. You know that."

He wasn't getting off the hook that easy. "Yes, but at my party, you made it sound like it was your first good look at the tea service. Why the act? And why didn't you bid on it yourself?"

"Why all the questions?"

"Because the service is a fake, that's why. It's no more a William Cripps original than I am. Or if it is, it's certainly not one of a kind. Mama gave me an identical tea service this morning for an early wedding present."

"You're joking!" Rob's voice registered surprise, but he blinked again. In my experience blinking often occurs in conjunction with lying. It isn't a foolproof test, however, since contact lenses and dust motes can produce the same results.

"I'm dead serious, dear. One way or another, I have an expensive copy on my hands."

"May I see the service you got from your mother?"

It was still in the trunk of my car, but I led him out to see it. Let Bob think what he wanted. After all, Rob and I were friends long before Bob showed up from Toledo.

I unwrapped the two creamers first and set them side by side on the floor of my trunk. "See any difference?" I demanded.

"Holy shit!" Rob said.

"You don't, do you? Now look at this," I said, and unwrapped the teapots.

There was more profanity, and although I was not offended, I was mightily annoyed. Rob seemed excited by what I showed him. He certainly was not embarrassed.

"So, Mister Expert, can you tell me which one is the original, and which isn't?"

Rob examined both pots carefully. If only he had been that careful the first time. A new Middle East Peace treaty was signed, broken, and signed again before he was through.

"Sorry, but it doesn't look good, Abby."

"They are both fakes, aren't they?" I screamed.

"Faux," he said calmly. "We call them faux, these days. These are damn good copies."

I gasped for breath. "How can you be so sure, when you pronounced one of them authentic just a few days ago? I bet you can't even tell them apart, can you?"

He shook his head slowly. "They both have soldered spigots and yellowed ivory handles. A knockoff imitator wouldn't have gone to all that trouble. He"—Rob looked pointedly at me—"or she, would most probably have cast the entire pot, so you'd end up with a sterling handle, and no seams.

"A first-class forger, however, wouldn't bother with casting. Copies are too easy to spot. Scratches and imperfections in the original show up in the reproduction. Anyway, these weren't cast, they were handmade."

"How do you know?" I am proud to say I kept the sarcasm in my voice to a minimum.

Rob smiled. "Feel the sides between your thumb and forefinger. What do you feel?"

"Nothing but damn silver. Or is that fake too?"

"It's sterling all right, but that's not my point. You can tell that this silver was hammered by hand. The bowls of the creamer and teapots are not uniformly thick. This is a damned good copy, Abby. "Or . . ." His voice trailed off, while my heart pounded.

"What?" I screeched.

Rob shrugged.

I grabbed his arm, and he nearly dropped a teapot. "Or they're *both* authentic?"

"Don't get your hopes up, Abby. That's highly unlikely. Unless someone with a great deal of money got old Bill Cripps to make an exact replica of one of his works—well, there's too much artistry here to produce it twice."

"The scratches," I said hoarsely, "let's examine them for scratches."

It was a sunny morning and we had no trouble finding the many little abrasions that even the best cared for objects will accrue over the length of two hundred years. But although corresponding areas on both sets showed wear, none of the marks were identical.

I was exultant. "Aha! Look there! That's a small dent. And see that long, thin scratch? This sugar bowl doesn't have a dent there. Or a scratch."

"Hold your horses, Abby. There could be another explanation."

"Like what?"

He shrugged.

"You're just jealous."

"That's ridiculous. What of? I could have bought one of these sets if I had wanted. Purvis gave me first option."

"It's not these damned tea sets. It's the fact that I'm marrying Greg and we're going to live happily ever after."

Okay, so I'd heard through the grapevine that the Rob-Bobs were having relationship troubles. Mandy Ferguson, who works as a cashier at Hannaford's, said she overheard them arguing in front of the bottled vinegars when she went to take her break. "I think a storm is brewing in paradise," she said to me as she rang up my stack of Lean Cuisine dinners.

At any rate, I didn't intend to be mean—well, maybe just a little. I'm not sure I believe in karma, but if I did, I assure you that my intentions were no tradeoff for the misfortune that befell me next.

5

Greg pulled up just as I slammed shut the trunk of my car. I wasn't mad at Rob, mind you, but at myself for being such a jerk.

"Where's Mama?" I demanded.

"Uh—well, the truth is, I never made it to the airport."

"*What*?"

"I got an important call from headquarters, Abby."

"And my mama—your future mother-in-law—isn't important?"

"I had to take care of department business."

"Gregory Washburn, I am your business! And now, thanks to you, my mama is getting fitted for her wimple. Well, you're just going to have to hop on the next plane to Dayton and talk her out of it. Who knows, maybe some of the other nuns will defect when they get a look at you."

The Wedgwood-blue eyes failed to dance with amusement. "This department business involved you, Abby."

"I paid those speeding tickets," I wailed. "All five of them."

My betrothed bent his long, lean body and retrieved a crumpled sheet of paper from the front seat of his car. His big hands took their time smoothing it flat against the windshield. Finally he handed it to me.

"This just came in from Elkin, up in Surrey County. You recognize it?"

I stared at the paper. It was a facsimile of my engagement announcement in the *Charlotte Observer*, complete with a picture of me. I had originally planned to have one of Greg and I together, our hands crossed, one over the other, like a four-layer lasagna, but since my intended is a detective, I was told that would be unwise.

"Oh, gross! Look at those bags under my eyes. A family of twelve could pack for a three-week vacation in those."

"Abby!"

I was surprised by the harshness of his voice. "I didn't say anything about your eyes, dear. They're gorgeous as ever."

"That's not it," he snapped. "Don't you ever listen to a single word I say?"

"Of course, dear. The *Surrey County Sentinel* picked up our announcement from the *Observer*." Something clicked. "But that's sort of unusual, isn't it? Our engagement is not exactly news."

"This didn't come from the *Sentinel*. This was found in the wallet of a crash victim along I-77. It was folded around an ad for some silver. You just bid on some silver, didn't you?"

My knees felt weak. "Not Mama! She was going to fly, not drive."

Greg briefly put his arms around me. Public displays of affection embarrass him. Apparently giving comfort falls into the same category.

"It's not your mother, Abby. As far as I know, Mozella is fine. The crash victim was a male, age thirty-five, from Bedford County, Pennsylvania. His name was Billy Ray Teschel. Did you know him?"

"No."

"You sure?"

"Pretty sure. A lot of my customers are tourists from

Pennsylvania, but they usually don't introduce themselves. Do you have a picture?''

Greg reached into his car again and extracted a second sheet of crumpled paper. He thrust it at me like a hot potato.

I glanced briefly at a photocopy of a Pennsylvania driver's license. I have a friend in Pittsburgh who claims her state's DMV trains their photographers at the Saddam Hussein School of Sadists and Torturers. Billy Ray Teschel's driver's license seemed to confirm that. But even allowing for the chicanery of a disgruntled government employee, the face on the license was not one I'd likely forget. Billy Ray Teschel was my vision of Satan on a bad hair day.

"I never saw him before in my life."

"You positive? Maybe you need a few more facts to jog your memory. Let's see now, the man was five feet eight and weighed one hundred and seventy-five pounds.''

I stared at Greg. "What are you driving at?"

"What are you hiding?"

"*Excuse* me? Is there something going on here that I don't know?"

"You tell me, Abby. Why would a good-looking guy like that be driving around with your picture in his wallet?''

It occurred to me for the first time that Greg might need glasses, because even a pit bull wouldn't consider Billy Ray Teschel good-looking. Then again, perhaps with a pair of specs—or maybe contacts—Greg wouldn't find me so ravishing. But unfortunately, it was beginning to sound like Greg's eyes were not the part of his head that needed examining.

"Look buster, I have no idea why he had my picture in his wallet. You tell me why. Your name is in that announcement too. Come to think of it, Greg, who sent it to you, and why?"

The muscles on Greg's left jaw began to twitch. "The

sheriff up there is an old buddy of mine. He read my name and thought I might be able to shed some light on the situation. Do you know how embarrassing this is, Abby, to have something like this flung in your face?''

I glanced around for something to fling in his face. Perhaps he could compare the two for me. Alas, I had only my key ring, and there was an open storm drain too close for me to take the chance.

"Are you implying that I and this accident victim were having some sort of tryst?" I hissed.

"If the shoe fits."

If there is one thing I learned from raising two kids and divorcing a lout like Buford, it is to simply remove oneself from a nonproductive argument. I got in my car, slammed the door, and drove away. I can't tell you exactly where I drove, because I didn't have a destination in mind. All I know is that two hours and a quarter of a tank of gas later I was back on Selwyn Avenue headed for my shop. I am pleased to report, however, that I hadn't racked up any new speeding tickets and I was a good deal calmer.

My serenity faded the second I saw Greg's car. It was still parked in front of my shop, and Greg was sitting inside eating something. I drove right past him and parked six spaces down. Then I walked back and rapped on the window. Apparently he hadn't seen me until then because he dropped the turkey sub he was holding into his lap. I heard a faint expletive before the window opened.

"Geez, Abby, don't scare me like that."

"If there's a better way to scare you, let me know."

He dabbed at some mustard on his khaki slacks. "We need to talk."

"I have nothing to say to you until you apologize."

He looked up from what I hoped was a permanent stain. "Okay, so maybe I got a little carried away back then."

I gave him my most penetrating stare. This, too, I

learned from my kids. Focus just above and between your adversary's eyes. It's guaranteed to drive them crazy. In this case it had a double benefit because it spared me from having to focus on those beautiful orbs.

"You were over the top and under the falls," I said. "Your insinuations hurt me to the quick. And I have yet to hear the words 'I'm sorry.' "

During the ensuing silence the population of China doubled and the Democrats came up with a workable welfare plan. I didn't dare shift my gaze, and I wasn't about to speak first. I may have learned how to walk away from verbal sparring, but I was still a warmonger when it came to a battle of wills.

"I'm sorry if I hurt you."

"If that's the best you can do—"

"Abby, I have to tell you something very important."

My gaze slipped a fraction of an inch. The blue eyes were definitely troubled.

"I'm listening."

"While you were gone—*wherever* you went—I got a call from the department. It seems that someone had it in for this Teschel guy. They're pretty sure the brakes on his car were tampered with. There's a nasty incline up there and apparently someone anticipated it and made sure his car couldn't slow on the way down. You know what this means, don't you?"

I shook my head.

"That somebody out there may have it in for you as well."

I should have been furious. The implication was there again that Billy Ray Teschel and I were an item. That there was a reason for our destinies to be intertwined. But much to my surprise, I wasn't mad at all.

"Where in Pennsylvania did you say this guy was from?" I asked calmly.

Greg gave me a "you ought to know" look. "Bedford County," he said quietly. "A little town called Hernia."

"Is that a joke?"

"Damn it, Abby. Isn't there something you want to say to me?"

Of course there was. I wanted to tell Greg that green did not match his eyes, that his jealous streak could be seen by astronauts on the space shuttle, that if his paranoia progressed, men in white jackets were going to take him away. But I said nothing more.

"Let me guess," Wynnell said. "You've had another epiphany."

I untangled the phone cord before answering. "Make that two epiphanies."

"Does one involve you-know-who?"

"It's all right to say his name, dear. Greg—there, I said it for you. As hard as it is to believe, that man is more insecure than a cat at a dog show. Who would have thought!"

"The cuter they are, the tighter they cling," Wynnell said, as if quoting from the Book of Proverbs. "Take my advice, Abby, and look for a man so ugly his own mama won't lay eyes on him. That is, if you value your freedom."

Wynnell ought to know. She's been happily married for thirty years to a man whose face could sink a thousand ships.

I promised that if and when I finally parted ways with my fiancé, I would let her fix me up with one of her many brothers-in-law.

She grunted with satisfaction. "Now tell me about the second epiphany."

I told her about Mama's early wedding present and the death of Billy Ray Teschel. It took much longer than it should have, because the puppets had returned and were banging on my shop door, even though the CLOSED sign was properly and prominently displayed.

"We know you're in there," one or both of them squealed in indignation. "We can see you sitting behind your desk." Then they went around and tapped on the side window. I was tempted to treat them to a very unladylike gesture, but fortunately good breeding prevailed.

Wynnell listened patiently to my fractured account. "Gracious me," she said when I was through, "you're not really thinking of going up to Pennsylvania, are you?"

"It's only a gut feeling, Wynnell. But that license plate Mama saw in Georgia, and now this Billy Ray guy—well, anyway, I haven't taken time off for a real vacation since I started my shop. I thought it would be fun to go up there and scout around for Amish antiques. Even if I just end up buying a quilt, I can use the change of scenery."

"Oh, Abby, take me with you!"

"*What*?" Wynnell is as fond of Yankees as she is lumps in her grits.

"You said the magic words, Abby—'Amish quilts.' Do you know how much the really old ones are worth? I heard that you can buy them straight from the Amish for a song. Lordy, could I make a killing with a pile of those. Please, Abby, can I come?"

I fingered an enormous Kashmiri sapphire I wear on my ring finger. It was a bequeathal from an elderly lady I hardly knew. In times of indecision, it functions much as Mama's pearls do for her.

"You're not serious, are you?"

"Are the Carolina Panthers the greatest football team ever?"

"Who will watch your shop?"

"Ed will. He's finding out retirement isn't what it's cracked up to be."

"I'm leaving tomorrow, Wynnell. I may be gone as long as a week. Are you sure about this?"

"Positive. It'll be fun, Abby. Sort of a girls' week away."

"Two very-long-in-the-tooth girls," I said, and believe me I was being generous. Wynnell has a dozen years on me.

"Hang up Abby, because I'm calling Ed right now." She hung up before I had a chance to.

6

I didn't have that much to do to get ready. Not with the shop, at any rate. There were a few invoices in my "in" box that needed attention, but outside of banking the contents of my register, that was it. Ever since I'd installed those new vent filters Paul Harvey advertises, my shop has been virtually dust free. As long as I pulled the blinds, there was no need to cover things with sheets.

The loud knock on the front door came at an inconvenient time. I had a right hand full of nickels, and a left hand full of pennies, and I was so startled I opened both. With all that change hitting the floor, I might well have been trying to flush out Republican spies at the Democratic National Convention.

Therefore, I will admit to being annoyed when the knocking continued. The puppet ladies were never going to get a price break from me.

"Go away!" I shrieked. "There are two dozen other antique dealers on this street to drive crazy. Try Major Calloway. He sells—"

"Abby! Abby!"

I looked up from the floor. It was the decidedly ample figure of Peggy Redfern on the other side of the door, not the two dehydrated matrons from Myers Park. Reluctantly I picked my way over and let her in. I was only slightly less irritated than before.

"Peggy, don't you have a business of your own to run?"

She was panting, which for Peggy is normal only in the bedroom—or so I've had the misfortune to hear. In all other pursuits Peggy moves with seductive languidness. I looked around for a man, but there were none in sight.

"Abby, can I go too?" she rasped.

"I beg your pardon?"

"To Pennsylvania. I was over at Wynnell's shop borrowing quarters when you called. She told me about your plans. So, how about it? I've always wanted to go to Pennsylvania."

I hate being put on the spot like that. Peggy is a nice enough woman—a friend even—but she's not on my list for sharing a vacation. The overage bag boy at Winn Dixie, the one who winks at me when he packs my bananas, is more likely to find his name there than is Peggy.

"I'd love to have you, dear, but my Grand Am really isn't that big and it clashes with your hair."

Peggy raked her hand through short but vividly red hair. "That's all right, we'll take my Town Car. It has oodles of room."

Leave it to Peggy to own a car with a back seat the size of a Japanese hotel room. There had to be another obstacle I could put in her way. I put on my thinking cap while Peggy panted.

"Your shop, dear. Didn't you say that both Christmas and Valentine's Day were unusually slow this year? I mean, you can't afford to be taking off for that long."

"But that's just it, Abby, with those quilts Wynnell was talking about, I could make up for those losses. Besides, I have an employee now. Didn't I tell you?"

You could have knocked me over with a goose quill pen. "Since when?"

"Since yesterday. Her name is Emma Jean Butler. She had a shop of her own in Waxhaw, but sold it when she retired. Then she got bored. She's only part time, but I'm sure she wouldn't mind taking over for a week."

"But—"

"Oh, Abby, *please*."

"Forgive me," I said, "but have you really thought this through? Amish men are not like the guys you meet at the Nascar races."

The blue eyelids blinked rapidly, but she kept her cool. "You remember my niece, Flora Mae?"

"The one who ran off to Memphis and became a barmaid?"

"That was Nashville, and she's a country-western singer. Anyway, she knows about this bed and breakfast up there where all these celebrities go. Real celebrities, like Tom Cruise and Brad Pitt."

I had only one excuse left. "Well, I'd be happy to have you along, but I'll have to ask Wynnell first." I lowered my voice. "You know how she can be."

Peggy beamed. "Oh, I already asked her. She said 'the more the merrier.' "

I smiled through gritted teeth. Wynnell was going to owe me big time.

When it rains it pours, they say. Given my life experiences I should carry hip boots and a bumbershoot everywhere I go. Maybe even an inflatable ark. I guess I should have expected the phone to ring the minute Peggy left. Believe me, I wouldn't even have answered it had not the optimist within me held out hope that Mama had finally come to her senses. At least I had the presence of mind to pretend I was an answering machine. In all modesty, I do such a good imitation that only the woman who potty-trained me can tell the difference. Or so I thought.

"You have reached the Den of Antiquity," I said in my best mechanical voice. "I'm sorry we are unable to come—"

"Abby?"

"Mama?"

"Don't be silly, Abby. It's C. J. What's this I hear about an all-girls trip to the Poconos?"

"It isn't the Poconos, dear. Just a little town named Hernia. There's nothing there."

"Then why are you going? And Wynnell? And Peggy? Abby, you promised to include me next time y'all got together and did something fun!"

"We're driving four hundred miles to buy quilts. I hardly count that as fun."

"Oh, Abby, everything you do seems fun to me. Did you know I think of you as the big sister I never had? Unless you count Ruebella. She was a monkey my parents got for a wedding present, but she died when I was only three."

I'll admit to being flattered. Nobody, including my younger brother Toy, has ever wanted me for a big sister. I put my hand over the receiver just long enough to let out a sigh worthy of a teenager.

"Do you really think you'd have fun cooped up in a car with three older women?"

"Oh, sure. My grandmother Parker, three of my aunties, and our minister's wife and I were all locked together in a linen closet—"

"If you don't finish that story, dear, you can come. We're leaving tomorrow morning from my house at eight sharp. There'll be room for you and the others to park your cars in the driveway if the first person pulls right up to the garage."

"Gee, thanks, Abby!"

"Eight sharp," I said, as sharply as I dared, and hung up.

The day was more than half gone and I needed to swing by Mama's house in Rock Hill to make sure she had locked it, and then say good-bye to my kids who were (*finally*, and only by the grace of God!) both enrolled in Winthrop University. Somewhere along in there

I needed to drop Dmitri off at Happy Paws Pet Motel on Arrowood Road. Then there were the minor things like stopping by the post office and filling out a "hold mail" card, and calling the newspaper to halt delivery. Never mind packing my clothes and watering my house-plants.

But when I closed the door of my shop behind me and turned smack into Purnell Purvis, I was too flab-bergasted to be annoyed. Purvis almost never leaves his happy little kingdom in Pineville. He certainly *never* makes personal appearances on Selwyn Avenue. I could hardly have been more surprised if Santa himself had shown up and invited me to tug on his beard.

I must hasten to assure you that I was not injured by my close encounter with the icon of the Carolina antique world. Purvis, like Santa, has a lot in common with an automobile airbag. Because I am vertically challenged, my face burrowed into his tummy—rather, his tummy billowed around it. Since my nose tends to be on the sharp side, it was not me, but Purvis, who took the brunt of the impact.

"Oomph," he gasped, but remained upright.

It took me a few seconds to recover my composure and to debate my course of action. They say the best defense is a good offensive, and I can be just as offen-sive as the next gal, but I really didn't have the time.

"Sorry, dear," I said as I tried to step around him.

"Abby, can we talk?"

"Here? Now?" Those were, or course, rhetorical questions. When the mighty Purvis leaves his ivory tower to talk, one listens. Either that, or one drives five hours to Atlanta to shop the auctions there. Besides, the autocratic auctioneer was wearing a pale blue summer suit and a cherry-red tie. I had never seen him so dressed up.

I led him into the shop and settled him into a sub-stantial eighteenth-century Italian baronial armchair. It was a piece acquired from a hefty Foxcroft matron who is almost as tall as Purvis, so I guessed that her weight would be about the same—give or take a ballpark. Still, I prayed that the piece would hold.

Then I excused myself and trotted off to my private storage area where I keep one of those refrigerators that is so small that you have to mash a loaf of bread to get it in. But there was nothing in there but an open package of three moldy slices of turkey bologna, and a jar of crusty brown mustard.

Frantically I rummaged in my desk drawers for some sort of libation, but alas, no bottle of Pernod magically appeared. It was not altogether a wasted effort, however, because I did find—mixed up with some rubber bands and paper clips—some candies I'd swiped from the bowl at Red Lobster.

"Peppermint, Purvis?" I asked politely.

He shook his massive head which, I noticed with dismay, was glistening with sweat. If any of that got on my baronial armchair, Purvis was going to pay. As for the consequences to me, in retrospect, five hours is not such a long drive with a good audio book along.

"What's this all about, dear?"

"I—uh—hell, Abigail, this isn't easy for me." Purvis extracted a white cotton handkerchief from his left pants pocket, and much to my relief, began mopping his brow.

"Take your time, dear," I said, glancing at my watch.

He mopped and swabbed in relative silence for several minutes, and then without any further warning, took the plunge. "I came to apologize."

There is no taking back a gasp, so I pretended it was the prelude to a yawn. "Pardon me. I guess I didn't sleep well last night. Now what was it you were saying?"

He crammed the sodden handkerchief back into his pocket. "You heard me, girlie."

"I liked it much better when you called me Abigail."

He stared at me. "You don't believe in cutting folks any slack, do you?"

I pulled up a Victorian side chair and sat down. "I believe in showing folks respect."

"Yeah, well, respect has to be earned."

I glanced at my watch again. "Let's not argue, shall we? So, you came to apologize. Well, apology accepted."

The porcine eyes blinked. "You did hear me!"

"Of course. I just wanted to hear you say it again. I would gladly trade that chair you're sitting in for a tape recorder. Now, what exactly is it you're sorry for?"

He took a dry handkerchief from his right pants pocket and mopped again before answering. "Maybe I was a little hard on you when you stopped by this morning. I guess I thought maybe you were blaming me for the tea set not being a genuine William Cripps."

"You said it was."

"I said that's what I *thought* it was. There's a big difference."

"That's easy for you to say, since you didn't lose any money." A twenty-thousand dollar goof allows one to be petulant, if you ask me.

"Abigail, you know my policy. It's standard for the industry. All sales are final. We don't guarantee the authenticity of any of our merchandise, because this business covers too many areas for any one person to become an expert on everything. That's why y'all get the opportunity to examine the merchandise before an auction."

Unfortunately I had no retort for that.

"However, I have decided to make an exception this one time." Purvis paused to attend to his personal needs. With both handkerchiefs soggy, he decided to use his shirtsleeves. "I paid five grand for that set, Abigail. How about I tear up your check, and you and I split the cost to me?"

To my knowledge, I have been that shocked only twice before. The first time was when Buford asked me for a divorce so that he could marry the Tweetie Bird,

and the second time was when Erica Kane was impreg-
nated by Dmitri. That's Dmitri on "All My Children,"
not my cat by the same name.

"Split the cost?" I sputtered. "*You*?"

Purvis waved a pudgy hand. "You're a good customer, Abigail. And like I said, this is a one-time exception."

I gave the side of my head a couple of hard raps with
the base of my palm. Something was not computing.
Purnell Purvis of Pineville was incapable of committing
random acts of kindness.

Purvis saw my gesture and had the temerity to
chuckle. "Truth is, Abigail, I've been wanting to do
something nice for you for a long time."

A really hard rap on the other side made no difference. "You have?"

He nodded. "I've had my eyes on you since the first
day you stepped into my auction barn. That little lady
is mighty special, I told myself."

"You did?"

"Yes, ma'am. I could see right away that you weren't
like any of the other women dealers in Charlotte."

"Leave my height out of this," I snapped.

He slapped a padded thigh. "That's exactly what I
mean. You've got fire in you, little lady. Spunk. That's
what I like in a woman."

That was certainly news to me. I suspected that Purvis
had been married at least once, maybe twice. He has
two loutish sons—as different from each other as rap
and music—and the word is they have separate mothers.
That was the extent of my knowledge. For all I knew
the man had a plethora of wives and concubines holed
up in the nether reaches of his auction barn, and they
kowtowed and catered to his every whim. I doubted if
any of them had spunk.

"Finding your harem ho-hum, dear?"

He laughed, and his eyes were replaced by a pair of
navels. "I'm not married. Haven't been for twenty years.

Of course now if the right woman came along—'' He leaned forward and deliberately touched me on the knee.

Of course I was shocked, but having been primed by his offer to help absorb my loss, I was not immobilized. I still had enough presence of mind to slap the offending hand away.

"If she was the *right* girl, she'd run for her life!"

"That's what I like about you, girlie. You give as good as you get."

"Then get this—get lost!"

"Yesiree, I like a woman with fire."

I stood up, and Purvis being a southern gentleman, born and bred, stood up as well. He had eyes again.

Suddenly it occurred to me that perhaps I had gone too far. "Did you mean what you said about splitting your cost?" I asked.

"I don't go back on my word, little lady. That's one thing you can count on if you hook up with me."

"Good, because I'd rather hook up with Godzilla."

"I love it!"

The exertion of standing had set off a new round of perspiring, and Purvis was now on his second sleeve. A good hostess would have offered him a box of tissues, but alas, the one on my desk was empty. Mama's unexpected departure had seen to that.

"Would you mind stepping outside, dear?" I asked politely. "This is a hardwood floor, and I just had it redone last summer."

"Anything you say, little lady." He stuck out his hand, which I had no choice but to shake. It felt like a clump of kelp fresh from the sea.

Purvis was halfway to his car before it occurred to me that I may just have been bought off. Hornswoggled by the best of them. What a clever ploy it was to offer me remuneration, even a partial one. And then the flirting! That was a stroke of genius. I had become so discombobulated that I had completely forgotten to press for a description of the mysterious vendor.

I raced after him and caught him just as he was opening the door to his Chrysler LeBaron. Without thinking, I put a restraining hand on a wet sleeve.

"Now that we have this special relationship," I panted, "you can tell me who the vendor was, can't you?"

He turned slowly. "What's the difference? You're only going to be out twenty-five hundred dollars."

"This could be the same man who sold the set to my mother. I'd like to ask him a few questions."

"Little lady—" Purvis said, and collapsed in the street.

7

I don't want you to get the wrong impression. Purnell Purvis did not hit the pavement with a thud. His collapse was slightly more gradual, like a soufflé settling when the oven door has been slammed. While he settled, I stood and stared with my mouth wide open. Needless to say, I am not particularly good with emergencies.

Major Calloway, whose emporium is just across the street, was the first one on the scene. The old goat can really sprint. He got there in time to cushion Purvis's head with his hands and guide it gently down to the hot pavement. A suspicious person might even assume that the major was watching and waiting for just that moment. Fortunately I am not the suspicious type.

"Call 911!" the major barked.

I did what I was told. It took only a minute or two, but when I returned a crowd had already gathered. Just where all these folks were until the major appeared, will always remain a mystery. Something similar happened to my Aunt Marilyn in Atlanta. A car smashed into a telephone pole in front of her house at three in the morning. Aunt Marilyn was the only one on the scene, administering first aid and getting blood all over her nightie, until the police showed up. Then every light in the neighborhood came on and the gawkers came pouring out of their houses like ants to a picnic basket.

Anyway, it was impossible for me to push my way through the band of rubberneckers that surrounded the fallen Purvis, so I wormed through at a lower strata. A woman yelled when her purse strap caught on my ear, and a grammar school boy kicked me in the ribs, but I ignored them.

Purvis was still prone, like a beached whale in a business suit. The major, dressed in a khaki uniform of British colonial issue, replete with pith helmet, was cradling Purvis's giant head in his arms and crooning something intelligible. Perhaps a Punjabi lullaby. It was a scene straight out of a Fellini movie.

"I'm back," I rasped.

The major didn't look up. "You call 911?"

"They said five minutes tops. Is he breathing?"

"Barely."

"Can't you do CPR?"

"It's been years since I took the course, but I'll give it a go," the major said.

He laid Purvis's head gently down on the pavement and straddled him. With his knobby knees protruding from the baggy khaki shorts, and a look of terror in his eyes, the major looked like a small child who had just mounted a pony for the first time.

Mercifully the paramedics reached us before the major could do any irreparable damage. And let me tell you this, these Charlotte guys and gals really know their stuff. By the time they were loading him into the ambulance, Purvis was fully conscious. Unfortunately he was articulate as well.

"Abigail," he whispered.

I looked around stupidly. The crowd was certainly large enough to supply two of us.

"Abigail!"

I edged closer. Sure, Purvis had plotzed on my pavement, but I had nothing to do with it. Now that I was in the process of breaking up with a Charlotte detective, a deathbed accusation was the last thing I needed.

"Closer," he croaked.

The paramedics waited patiently, the stretcher half in and half out of the yawning ambulance. Apparently this sort of drama was routine. I gave the throng my best nonchalant shrug and took a full step closer.

"Abigail, remember our little arrangement?" Purvis asked in a voice loud enough for even those at the back of the mob to hear.

"Yes," I mumbled, but my lips were as tightly sealed as Howdy Doody's.

"Well, it's off!" he practically shouted.

"You lying snake!" I hissed.

Purvis slowly raised himself on his elbows. At the angle he was pitched, it was a wonder he didn't topple facedown on the street.

"You—" he said, and fell back against the stretcher. His eyes were closed.

"Thank God he didn't die." Wynnell wiped the corners of my mouth with the hem of her blouse. Since her homemade outfit was made from pinned-together table napkins, it didn't matter.

I looked past her and through the front window of Applebee's at Carolina Place Mall. Not a mile away Purnell Purvis was resting quietly in the cardiac ward of Mercy Hospital South. His prognosis was good. The man had had a mild heart attack, but there were no complications. In fact, and this puzzled his doctors, portly Purvis had no history of heart disease. His vast bulk aside, there was no reason for him to have had one on Selwyn Avenue.

Peggy put a fist-size bite of quesadilla into her mouth. She'd been the first to arrive, and hadn't waited for anyone else before she ordered. This was vintage Peggy who was addicted to both food and sex and obviously wasn't getting any of the latter.

"Abby," she asked, "that wasn't you Purvis was talking to, was it?"

"Don't be silly," Wynnell said loyally.

"What do you mean?"

"Our Abby doesn't get along with Purvis. Everyone knows that."

I turned from the window and shot my friend a warning look. It was in vain. Wynnell, bless her heart, is a woman without guile. This is possibly an admirable quality, but it can be hazardous when in the hands of unprimed friends.

"Exactly what I was getting at," Peggy said, and treated me to a glimpse of masticated Mexican. "I mean, don't you think it was odd that Purvis wandered down to Selwyn and just happened to have his heart attack in front of Abby's shop?"

The major snorted. "It wasn't odd at all. Purnell Purvis didn't just happen to collapse in front of the Den of Antiquity. He went in to see Abby first."

All eyes turned to me. There were seven pairs in all. The entire gang had assembled for supper at Applebee's to talk about the day's happenings, Purvis's heart attack in particular. This alone struck me as strange, since a communal supper was not a regularly scheduled event for us. What made it even stranger was the fact that the major had been the one to suggest it.

"I didn't do anything to him," I wailed. "I'll swear on a stack of Bibles. I'll even wear white after Labor Day if I'm lying."

C. J. gasped. "Never wear white after Labor Day, Abby. My mother did that once when I was in the seventh grade, and the next thing I knew she was gone. Poof, just like that. I didn't see her again for several days."

"What happened?" Bob Steuben won't admit it, but he has a soft spot for our junior member. I think she reminds him of his little sister up in Toledo. He is also keenly aware that Rob finds C. J.'s yarns as irritating as a stiff label in a new shirt.

"She stepped outside and got lost in a snowstorm."

"In Shelby, North Carolina?" Rob asked. For the first

time I could remember the Rob-Bobs were not sitting together. In fact, they were seated at opposite ends of our double table.

Calamity Jane nodded emphatically. "It was the worst winter in a hundred years. Snow was already up to the top porch step, and it was blowing so hard you couldn't see past your outstretched hand."

"Lord have mercy!" Bob brayed. I had to give him credit for trying to sound southern.

"Oh, Mama was all right," C. J. hastened to assure us. "She'd just gotten done pouring brandy on our Christmas fruitcakes—Mama always made them from scratch—when she heard what sounded like a knock on the kitchen door and went to answer it. She was holding the biggest fruitcake when the wind blew her away. It didn't blow her very far, of course. Just off the porch and into a snowdrift. But then she got turned around and headed for the barn instead of the house. We found her three days later when the weather cleared. Not only had Mama eaten all of the fruitcake, but she was still a little bit tipsy from the brandy. She had no recollection of what happened."

"The poor dear," I said against my better judgment.

"Oh, she was fine—honest. She had Moonjumper, our cow, to keep her warm. She smelled a little funny, though, until we made her take a bath the next week. Moonjumper, I mean, not Mama."

Rob rolled his eyes. "I thought you said she ate the biggest fruitcake."

"Rob!" Bob boomed.

It was time to do a little diffusing. "What do you recommend?" I asked Gretchen, who was scanning the menu through horn-rimmed spheres the diameter of my water glass.

Gretchen's gaze shifted from the menu and slowly focused on my face. In the meantime, six pairs of eyes focused on Gretchen. Our taciturn troop leader was about to dispense another pearl.

"What sort of arrangement did you and Purvis have, Abby?"

"What arrangement?" I croaked.

"I was standing close to the ambulance. Purnell Purvis said for you to remember y'all's little arrangement."

"Do tell," Peggy squealed, unnecessarily spraying me with quesadilla crumbs.

I looked frantically at Wynnell for help, but she was giving me the fish eye. My friend claims that I never confide in her until the entire southern half of Charlotte knows my business.

"Yeah, tell," Rob said. He was clearly miffed at me for having called him jealous earlier.

I was trapped. To stall further, or deny the conversation, was to dig my way deeper into the quicksand of suspicion. "If you keep your curtains open," Mama often said, "folks don't need to wonder what's inside your house." It was time to open the drapes as wide as I could.

"Purvis did come by to see me this morning—"

"Aha," the major barked, "I told you so."

"He offered to return the money I paid for the William Cripps. Well, not *all* of it. The arrangement is we split his cost."

"Then who gets to keep the set?" Rob asked.

"I do."

"Hey that's no fair. *I've* never been allowed to return an auction item."

Of course Rob was absolutely right. It wasn't fair. And if anybody deserved a break on returns, it was Rob. As owner of the Finer Things, truly the finest shop in Charlotte, he handed over a fortune each week to pertinacious Purvis.

"He's right," Bob grunted.

Rob cast his life-partner a grateful look. Alas, it was too fleeting to lead to reconciliation.

"Isn't there something in our by-laws that forbids favoritism?" the major whined.

The six pairs of eyes returned to Gretchen, who ceremoniously closed her menu, pushed the horn-rims back into place, and then cleared her throat.

"No," she said.

The major has a clipped mustache, not unlike Hitler's, except that a few hairs on each end are allowed to grow. He was twisting these furiously.

Gretchen held up a calming, well-manicured hand. "But Purvis can't claim a no-return policy that doesn't apply to everyone. Either he changes it, or we boycott him."

Our leader had spoken. Everyone nodded, including Wynnell. Then everyone turned and stared at me, as if I was somehow responsible for Purvis's bias.

"Don't look at me," I wailed. "Purvis has a crush on me, that's what."

Several mouths gaped. Mercifully Peggy's was not one of them.

"It is not reciprocated!"

They continued to stare.

"All right, I'll tell you everything. I went to see him this morning about the vendor of my silver, and he was really nasty. Then he came over this afternoon to apologize, and that's when I asked for my money back. I was just as surprised as you that he cut me a deal. And I was even more surprised when he said he had a crush on me. I didn't even have an inkling about it until then. In fact, I thought he disliked me. He always growls when I'm around."

"That's a sure sign of affection," Bob growled, and he stole a glance at Rob.

Peggy swallowed the last of her quesadilla. "How long has this favoritism been going on?"

Our waitress appeared then, pad and pen in hand, but I vigorously waved her away. "It hasn't! And just to show my solidarity with y'all, I'm not going to accept the partial refund.''

There were several murmurs of approval. I tried not to detect their sources. Few things can stand more solidly between friendships than twenty thousand dollars.

''I'll bite the expense,'' I wailed bitterly, hoping that someone would rush to my defense. No one did.

I tried to force a few tears to illustrate my anguish, but Peggy had moved the pepper out of sniffing reach. And while pinching myself in the soft spot behind my knee sometimes helps keep me awake, it did nothing to stimulate my ducts.

Gretchen tapped on her half-empty tea glass with her fork. ''Enough business. Let's order.''

''I'll second that,'' Peggy said, and ordered seconds.

The trip to Pennsylvania was still on. Purvis was getting the best care available at Mercy South. There was certainly nothing the four of us could do to help. His two sons, Jimbo and Skeet, could run the business for him until he was back on his feet—well, actually they couldn't, but Purvis sure the heck wasn't going to allow any of us to prowl around his auction barn in his absence.

Unfortunately, our supper at Applebee's, as emotionally necessary as it was, had taken far too much of my valuable time. Dropping Dmitri off at Happy Paws Pet Motel was out of the question. It was already closed for the day, and Miss Kitty Blattner, the woman who runs it, never accepts ''guests'' before noon. Dmitri adores Miss Kitty's establishment with as much fervor as he abhors every other kennel I've ever tried to leave him with. Since we wanted to leave Charlotte by eight, that meant my ten-pound bundle of joy was going to get his first trip north of the Mason-Dixon line.

I still had to drive down to Rock Hill and check on Mama's house and the kids. A lot of folks prefer to take I-485 to I-77 south, but I find that it takes no more time, and is just as pleasant to turn left out of Applebee's parking lot and take State Route 21 straight down to Rock Hill, where it becomes Cherry Road, the town's main drag. Sure, there are some stoplights and a few stop signs between Carolina Place Mall and Rock Hill, but there is a lot less traffic. There is certainly more to see along the state route.

It was dusk when I got to Rock Hill and the bright lights of Cherry Road made my hometown seem much larger than it is. Rock Hill may have only forty-five thousand people, but it has everything a body could want. Howard Johnson's, Denny's, Holiday Inn, Shoney's, Office Depot, K-Mart, Payless Shoes—you could have plonked me down in Las Vegas and it would have taken a couple of minutes to figure out I was somewhere else.

I turned left at Love's Plaza and then made a right on Eden Terrace. Mama lives on down past Winthrop Stadium, near the intersection with Myrtle. It is the same house my parents bought after they were first married, and the place I was born. While it may be one of the more modest houses on the street, it is still a desirable address. Eden Terrace and Myrtle are the dwelling places of the Old Guard of Rock Hill. These are not necessarily rich folks—although some are—but people whose Rock Hill roots go back at least two generations. And because it is the South, it is generations, not years that count. Mama claims to have befriended an octogenarian widow who moved to Myrtle Drive from another part of Rock Hill and was very well received. When the silly woman revealed that she had been born in Michigan, and moved to Rock Hill as an infant, you would have thought that Sherman had been resurrected and was planning a second coming. Mama's new friend had to sell her Myrtle Drive house and move to the Meadow Lakes II subdivision in shame.

That said, I was disturbed by the number of cars I saw parked along the street near Mama's house. Folks on

Eden Terrace are not given to partying during the week.
Either someone died, or someone was about to. Then I
saw that Mama's driveway was not only filled with cars,
but there was one parked on the lawn in her petunia bed.
Of course I panicked. But the second I opened my car
door I could hear, as well as feel, the pulsating bass of
rock music.

So Mama had not run off to Dayton to become an
Episcopal nun! I should have been that lucky. To the
contrary, Mozella Hayes Wiggins had become a party
animal. Her dramatic good-bye had been a ruse, the silver tea set nothing more than a balm to assuage her
guilty conscience as she desecrated my father's memory
by turning their home into a den of iniquity.

I double-parked beside a Ford Festiva that had seen
better days and strode across the lawn like an avenging
angel. Had there been a stick lying around I would have
snatched it up with the intention of driving the money-
changers from my daddy's temple. You can bet I didn't
ring the doorbell.

8

I t was my turn to have a heart attack. Those weren't
Mama's friends bebopping around her living room—
not unless she had slipped further than I thought. My
mother might be a bulb short of a chandelier, but she
wasn't so far gone that she would mess with jailbait.
The lithe male body gyrating shirtless just in front of
me was less than two decades old. I was on the verge
of backing out quietly and then fetching the police, when
I noticed that the attractive girl mirroring his undulations
resembled my daughter, Susan.

First I prayed for patience, and then I flipped the light
switch several times.

"Raid!" someone shouted.

There was an assortment of cries and a scuffling of
feet as over fifty young people, unfamiliar with the lay-
out of Mama's house, stampeded for the back door.
When the dust had settled, so to speak, only two delin-
quents remained.

"Charlie?" I asked, blinking in disbelief.

"Mama!"

"It isn't what you think," Susan wailed.

My hands took familiar positions at my hips. It was
worse than I had initially thought. Never mind the cellophane cyclone that had obviously hit the room, spew-
ing chips and nachos on every surface, only to have
them ground into the couches and carpet by denim-clad

buttocks and odiferous sneakers. Forget the smorgasbord of salsas and dips that followed the chips. Ditto for the soft drink cans. What really mattered was the flotilla of beer cans and the armada of cheap wine bottles.

I picked up a Coors Light can. It wasn't quite empty and warm beer dribbled off my fingers and splashed on the floor. The suds on the rug more likely helped than hurt.

"Can you explain this?"

Charlie was as white as the inside of my elbow in January. "It was all Susan's idea."

"Bastard rat fink," she hissed.

"Just like Adam blamed Eve," I said to Charlie.

Susan took that as a sign of encouragement. "He put up half the money and made some of the phone calls. In fact, he wanted to hire a stripper, but I said no."

Charlie turned the color of an uncooked shrimp. "Liar. I didn't say anything about a stripper. That was Jason's idea."

"Children!"

My two college students snapped to attention, proving that it's all in the tone of the voice—that, and an unspoken threat to call their father, Buford the Money Bags. I wanted desperately to sit now, but not desperately enough to act as a canvas.

"How long has this party being going on?"

Susan shrugged. "Just after my third period class, I guess. Grandma stopped by before that and told me she was leaving. Is that cool or what? My grandma the nun!"

"It's as cool as a jalapeno in hell."

My sarcasm was lost on Susan. "Does this mean I get to call Grandma 'Sister'?"

"Speaking of your grandma, does she know about this?"

Charlie shook his head. "Susan made us wait an hour to make sure Grandma was on her way to see you."

"Fink! Fink! Fink!"

"Liar! You said we wouldn't get caught, Susan."

"I'm surprised you didn't get caught hours ago. It's only because your grandmother is so well liked that you got away with it this long. The neighbors undoubtedly thought this had something to do with her. If they had known it was just you kids, they would have called the police right away."

"Oh damn," Charlie said. "The booze."

"Ah, back to the booze," I said, searching for a tone they wouldn't tune out, "I am really very disappointed. In *both* of you."

"I'm almost twenty-one," Susan said, digging her toe into the crusted carpet.

"Your birthday is eight months away, dear. Charlie is just barely nineteen. Besides, that really isn't the point. All those cars out there"—I waved my arms—"had North Carolina plates. Those weren't Winthrop kids, were they?"

"Some were," Charlie said. "My roommate was here. And my biology lab partner and her roommate."

"We grew up in Charlotte," Susan said, her eyes half-closed in defiance. "Where do you think most of our friends live?"

"So, they're driving home now with a few beers under their belts? They could kill somebody, or get killed themselves, you know. How would you feel then?"

Charlie hung his head. Bless his heart, he has always been fairly easy to shame.

Susan opened her eyes. The muscles along her jaw were twitching.

"Then that's your fault, Mama. You're the one who scared them away."

I took my own oft-given advice and counted to ten under my breath. I did it again in Spanish. Then I tried it in German but only got as far as five.

"Did Grandma give you permission to have a party?" I asked quietly.

Susan squared her shoulders. "She gave me a key."

"I see. And what did she say when she gave it to you?"

"She asked me to water her plants and bring in the mail until you had a chance to get down here. *And* she said I could come over and chill out if I needed to. The dorm gets on my nerves."

I remembered six through ten in German. "But she didn't give you permission to throw a party, did she?"

"She didn't say I *couldn't.*"

Charlie raised his head. "You said she did!"

My daughter's eyes became mere slits. "I hate you, you spoiled little mama's boy. I shouldn't have even told you."

"Shut your big fat mouth!" Charlie screamed.

They were seven and nine again. Their adult bodies sat in classes where Proust was discussed, and examined tissue samples under microscopes, but within the petri dish of the family, they were fighting over who broke the knob off the television and who ratted on whom. And here I was still moderating—no, make that facilitating—their fights.

I sat down on Mama's newest sofa. It had originally been powder blue to harmonize with everything else in the pastel room. Frankly, the guacamole and salsa made it come alive. No doubt they would do the same for my khaki skirt. So be it. I was just too pooped to pop.

My disregard for my clothes amused Charlie. Susan was a harder nut to crack, but that didn't matter. I neither wanted to amuse nor mollify them. There was a job to be done, and by golly, they were going to do it.

"Look for leaf bags in the garage," I said to Charlie. "You," I said to Susan, "get Grandma's vacuum and bring all the attachments."

They both stared, their mouths wide open.

Susan was the first to recover. "Is that it?"

"Don't be silly, dear. You'll be scrubbing and cleaning 'til the cows come home. The wild horses too."

"Aren't you going to punish us or anything?" Charlie asked.

"How? Send you to your dorm room?"

"You could tell Daddy," Susan said warily.

I smiled. "I could. And maybe I will. But let's see how this goes first. Telling Daddy isn't going to get Grandma's house back in shape."

Charlie pointed to the couch and shook his head. "That's never coming clean."

"Then I guess y'all are going to have to save up your spending money and buy her a new one."

"No fair," Susan said, and then clamped a hand over her mouth.

"Clean!" I ordered.

They got back to work. Four hours later Mama's house looked like it had been hit by Hurricane Hugo, instead of fifty college-age kids. It was a definite improvement. The rest of the job just had to wait until I returned from Pennsylvania.

Before I kicked the kids out and locked the door, I told them each that I loved them. I added that next time I would not hesitate to call the Rock Hill police. Then I pocketed the key.

The midnight phone call began as part of my dreams. It was a call from Mama. She said she was calling from Caesar's Palace in Las Vegas. She had both kids with her. Susan and Charlie had been recruited by the Mafia to infiltrate the blackjack tables, posing as dealers. Somehow, at a given signal, my children were to rob the casino and escape in a hot air balloon shaped like a woodchuck. In the meantime Mama was going to distract everyone by doing a striptease act to songs from the forties. Did I want a piece of the action?

I only briefly considered it and then remembered that Caesar's Palace had been torn down. The dream rapidly dissolved into a realization that a real phone was ringing beside my bed, and since it was so late, something awful had surely happened.

"What's wrong?" I practically shrieked into the receiver.

"Abby, we need to talk."

"Greg?" I glanced at the clock. "It's one-thirty in the morning!"

"Oh, did I wake you?"

There was no time for sarcasm. "Is it the children? They promised—"

"No, and it's not your precious mama, either. It's us."

"Us? You woke me up in the middle of the night to talk about *us*? Do you have any idea how frightening it is to wake up to a ringing phone?"

"That's part of the problem, Abby. If everything was like it should be, I'd be there beside you. I wouldn't need to call."

"We've been over that a million times, Greg. I don't want to sleep with you until after we're married."

Actually, I did want to sleep with him. I had never desired anyone as much as I did Greg, and that included Buford back when I was a walking collection of collegiate hormones. My urges, however, were going to wait until after that plain gold band was officially slipped on my finger.

"Yeah, well, I've been thinking that maybe you and I need to take a little break from each other. I have a lot of vacation saved up, so I thought maybe I'd head on down to the Keys and fish for grouper."

I sat up in bed and turned on the light. This was not lying in the dark kind of news.

"What does that mean?" I asked.

"Grouper is a kind of fish, Abby. They're—"

"I know what a grouper is," I snapped. "What do you mean about us needing a break? And what about our honeymoon to Jamaica? We can't go if you use up all your vacation time."

I hate to admit it, but I was both hurt and excited. How dare the man need time away from me? But since he did, he could hardly object to my jaunt up to Pennsylvania.

"Jamaica will use up just a week," Greg said. "And Abby, you know that we've been missing more than hitting lately. I think that being apart might give us a new perspective."

"I see. Well then, if you're going to be deep-sea fishing in the Keys, you won't have any objection to me taking a trip to Pennsylvania."

In the ensuing silence the population of India doubled and Michael Jackson learned to sing bass.

"You're not going to Hernia, are you?"

"It's a quilt-buying trip, Greg. Wynnell and the girls are coming with me."

"Abby, keep your nose out of police business."

"I'm a big girl. I can take care of myself. You just make sure you keep your nose in a bait bucket."

"What the hell is that supposed to mean? And when are you taking this trip? Is this something you've been planning all along?"

"I started planning it yesterday, and we leave"—I glanced again at the clock—"in just over six hours. So, dear, I really have to get off the phone."

"When were you going to tell me? Before or after I worried my head off and got the SWAT out there to break down your door?"

"Don't ever worry your head off, dear. It's too cute. You'd be hard put to come up with a quality replacement. Now, if you'll excuse me, I really have to go back to sleep."

I hung up. Then I did something I'd never dare do before—I unplugged the phone.

I assure you that I set my alarm clock. It just didn't do any good. Somehow I managed to shut it off and I was sound asleep when the doorbell rang promptly at eight. I didn't hear that either.

Wynnell has a key and took the liberty of letting herself in. She claims she called my name loudly before laying a hand on me, but all I know is that when I woke up I was being shaken like the paint mixer at Home Depot. It was not a good way to start the day.

"You said eight o'clock, Abby. It's already five after and you're not even dressed."

I groaned. "Perhaps I was being a bit optimistic about our departure. How does ten sound?"

"But we're all ready, Abby. Peggy and C. J. will be here in a minute. Besides, I want to get there well before dark."

"It's only a nine-hour drive, Wynnell, and it doesn't get dark until seven."

Wynnell shook her head. "My neighbors, DeLand and Corky Ledbetter, drove to Ohio last summer. They said you have to drive real slow up north if you don't want to get caught in those speed traps."

"Speed traps?"

She nodded with the power of second-hand conviction. "Every little town has them. Some skinny Yankee sheriff sits off to the side of the road just waiting for a car with southern plates to drive by. Well, if you aren't going the *exact* speed, or maybe even a few miles under, they haul you off to jail."

"And you don't get to pass 'GO'?"

She stared at me blankly.

I sat up. "You mean they don't even give you a speeding ticket first? They haul you straight to jail?"

Wynnell frowned. "That does seems a little harsh, even for Yankees, doesn't it? Maybe the Ledbetters left something out of the story. But I do know that northern jails are no place for a southerner. Both Deland and Corky said it was the worst food they'd ever eaten."

"Do tell, dear."

"Well, for one thing, they don't eat grits up there."

"Lord have mercy."

"And they put sugar in their cornbread."

I feigned gagging.

Wynnell looked at me sternly. "Abby, are you mocking me?"

I stretched. "Guilty, dear."

Mercifully the doorbell rang and Wynnell trotted happily off to get it. By answering my door, Wynnell would once again prove to the others that she was indeed my best friend. Not that I am such hot stuff, mind you, but since this trip was my idea, that put me in charge. In our little world, where friendships and business relations are as intertwined as a cat's cradle, the pecking order has to be preserved somehow, and Wynnell, bless her heart, was eager to establish her place.

While Wynnell pecked, I slid back down between cool sheets and grabbed another wink.

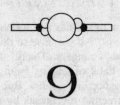

9

Peggy and C. J. were not nearly as patient as dear Wynnell. They too had heard the horror stories of gaunt Yankee lawmen who preyed on innocent southerners.

"And don't you dare try and pass for a Yankee," C. J. said to me. "That only makes it worse. My cousin Elmo was hired to drive a car to Chicago that had Illinois plates. They stopped him at the border and made him say his 'ahs.' "

"I beg your pardon?"

"You know, the alphabet letter that comes before 's.' "

"Get out of town!"

C. J. shuttered. "It was terrible. Not only did Cousin Elmo flunk that test, but then they tried to get him to spit on a picture of Jesse Helms."

"No way, Jose! Well, did he?"

"I hate to interrupt," Peggy said, "but if we don't hit the road soon, we won't make the border before dark, and I am not driving around Pennsylvania at night. If we hit an Amish buggy we'll end up in jail for sure."

I ran fingers through my wet hair. My friends had literally thrown me into the shower. Worse, they had refused me the time to eat—even a bowl of *instant* grits, may Granny Wiggins rest in peace.

"Well, I'm ready," I said, picking up the hastily assembled collection of clothes and toiletries Wynnell had laid out on the bed. "All we have to do is find Dmitri."

My cat eschews strangers. Thank goodness I finally broke him of the habit of leaping from high places onto the backs of unsuspecting visitors. But alas, he is still a long way from greeting my guests by purring and rubbing against their legs. The last time I had company it took me a day to find Dmitri. If it hadn't been for that foul odor coming from the linen closet, I am sure it would have been much longer.

Peggy froze. "You weren't planning to take that mangy mutt with you, were you?"

I forced a pleasant smile. "Dogs are mangy mutts, dear. Felines are pathetic pussies. And yes, I'm afraid we have to, if we plan to leave anytime soon. Happy Paws Pet Motel doesn't open until noon."

"There are lots of other kennels," Wynnell said. "I'm sure some of them open early."

I shot her a warning glare. "My shnookums wouldn't be caught dead in one of those."

My friend recovered quickly. "Ah, yes, I forgot. So many people travel these days that you have to make reservations days in advance. We have to take him with us, all right."

Peggy paled. "But aren't we taking my Lincoln Town Car?"

"Absolutely, dear. The five of us will be ever so comfortable."

"But—"

"Or, we could take my little Grand Am. Of course Dmitri thinks the front seat is his. But that shouldn't matter too much, since y'all are wearing slacks, and I trimmed his claws just last week."

There was a hasty conference and from the get-go the pressure was on Peggy. While she protested, I searched Dmitri's favorite haunts, starting with the microwave— don't get me wrong, he is a smart kitty, just not brilliant—and ending with the dishwasher.

"Oh, there you are, you naughty boy!" I cried, genuinely glad to see him.

Dmitri was so grateful to be rescued he didn't even hiss, but purred contentedly in my arms as I started the empty washer. Rest assured that I set it on the pots and pans cycle, with the water as hot as possible. I even used extra detergent.

By the time I returned to the living room the palaver had been settled. Dmitri could come, but he would be restricted to my lap. At night he would sleep in my bed. If there were any accidents, I would have to clean up.

"Understood," I said, perhaps a bit smugly. Happy Paws Pet Motel was not cheap, and Kitty Blattner refused to give me a price break even though I once sold her a cast-iron Scotty bank at cost.

I am proud to say that Dmitri behaved very well—much better than we. Peggy has a preference for meat-locker temperatures. I am convinced that she plans to have her body cryogenically preserved when she dies, and she is practicing for that occasion. We mumbled and grumbled until we were blue in the face (given the temperature setting that didn't take long) and by the time we reached the interstate had worn her down to the point of compromise. She turned the knob to a setting that might put an ice sculpture at risk, but was still no danger to milk, and we shut our mouths gratefully.

Peggy eased the Lincoln on to I-77 at Tyvola and by the time we passed the Metrolina exit Dmitri was fast asleep, his tail curled snugly around his nose. By the time we hit Statesville I nodded off and slept three hours straight.

I woke up to Peggy poking me in the ribs. I grunted and slapped her hand away.

"Lord have mercy," Wynnell cried gratefully. "I was beginning to think you'd been drugged."

"Or frozen to death," C. J. said through chattering teeth.

"Where are we?" I slurred. I had a gut feeling that

we had already passed the spot where Billy Ray Teschel became a buzzard buffet. I know it sounds morbid, but I had really wanted to see it.

"West Virginia, hon. That's Beckley right up ahead. There's a Cracker Barrel just on the other side, and we voted to stop there for lunch. That all right with you?"

"Fine. Just as long as it has a bathroom."

We found the Cracker Barrel. I let the others go on in while I apologized to Dmitri for having to leave him in the car. The poor dear was obviously miffed, because as soon as the car stopped, he jumped off my lap and crawled under the seat. It took me forever to coax him out, and I wouldn't have bothered, except he appeared to be wedged in there tighter than summer feet in new fall shoes. Finally he forgave me, and we struck up a deal of sorts. He promised not to rip up Peggy's leather seats if I brought back a piece of chicken. By the time I joined the others they had already been seated and were poring over their menus.

"Looks like the exact same menu they have back home," Peggy said. She, for one, would know.

Wynnell scanned the breakfast portion. "Well, I'll be. They even have grits. I wonder if they put sugar in their cornbread."

"Is West Virginia a southern state?" C. J. asked. "I mean, we've gotta know, because this is where we get off the interstate and catch Route 19. It'll save us a lot of time, and we'll get to see New River Gorge. Of course we shouldn't take the shortcut if this is a northern state."

"But we must see New River Gorge," Peggy cried. "Folks who've been up this way say it's spectacular. I was going to come up here on my honeymoon, but Danbo broke his leg at the bachelor party."

We stared at her, open-mouthed and wide-eyed.

"I didn't know you were married," I said.

"*Was*. It lasted three months. I was seventeen. That doesn't count, does it?"

"Seventeen is just a baby," C. J. said. She could afford to say that now that she was twenty-four.

"Anyway, I've always wanted to see it, and I don't think I'll ever get to the Grand Canyon. This might be as close as I come to ever seeing a big hole in the ground."

Wynnell shuddered. "But what about the speedtraps? Just thinking about those gaunt Yankee sheriffs gives me the creeps. I'm not sure even the Grand Canyon would be worth a night in a Yankee jail."

"Yeah," I said, "and never mind about the bigoted lawmen, it's the people in general that give me the creeps. It must be all that outbreeding. Did you know that up here folks sometimes marry complete strangers?"

Wynnell looked shocked. "You're kidding!"

I nodded solemnly. "Just look around you, dear. Have you ever seen so many full sets of teeth?"

Wynnell's hand flew up to cover her mouth. "Lord have mercy! This *must* be a northern state!"

We were just kidding, of course. At least I hoped we all were. Still, it was an interesting question. Was West Virginia a southern state—it had once been a part of Virginia, after all—or was it, as some cartographers claim, a mid-Atlantic state? If the latter was true then where, pray tell, was West Virginia's coastline? Our map didn't show it. We decided to ask our waitress for her opinion.

The woman who brought me my tea—I had to ask for it sweetened—had beautiful teeth. She was tall, and thin, and her waitress uniform did nothing for her. That woman was flat as a shuffleboard court. I guessed her to be about thirty-five. Her name was Susannah and she seemed about as interested in her job as I was in the Lithuanian stock market.

"Excuse me, dear," I said. "Do y'all consider yourselves Yankees or southerners?"

Susannah shrugged. "Beats me. I'm from Pennsylvania. I'm only here because I broke up with my boy-friend and this is as far as I could hitch in one day.''

"Where in Pennsylvania are you from, dear?"

"Oh, you wouldn't have heard of it. Nobody has. It's a dinky little town in the mountains called Hernia."

"Well Lord, Abby, isn't that where we're headed?" Wynnell asked.

I nodded.

Susannah's jaw dropped. "No way! Whatever for?"

"We're antique dealers," I said. "We're headed up there to buy Amish quilts."

"And," Peggy said, sucking back the drool, "we're going to be staying at a famous bed and breakfast where movie stars stay. I heard that Brad Pitt was there recently."

"Down, girl," I said.

Susannah rolled her eyes. "Do you have reservations?"

"No, dear," I said. "This trip has been a little last minute."

"You *are* talking about the PennDutch Inn?" Susannah asked.

"Yes. Is it hard to get a room? I mean, because we could share one if we have to."

Susannah's eyes rolled so far back in her head I was afraid they would get stuck. Apparently C. J. shared my concern.

"You really shouldn't do that," she said. "My niece Betty Mae, back in Shelby, North Carolina, did that once to her eyes and they stayed that way. We thought sure she was going to be blind for the rest of her life, but then a surgeon up in Raleigh figured out a way to drill two holes in the back of her head so she could see. The thing was, she had no eyelids, and she had to walk back-wards from then on. But it made her a terrific slow dan-cer because she never backed into anyone."

"You'll have to forgive her," I said. "Her mama dropped her on her head when she was a baby."

C. J. stared at me. "How did you know?"

"Lucky guess, dear." I turned to Susannah, who was mercifully sporting irises again. "I take it we'll have to find another place to stay. Isn't the town of Bedford nearby?"

"Bedford is twelve miles away. But—and I'm not promising anything—I'll see what I can do about you getting someplace to sleep at the PennDutch."

"You know the owners?"

Susannah smiled. "My sister is the owner. However, she and I don't get along as well as we should. Still, there's always the chance that somebody canceled. If so, I'll try and convince Mags to fit you in instead of going down her waiting list. Don't hold your breath though."

Peggy exhaled. "We understand. Just do your best. Is it true that Tom Selleck swims naked when he stays there?"

The eyes began an upward turn, but, thanks to C. J.'s story, Susannah caught herself in time. "We don't even have a pool, and if we did—well, you don't know my sister."

We placed our orders—none of us had the nerve to order the cornbread—and Susannah sauntered back to the kitchen. Halfway there she turned around and sauntered back. I realize it isn't my place to complain, but the woman moved with all the rapidity of a teenager sent to clean her room.

"Yes?" I said, perhaps a bit testily. I was hungry, after all, and as long as our orders had yet to reach the kitchen, nothing was being done to remedy the situation.

"Well, ladies, as long as I'm doing you a favor, how about you doing one for me?"

"You mean a finder's fee?"

"Ah—that would be nice too, but I was thinking more along the lines of a ride."

"We're really on a tight schedule," Peggy said. "We want to have time to stop at New River Gorge."

Susannah yawned. "Whatever for? It's just a hole in the ground with a river at the bottom."

"I want to see it," Peggy said stubbornly.

"Hey, that's cool then. Whatever you say. New River Gorge is right on the way."

"Where is it you want to go?"

"To Hernia, of course. I know I've only been gone five days, but I miss my Melvin. Maybe if I beg, he'll take me back."

Despite Wynnell's warning look, I had to speak my peace. "Never give a man that much power, dear. Besides, they don't respect a woman who begs."

"Speak for yourself," Peggy said.

I don't think Susannah even heard us. "Well? How about it? Can I hitch a ride? As it just so happens I brought my luggage with me to work today."

I stroked the rock on my ring finger. "You mean you'd quit your job just like that?" I asked.

She shrugged. "Sure, why not? I've done it oodles of times."

I told her we'd think about it while she placed our orders with the cook. That seemed to light a small fire under her. At least she made it as far as the kitchen that time.

Since the four of us were kind, southern women, well schooled in the art of hospitality, we agreed to take her with us. She would have to sit in the middle of the back seat, of course, and there would be no smoking. We had all smelled smoke on her.

We had agreed to meet Susannah on the porch in five minutes, and by some miracle we found four empty rocking chairs in a row. We settled into them and were quietly and contentedly digesting a mighty good lunch when fifteen feet of filmy fabric floated out the door. It took me a second to realize there was a person somewhere inside that swaddling swirl.

"Gotta love that woman," I whispered to Wynnell.

Wynnell frowned and smoothed the bodice of her creation of the day. Actually it was a fairly substantial outfit, because in addition to the usual plethora of pins, it contained a few scattered stitches.

"You're just jealous because you can't sew, Abby."

"You're absolutely right dear."

The walking bolt of cloth headed in our direction and I briefly contemplated fleeing. The last time someone dressed like that approached me I ended up paying ten dollars for a single, wilted rose. Call me a sucker for the freedom of religion.

"Hi," the material girl said.

We all stared at her.

"It's me, Susannah. You know, from Hernia."

We eventually closed our mouths.

"Don't I look a hundred times better?"

"You certainly look different," I said quickly. No telling what the others would say if I gave them a chance. "What about your luggage?"

For the day's second miracle Susannah whipped out a pink American Tourister train case. Who knew what else the folds of her garment hid?

"That's it?"

She giggled. "I like to travel light."

I, for one, was beginning to have second thoughts. The woman might have all her teeth, but it was beginning to look like she was a page short of a chapter. Dmitri definitely didn't like her. He hissed like a steam iron on a corduroy shirt. Then he slunk under my seat and refused to even look at the chicken I'd brought him.

With a great deal of effort we managed to arrange our guest on the back seat between Wynnell and C. J. and not have her smother them. Fortunately she didn't have any suitcases.

It was a surprisingly brief but pleasant ride from Beckley to New River Gorge. On the way there Susannah regaled us with tales of the famous people who had slept in her sister's inn. Several times C. J. tried to interrupt with tales of Shelby, but Susannah wouldn't have it. She was clearly a one-woman show with a captive audience. C. J., bless her heart, finally gave up.

When we got to the gorge everyone tumbled out except for Susannah. I suppose that was just as well, since getting her resituated would have been too time consuming, but still, I worried for Peggy's sake. The overlook for the gorge is a long way from the parking lot, and we barely knew Susannah. Any woman who can transform herself from a waitress into an unwrapped mummy within minutes is undoubtedly capable of hot-wiring a car.

The gorge was indeed breathtaking and well worth the stop, but needless to say I was relieved to see the white Lincoln Town car right where we had left it. Susannah, however, was gone.

10

There is a small museum with an information desk at New River Gorge, and we did a thorough search of it, including the men's room. The latter was Peggy's idea, as you might have guessed, and totally unnecessary. When Wynnell asked the girl at the information desk if she'd seen someone answering Susannah's description, we were immediately handed a note. Actually it was a length of toilet tissue with a lipstick message in two colors.

"She said to give you this."

I took the paper from her with the tips of two fingernails. "She say anything else?"

"No, but I can tell you what happened. I was just getting off my break when you guys pulled up. I saw the rest of you head to the overlook. Just about a minute later this Jaguar pulls up with this real handsome guy in it. About five minutes later she comes inside, goes into the bathroom, and comes out with that." She pointed to the tissue. "You can bet she rode off with him."

"Do you know which direction they went?"

"South. The Jaguar had Florida plates. You wouldn't believe though some of the things I've seen working this job. Like one time—"

I thanked her politely and reluctantly called the number Susannah had left. I placed the call from a pay phone that had seen better days and the reception left something to be desired.

"PennDutch Inn," a less than cheery voice answered.

"Hello. My name is Abby—"

"Abby Van Buren?" The voice was suddenly ebullient.

"No, Abby Timberlake."

"Ach, I should have thought of that. Just like your sister's real name isn't Ann Landers."

"I don't have a sister, ma'am—"

"That's all right, I understand. There are people around you, right? Believe me, I know all about that. Here at the PennDutch we are used to celebrities. So, Abby, you got my letter?"

I was on the verge of hanging up. The static sounded like someone was running an electric razor over a high school gymnasium microphone. But something—call it gut instinct—told me this woman would somehow figure prominently in the drama that was my life.

"Do you have a sister named Susannah?" I asked.

"Of course. That was in the letter, wasn't it? I tell you Abby, that woman drives me crazy. If I hadn't promised Mama and Papa"—she was drowned out by the static for a few seconds—"so you see, all I can do is take one day at a time."

"That's all anyone can do," I said. "That, and don't sweat the small stuff."

"Ach," she said, "you are so wise."

I am ashamed to admit what happened next. I can assure you it never would have happened if I hadn't been cheated at an auction, had my mother run off to a convent, had my picture found in the wallet of a dead man, and found my underage children boozing it up in their grandma's house. It was the stress that broke this camel's back and made me take advantage of a simple Mennonite woman with a lap full of problems of her own.

"You wouldn't happen to have any vacancies in your inn?" I asked.

"Well, normally—but Dear Abby, of course I'll find a room."

"What are your rates, dear?"

"Ach, for you, nothing."

"I have three friends with me."

"Hmm. Do you mind sharing a room with your staff?"

"No," I said, and hoped that Mama would say an extra prayer for me that night in her cell.

We made good time getting to Bedford, Pennsylvania, but had a devil of a time finding Hernia. Peggy had directions in her guidebook but they were about as clear as tomato soup. That portion of Pennsylvania is traversed by parallel ridges and the roads run *between* them. For some reason—and I do not take responsibility just because I was the navigator—we were always one ridge away from Hernia. When we finally found the town we realized that we had driven through it at least two times already. Apparently we blinked.

So it was well after dark when we pulled into the gravel drive that leads to the inn. The lights on the front porch were burning, and I could see a row of rocking chairs just like at the Cracker Barrel. In each of the tall, narrow windows light bulbs masqueraded as candles. The inn looked cozy and inviting.

"What a dump," Peggy said. "I can't believe people spend hundreds of dollars a night just to sleep in an old farmhouse."

"It's the atmosphere," Wynnell said sleepily.

"Lord have mercy!" C. J. cried. "This looks just like my granny's farm near Shelby."

Peggy craned her neck, studying the cars in the small parking lot. "None of them have California plates. I don't think Brad Pitt is here. Or Tom Selleck either."

I gave her a comforting pat and turned in my seat.

"Now, remember what I told y'all. Susannah's sister—Miss Yoder—thinks I'm you-know-who. Y'all promise not to give me away, right?"

"Right," they chorused. They may as well have been ten-year-olds promising to brush their teeth at camp.

I was understandably nervous as I led my troop up the walk and to the door. I hesitated before ringing the doorbell and just as I got up the nerve, the door swung open and a woman in Amish-looking clothes greeted us.

"Welcome to the PennDutch," she said. "I'm Magdalena Yoder. I'd prefer it if you call me Magdalena."

I gazed up at her with the awe I reserve for those people who extend through several climate zones. But not only was Magdalena tall, she was angular as a geometry problem and sported a nose that would have made an eagle proud. This aquiline proboscis was all the more prominent thanks to her hairstyle, which featured muskrat brown hair pulled severely back from the face and knotted in a bun. And to be perfectly honest, she suffered from a deficit of chin.

Her clothes fit her physiognomy. A plethora of tiny pleats gave structure to her dark blue dress, which fell midway between her ankles and her knees. Her black leather shoes were the kind of lace-up pumps I remember Granny Wiggins wearing when I was a little girl, and which I thought had long gone the way of smelling salts and lavender bath powders. Yet despite this somewhat harsh description, she was not unattractive. Her dark eyes were full of life.

I extended my hand. "Hi. I'm Abby."

The dark eyes flickered. "You really should have a new picture taken, dear. The one in the paper doesn't do you justice."

"Bad hair day," I mumbled.

She nodded and gestured to my friends. "Your staff?"

I sheepishly introduced Wynnell as my personal assistant, Peggy as my chauffeur, and C. J. as my hairdresser. Those were only white lies, mind you, and therefore not prohibited by the Big Ten. Besides, Wynnell has at times brought in my mail and made me tea, and I once allowed C. J. to streak my hair. The Peggy part was, of course, the gospel truth.

If Magdalena saw through our little deception, she didn't let on. She proudly ushered us in and immediately commenced with the fifty-cent tour. She even introduced us to several of the guests, none of whom I recognized— although Peggy later told me that the tall skinny woman with frizzy blond hair was a famous mystery writer. I remembered then having read some of her books, and they were really pretty good.

I must say that I agreed with Peggy's initial assessment. If I'm going to shell out an amount equivalent to my monthly mortgage payment for a single night's lodging, I want some bang for my buck. The PennDutch Inn, however, didn't even pop. It was just as plain as the proprietress. No private Jacuzzis, no big screen TVs. It didn't even have a gym.

But the furniture, now that was another story. I had never seen such a handsome collection of seventeenth- and eighteenth-century pieces outside of a museum. The dining room table in particular caught my eye.

"Oh, *that*," Magdalena said modestly. "That was made by my great-great-grandfather, Jacob the Strong. He made it so large because he had sixteen children."

"Would you ever consider selling it?" Wynnell asked, reaching for her checkbook.

Magdalena laughed, sounding just like the wild turkeys I'd seen on the Discovery Channel. We interpreted her answer as "no."

The room we were given contained one double bed and two army-style cots. Because the trip was my idea, I would have thought the bed—at least half of it—was mine for the taking. My companions, however, had other thoughts. After a lengthy discussion it was decided that

Peggy would get half of the bed as a reward for driving. The other half was to be decided by guessing a number Peggy chose. Alas, young, hearty C. J. was the winner.

For the record, I barely slept a wink, thanks to the sagging cot and the peculiarities of my three roommates. First, Peggy selfishly and unabashedly kept us up late giving herself a facial. Then when we did hit the sack— and I meant that literally—Wynnell's snores made it impossible to fall asleep. A couple of times I actually drifted off, only to be awakened minutes later by muffled screams. C. J., as it happens, suffers from chronic nightmares, and Peggy, bless her heart, is able to muffle someone without waking.

The next morning I stumbled downstairs for breakfast at the last minute. Morning carbohydrates are a must for me. Magdalena had made it very clear the night before that breakfast was a set meal, served at a set hour. Either we showed up in time and ate what was served, or we did without. My three roommates chose to do without.

Magdalena was sitting alone at the massive table. Her outfit was identical—if not the same—to the one she was wearing the night before. The only difference was an organza cap, barely larger than a muffin, that was perched atop her bun.

"Good morning," I said.

"Ach, good morning." She seemed surprised to see me.

"I hope I'm not too late."

"My paying guests have already eaten, but there's still something in the kitchen. Will your staff be joining us?"

I shook my head. "I'm sorry, but they're not morning types."

She rang a little brass bell that was shaped like a plantation belle in a hoop skirt. A few minutes later the kitchen door opened and a short, stocky woman with gray hair and enormous bosoms bustled in bearing a plate piled high with every fried breakfast food imaginable. When she saw me, the portly woman scowled.

Magdalena flashed her a wry smile and turned to me. "This is Freni Hostetler, who is both my cousin and my cook. Freni, this is—"

"Ach, I don't have time to chit-chat, Magdalena." With that the cook plonked the platter of grease on the bare table in front of me, and bustled back to the kitchen.

I ate hungrily of the repast which, because of its fat content, was just about the best food ever to pass these lips. Only Bubba Wong's chicken fried steak with gravy has earned more stars from my palate.

"Well, Abby," Magdalena said when I was almost done, "what are your plans for today?"

I chased some half-congealed butter around with a scrap of French toast. "You mean after I write my morning column?"

"Yah, after that."

"Well, after that I thought I would take a little time off and explore the countryside. After all, man does not live by bread alone—even French toast." I chuckled pleasantly.

Magdalena's dark eyes—which, to my surprise, were blue—bored into me. "Look dear, I may be a simple Mennonite woman, but you can't pull the wool over my eyes. You're no more an advice columnist than I am. You're certainly not Abigail Van Buren!"

My throat constricted. "I'm not?"

"Susannah called late last night to let me know she was on her way to Orlando. She told me how you met, and that I should expect you. Besides, I had my suspicions from the moment I saw you."

"The hair, right?"

"Your face, dear. You're no older than I am, and I've been reading Dear Abby since I was fifteen. I cater to the rich and famous and I can spot a knife job at a hundred paces. Most of my guests have to close their eyes just to open their mouths."

"Must be hard to eat," I said.

She nodded vigorously. "How else do you think that crowd stays so slim?"

"So that's why there's no tablecloth!"

"You're a smart woman, Abby. So don't underestimate me. What is it you're really up to? Who are those three English women with you?"

"English?"

"Ach, that's anyone who isn't Amish or Mennonite."

"They're my friends. We're antique dealers. They came up here to buy old Amish quilts and furniture. I came primarily to do some research on a man named Billy Ray Teschel."

Magdalena frowned. "What kind of research?"

Already I knew better than to try and put one past her. "Let's just say that I was cheated out of a lot of money and this Billy Ray guy may have something to do with it."

"I see."

There was a caginess to her tone that I didn't like. It reminded me of my children's promise not to throw any more wild parties in my absence.

"Do you know this man?"

"No, we've never met."

"But you know of him?"

She shrugged. Her shoulders were so bony they looked like they might pierce the thick, starched fabric of her dress.

"As you know, Hernia is a small town. I went to school with some Teschels, but I don't remember a Billy Ray. Did you look in the phone book?"

"Not yet. There wasn't any in our room. Come to think of it, there wasn't even a phone."

She smiled, and I was struck by how straight her teeth were. "That's my room. I took the phone out when I let you have it. I don't supply my guests with phones. They actually seem to prefer it that way."

"*Your* room?"

She nodded. "That's only because I thought you were Dear Abby, of course—well, that is until I met you. You didn't honestly think I had an empty room?"

"Well, I—"

Magdalena gobbled like one of the turkeys on Discovery Channel did when he discovered the joys of procreation. "I'm booked up solid for three years."

"Did you say three *years*?"

The shrewd eyes were scanned me. "Besides, dear, I don't think you could afford my rooms."

I straightened. "The Den of Antiquity does very well, thank you." I waggled the enormous sapphire. "I am not hurting for money. So, how much does one of your rooms cost per night? *If* one were available, I mean?"

Magdalena named a sum that was equal to the gross national product of at least seven Third World countries, or the cost of three government-made screws, take your pick.

I threw back my shoulders. "We'll stay in Bedford."

"Not this week, dear. It's the Bedford Third Annual All-Star Golf Tournament. You'd have to go all the way to Somerset to get a decent room. That's a forty-five-minute drive." She cocked her head. "Don't people in the Carolinas call ahead for reservations?"

The arch disappeared from my back and I hung my head in shame. We four were not fit to be ambassadors of the South. We should turn in our hoop skirts and drop a vowel from each word.

"On the other hand," Magdalena said slowly, "if you're *really* desperate—"

"We are!"

"Well, there's the Motor Coach Motel on Old Business Route 220. I'll call them for you if you want me to."

"Yes, please. But tell me, why did you give us your room if you had us figured out?"

"Well, I almost didn't. But you looked so pitiful—like something the cat dragged in—"

"Oh, my God!" I shrieked. "Dmitri!"

I knocked over my chair and nearly tipped Magdalena backwards in hers in my haste to get to the door.

11

Dmitri was thirsty, but fine—certainly in far better shape than Peggy's car. Unfortunately I had forgotten to set out his litter tray. Fortunately Magdalena had cleaning supplies and a powerful disinfectant. Dmitri was, of course, thoroughly vexed with me and vowed to stay in a huff for the rest of the trip.

The day went downhill from there. My three roommates were harder to rouse than a teenager the morning after the prom. I had to resort to all the tricks and threats I once used to get my kids off to school, and then some. By the time I got them up, showered, and dressed, I was ready to go back to bed—just not one of Magdalena's beds.

"Now, I've got good news and bad news," I said, eyeing the disarray of clothing and toiletries that only four southern women are capable of producing. "Which do you want to hear first?"

C. J. gave me a "you should know better than to ask" look. "Never tell the bad news first, Abby. My Uncle Remus bought an orchard near Shelby, but he had a devil of a time raising peaches. No matter how much he fertilized his trees, the peaches never grew larger than an egg, and they were always as hard as rocks. Every October the stunted things shriveled up altogether and fell to the ground. Finally Uncle Remus sent a couple

89

of peaches to the County Agricultural Extension for analysis. They sent him back a letter saying that the trees in his orchard weren't even peach trees. Uncle Remus dropped that letter like it was a hot potato and ran out to the orchard and cut every last one of those trees down. Then he read the second half of the letter—" C. J. paused dramatically.

"What did it say?"

"It said 'Congratulations, Mr. Cox. Your pecans were the finest we've ever seen.' "

"Give me a break," I moaned. "Nobody is that stupid."

C. J. nodded vigorously. "Did I ever tell you about my Auntie Agnes?"

"Please," Wynnell begged. "No more Shelby stories until after breakfast."

I shook my head. "She's stopped serving breakfast. The kitchen is closed."

"What do you mean the kitchen is closed?" Peggy hissed.

"This isn't a restaurant, dear," I said. "And anyway, we can pick something up on the way to our new digs."

"Our new digs?"

"That's the good news, dear. Apparently there is some kind of golf tournament going on in the area and rooms are scarce, but Magdalena was able to get us a couple of rooms at the Motor Coach Motel in Bedford."

"So the bad news is we've been kicked out of here?"

I hung my head in shame. "She pegged me for the impostor that I am."

C. J. shook her finger at me. "You were a pecan pretending to be a peach?"

Wynnell, loyal friend that she is, patted my arm. "Well, you'll always be a peach in my book, Abby, and frankly, I'm glad we're moving out. This place is a dump, if you ask me."

I'm not claiming that Magdalena Yoder bugs her own room at the PennDutch, although I wouldn't put it past her. I am merely suggesting that the woman has the hearing of an owl. When we said our thank-yous and good-byes Wynnell was treated to a glare that could have withered the peaches off a real peach tree at fifty paces. C. J. and Peggy were lucky to escape with frowns.

As the others were loading up, Magdalena took me aside. "I've been doing some soul-searching Abby, and there's something I have to tell you."

"You're not a Mennonite woman after all, but an ex-Mafia hit man in a witness relocation plan?"

She blinked. "Ach, you English say the strangest things. I just wanted to warn you to stay clear of the Teschel clan."

"So you do know them!"

"Ach, like I said, not personally. But I've heard *certain* things."

"What kind of things?"

Alas, Magdalena's lips were sealed tighter than a clam at low tide.

The Motor Coach Motel made the PennDutch Inn seem like the Taj Mahal by comparison. Perhaps we should been tipped off by the fact that only the letter "r" remained in the word "Motor," and the "c" was missing from "Coach." Sensible folks would have kept right on driving.

"I didn't drive five hundred miles to stay in the Roach Motel," Wynnell whined.

I turned and flashed her a smile. Then I fished a folded paper out of my bottomless purse and handed it back.

"Magdalena gave me this. It's the inventory of an Amish estate sale that will be held this afternoon at two o'clock. She said hardly any tourists will be there— they'll all be watching the tournament. She's sure there'll be lots of bargains. She'd go to the sale herself, but she has to drive into Pittsburgh to pick up a VIP customer."

Peggy turned off the ignition. "Who?"

"She didn't say, dear. Well—just that normally her guests have to make their own arrangements, but this was somebody really special."

"That's all she said?"

That was indeed all, but with Mama in a convent with nothing better to do than to pray for me, I could afford to embellish the truth a little, couldn't I? Besides, lassitude had kicked in, and I was counting on the moral latitude to perk me up.

"I forget his name," I said. "But she said something about him frolicking naked with coyotes."

"*Dances With Wolves*? You mean Kevin Costner!"

"*You* said it, dear."

"Never dance naked with wolves," C. J. declared pompously. "My granddaddy did that. The next thing you know my Uncles Romulus and Remus were born. Of course granny—"

"C. J.!" Wynnell said sharply.

But the girl was on a roll. If I was going to escape the weird tale of her forbear and his lust for lupines, I had to act fast.

"I'll go check us in," I said, and fled from the car like a rat from a burning corncrib.

The motel's office was darker than my ex-husband's heart, and just as stifling. I was gasping for breath by the time I spotted the round bell with the PLEASE RING ME sign taped across it. I rang it. When there was no response after a reasonable period of time, I banged on it with my fist. Then again and again.

"Hold your horses, lady. I'm right here, for crying out loud."

I peered through the gloom. Sure enough, a little man, not much taller than I, was hobbling slowly towards me. He was as bald as a mushroom, and when he got closer I could see that he didn't have any visible hair—no eyebrows, not even a single eyelash. His smooth visage had the pallor of prepackaged mushrooms that were a few days past their expiration date. The musty odor he exuded, however, reminded me of artichoke dip made with Parmesan cheese.

I smiled warmly. "Hi, my name is Abigail Timberlake and—"

"We don't have any vacancies."

"But surely you must. A Ms. Yoder called and reserved two rooms in my name."

"Just a minute." Mushroom Man turned on a small lamp that was shaped like a belly dancer, with a switch for her navel, and a shade for her veil. "I'll have to check my ledger."

"She called just this morning," I said, trying to be helpful.

Mushroom Man ignored me and opened a giant tome that had ragged pages the color of saffron. Then he licked a pale finger and began slowly tracing it down the columns of names. Each time he came to the end of a page he sighed, and then flipped the page with so much vigor I thought it would rip from its binding. I might have been impressed at the theatricality of his performance, had I not noticed the dates on the upper right corners. The earlier entries were over three years old.

"Ah, here it is," he said. His hairless finger had paused on a mostly blank page. The entry above mine was dated the week before.

"Wonderful," I said. "You have us down for two rooms, right? Two beds in each room?"

His forehead composed itself into a browless frown. "She didn't say nothing about that. All's I can do is give you'nz two rooms with kings. What with the tournament and all."

I breathed a brief prayer of thanksgiving that Peggy didn't snore, scream, or grope in her sleep. If at all possible, I would bunk with her.

"That will do."

He leaned forward, his mouth partly open. The smell of artichoke dip was stronger.

I took a step back. "Yes?" I asked politely.

"You don't have any children or pets along, do you? 'Cause I don't allow those."

I chuckled. "You flatter me, sir. Do I look young enough to have a child with me?"

He slammed the ledger shut, and a dust cloud rose and temporarily veiled the belly dancer. We both sneezed.

"Rooms thirteen and fourteen," he said. "I don't have cable, so don't even ask. You'nz will find a pop machine down by the Exxon station on the corner. But no bringing back food. Is that clear?"

"Yes, sir. Do the rooms have phones?"

He gave me a pained look. "Rooms fifteen and nine then. But you'nz will have to leave a twenty-five-dollar deposit against long-distance charges."

I nodded.

"That's a twenty-five-dollar deposit per room."

I resisted my temptation to argue, but asked to see the rooms. Mushroom Man grumbled, but handed me the keys. Perhaps the Pennsylvania sunshine was too much for him. At any rate, it was just as well that he stayed behind, because Dmitri was stretched out in the rear window of Peggy's town car having a solar bath.

We took the rooms. A cursory inspection had failed to uncover any roaches, the reddish-brown stains on one of the sinks were, we concluded, caused by rusty pipes, and both phones produced dial tones if held upside down. As for the footprints on the ceiling of Room #15—well, what is life without a little mystery?

At the last minute I backed out of the trip to the Amish estate sale. I've had a lot of practice in my time with headaches, both real and imagined. On rare occasions I have even been a headache. At any rate, and at the risk of sounding vain, my headache-faking skills are unsurpassed, and I had the gals thoroughly bamboozled.

"Then I won't go either," Peggy said. "Someone needs to stay behind and keep an eye out on you."

"Then who will drive, dear? You won't let anyone else touch your car."

"We'll all stay," Wynnell said. "One for all, and all for one, right?"

"Ah," C. J. said, "I really wanted to go to this auction. I've been looking at this inventory sheet Ms. Yoder gave Abby and there is some really neat stuff."

"C. J.!" Wynnell said sharply.

I pressed my fingers to my temples. "Please," I moaned. "What I need is a nice long nap, not three nannies hovering over me."

That's all it took. Well—that and allowing them to lead me to the bed, remove my shoes, and close the moldy drapes. They wanted to tuck me in under the covers, but I refused on the grounds that the air conditioner was thermostatically challenged. It was all I could bear just to have Dmitri lying on my chest. When they were satisfied that they had done their best to insure my recovery, they bounced off with glee, images of Amish bargains dancing in their heads.

As soon as Peggy's car cleared the Exxon station I turned the telephone upside down and called all the car rental agencies listed in the Bedford telephone directory. They snickered politely when I inquired about renting a car. Thanks to the tournament, only one had any vehicles left on the lot, and that turned out to be a pink stretch limo.

It was not a hopeless situation, however, because I had noticed a pale yellow car parked behind the motel office that looked like just the sort of car Mushroom Man would drive. Although he was just as difficult to deal with the second time, Mushroom Man knew the value of a dollar, and after I had parted with a few more of those I was the not-so-proud driver of a yellow 1978 Mercury Comet. My new wheels were only slightly less conspicuous than the pink stretch limo, but they were cheaper, and easier to drive on the mountainous roads of central Pennsylvania.

At the risk of making myself sound like a cruel mother, I will confess that before leaving the motel room for the last time, I shut Dmitri up in the closet. This time, however, he had his litter pan, a full dish of food, and plenty of water. He also had a nice thick bed made out of a folded blanket.

"You be quiet," I warned him. "If the Mushroom Man finds you, he'll skin you alive. He eats kitties for supper."

Dmitri purred contentedly.

Yoder's Corner Market was the only place in Hernia that had a public phone, and it was tucked back between a cooler full of head cheese and fresh pig's feet, and a tower built out of fifty-pound sacks of unbleached flour. A hand-lettered sign taped above the phone informed me that the directory was available upon request at the checkout counter.

Sam Yoder, the proprietor, struck me as a very pleasant man. I took him to be about my own age. He was neatly dressed in khaki slacks, a blue-and-white pinstripe shirt with a button-down collar, and a navy blue tie. His most distinguishing feature was his nose, which was identical to Magdalena's.

He caught me stealing a peek at his remarkable proboscis. "It's the Yoder nose," he said.

I blushed, embarrassed to be caught noticing something so personal. "Are you related to Magdalena Yoder?"

He chuckled. "Which one? There are three Magdalena Yoders in Hernia, five in the county altogether."

"Oh, my. Well, the one who owns the PennDutch Inn."

"Actually, I'm related to all of them in some way or another. Virtually all Yoders are descended from a pair of brothers who came to this country in the early seventeen hundreds, but the Magdalena Yoder of which you speak is my first cousin."

I asked to use the phone book. Sam Yoder made an exhaustive search for the book, but came up empty-handed. He shrugged.

"There really is a Hernia phone book—of course it's not much thicker than a comic book—but I have this high-school girl who comes in three afternoons a week. Sometimes things grow legs when she's around, if you know what I mean."

I knew exactly what he meant. Lots of things in the Den of Antiquity grew legs, but they were always more valuable than a telephone book.

"Who are you trying to look up?"

Like I said, he seemed pleasant, the kind of person you just know you can trust. Call it a gut instinct if you will.

"A family by the name of Teschel," I said, trying to sound casual.

A cloud passed over Sam's face. "You related?"

"A very distant cousin," I mumbled. All right, so it was getting easier to lie. But I promised myself that I would adhere rigidly to the truth once I got back to the Carolinas.

"So, you're here for the funeral."

"Yes, the funeral."

Silly me, I hadn't thought about the funeral taking place in Pennsylvania. Billy Ray had died along a North Carolina highway, in bits and pieces. I had just assumed they would bury him there. Maybe in Elkin, the town nearest the accident. I certainly hadn't come prepared to attend a funeral, not that day at any rate. I was wearing a pink and white gingham sundress and white, open-toed sandals.

"Well, it's the cemetery you're looking for then, isn't it? Just keep going down Main Street until you hit Woodlawn Avenue. Make a left, and its only about half a mile. You can't miss it. It's Hernia's only public cemetery."

I was sure it wasn't my imagination. Pleasant Sam

was no longer quite as pleasant. The name Teschel had not struck a happy chord with him. I cast about for something to say. I would probably never see Sam Yoder again, but it was somehow important that he not think ill of me.

"You see, I'm really a *very* distant cousin. I haven't been in touch with the family for years."

"Go on," he said. "The procession passed by here an hour ago. You don't want to miss one of the happiest events in Hernia's history."

12

"I beg your pardon?"

Sam turned and fiddled with a display of breath mints. "Sorry about that. I was out of line."

I waited quietly. It has been my experience that nothing draws words out of angry people quite like silence, and the once-pleasant Sam was obviously very angry.

"Of course you're not a close relative. You said so yourself. And anyway, the truth's the truth."

"That it is."

He faced me again. "You don't even look like a Teschel. That's kind of funny, because they all look the same."

"Kind of like you Yoders?"

"Yeah. Only the Teschels remind me of catfish."

"I shave my whiskers daily."

He smiled. "I meant slippery."

"Oily? Wet?"

"No, it's not how they look so much as it is how they look at you. It's like they have slippery souls. You can see it in their eyes."

I took a deep breath. "I have a confession to make—"

The door to Yoder's Corner Market opened and two women entered. By their dress I judged them to be Amish, or else very conservative Mennonite women.

They looked almost identical enough to be twins, but my guess was that they were mother and daughter. Both women nodded when they saw Sam, but they didn't even pause in the flow of their conversation.

"—and she's not supposed to cook anything salty on account of his gall bladder."

"Are you sure it's his gall bladder? I thought low-salt diets were for hypertension."

"Maybe that's it then. Anyway, I told her to talk to you—"

"Nice meeting you, Mr. Yoder," I said, and slipped out the door.

Sam was right. As long as I turned left on Woodlawn Avenue, I couldn't miss the cemetery. What Sam had neglected to tell me was that Woodlawn Avenue dead-ended into the cemetery which, in fact, was called Woodlawn Cemetery. Wrought-iron letters about three feet high and suspended by a wrought-iron arch, which was in turn supported by two stone pillars, identified the place clearly.

My problem was locating the funeral itself. Wood-lawn certainly lived up to its name, a multitude of ma-ture maples and oaks dotting a vast grassy lawn. It looked more like a park than a burial place. A coarser person than I might even joke that you couldn't see the headstones for the trees.

Much to my relief there appeared to be only one road, which split just inside the gate and looped through the cemetery. A sign directed me to keep to the right, so that's what I did. But I didn't see any mourners, and I certainly didn't see any cars.

Lord knows I've been known to overlook important things before—like Buford's scales and fangs—so I took a second circuit, and that's when I noticed the single woman sitting on a metal folding chair in the shade of a red maple. If it hadn't been for the distinctive color of the tree which attracted my eye, I never would have spotted her.

I parked along the side of the drive and picked my way through a maze of stones. Some were small and hugged the ground, but others were true monuments, marble play houses with stained-glass doors, and topped with chiseled cherubs, or angels armed with swords. The dates on these varied markers spanned almost two hundred years, but they were mixed as thoroughly as a good set of Scrabble tiles. The rich and the poor of Hernia, the young and the old, Woodlawn Cemetery was where they all came together in the end.

The woman saw me coming. She never looked directly at me, but I could feel her monitoring my progress. She straightened, recrossed her legs at the ankles, and folded her hands in her lap. The corners of her mouth prepared themselves for a welcoming smile.

She was older than I, but younger than Mama. I guessed her to be in her mid-sixties, of medium height, perhaps a bit on the heavy side. Unlike Mama, she wore no makeup. Not even a trace of old lipstick. Although her gray hair was worn in a tight, carefree perm, it did little to flatter her full cheeks—jowls, a less charitable person might call them. Her shirtwaist dress was two shades lighter than black, and I had the impression it had become faded through frequent washings. Her sensible shoes were black, but made out of plastic, as was the valise-size purse parked by her chair. A single strand of small pearls was her only adornment, and they were all but lost against her pale skin.

"Welcome," she said. "It was nice of you to come."

I was at a loss for words.

She stood carefully and extended her right hand. "I'm Leona Teschel," she said.

I hesitated, and then reached for her hand, which was waving like a tendril in a gentle breeze. I wondered if she was drunk, or suffering from palsy.

"Hi, I'm Abigail Timberlake." I hadn't meant to divulge my name. At least not so early in my investigation. When I spoke she adjusted her stance and her eyes raised to find mine. I realized with a start that Leona Teschel was blind.

"You a friend of Billy Ray's?" she asked. A milky film covered her blue-gray eyes, but they seemed to be fixed on mine.

"Well, not exactly. I mean—"

"From North Carolina? South?"

A chill ran up my spine. "How did you know?"

"Your accent, child."

For the first time I heard the faint dulcet sound of Carolina in her voice. In a reverse way she reminded me of a neighbor of Mama's who moved to South Carolina from Chicago when she was thirteen. Most of the time Dorothy Mitchell sounds like a native of Rock Hill, but every now and then a strong "r" escapes her transplant lips.

Perhaps I should have been wary of establishing a stronger connection. Since I assumed Leona was Billy Ray's mother, I should have offered her my condolences and left. I wasn't expecting to share a private graveside moment with her. I was, in a nutshell, woefully unrehearsed.

"I'm originally from Rock Hill," I heard myself say. "But I live in Charlotte now."

She smiled broadly. "I'm from Gastonia. I'm sure you know where that is."

I nodded foolishly. "Yes, ma'am."

"And you came all the way up here for Billy Ray's interment?" She said "interment" with the same care I would use in trying on a diamond tiara.

"Yes, ma'am." Okay, so there wasn't even a smidgen of truth to that. But I had very little experience lying to the disabled.

"Mind if I sit?" she asked.

I motioned that it was fine. One of the advantages to being vertically challenged is that I don't feel like a towering idiot when others are sitting. Suddenly I remembered that she couldn't see. "Please. Go ahead."

She sat with a sigh. "I'm sorry I can't offer you a chair. I only brought this one."

"That's all right, Mrs. Teschel. I can't stay long anyway." I slipped off my sandals and let the grass caress my feet. She wasn't going to know the difference. "Excuse me, ma'am, but when exactly will the service be?"

"There won't be no service," she said quietly.

"I see." Of course I didn't.

"My son"—that was the first confirmation I had of their kinship—"didn't want no funeral. And there weren't any need for a burial. He was cremated, you know."

Of course. That made sense. From what Greg described, there wasn't enough of Billy Ray Teschel left to fill a lunch box. It was a miracle that his wallet survived.

"I'm sorry," I said.

"You're the only one who showed up—and you came all the way from Carolina."

"The *only* one?" I didn't mean to sound so dramatic.

"A body doesn't need company to distribute the ashes. There"—she pointed in the general direction of the red maple's trunk—"is where I put him. All around the base of this tree. And I didn't just scatter them ashes either. I interred them."

I said nothing. In the distance a crow cawed.

"In here"—she leaned over and patted the valise—"I brought my gardening tools, you see. I dug little holes, and poured my Billy Ray's cremains into them. Then I covered them. The wind ain't going to blow my Billy Ray around no more."

I glanced at the base of the tree. Sure enough, the grass had been disturbed in spots, but it would have been reasonable to guess that a squirrel had been busy burying nuts.

"You picked a lovely place," I said. "This is a beautiful tree."

"My Artie planted it—Billy's daddy. This is the Teschel family plot. Once there were lots of Teschels hereabouts.''

I looked around. Indeed, the Teschel name seemed to be everywhere.

''But now there is only me,'' she said with a little laugh, ''and I ain't even a Teschel by blood.''

''Blood isn't everything,'' I said.

''You couldn't tell that to a Teschel.'' Tears escaped from the sightless eyes and began slowly tracing their way down and over the ponderous cheeks.

I brushed a cloud of gnats away from my face. ''Mrs. Teschel, how did you get here? I mean to the cemetery. There isn't any car. Did someone drop you off?''

''I took me a taxi.''

I was both saddened and intrigued. ''Hernia has a taxi service?''

She shook her head. ''I called the one in Bedford.''

''How were you going to get home?''

She tilted her chin, temporarily disrupting the flow of tears. ''Walk. I can do it if it's just one way.''

''How about if I give you a ride back?''

She turned her head away. The tears had begun to flow faster.

''That would be mighty nice, Miss Timberlake. Thank you.''

''You're quite welcome.''

''And then maybe you can stay for tea,'' she said.

I rolled my eyes. It was practically an involuntary action. I certainly meant no disrespect. Besides, she couldn't see me, remember?

''That would be lovely,'' I said. Once again I proved that I can get myself into an infinite number of jams.

Mrs. Leona Teschel lived on Eighth Street in a two-bedroom home with white aluminum siding and one scraggly Japanese yew planted by the front door. A six-inch stump was evidence that there had once been a pair. In the side yard, which needed cutting badly, four con-

crete blocks supported the body of a 1962 Chevy Bel
Air. The once blue car—now predominantly rust-
colored—had no doors, and since Mrs. Teschel had no
garage, the former vehicle made a handy, if somewhat
crowded, storage shed. I couldn't help noticing several
mops, a rake, a reel push-mower, and a badly dented
barbecue. Clearly this was not Hernia's high-rent dis-
trict.

My hostess put her folding chair and tools in what
remained of the back seat, and then, carrying the empty
bag, led me up the cracked driveway, along a narrow
sidewalk in even worse condition, and to the front door.
She seemed to know exactly where to put her feet.

"Watch the top step," she said. "It's broke."

"Thank you."

"And be careful not to lean on the railing. It's loose."

We got inside without incident.

Mrs. Teschel set the valise down beside the door.
"Please sit there," she said, pointing directly to a walnut
rocking chair with a worn needlepoint seat. Then she
gestured at the window. "I keep them curtains closed,
because it's cooler this way."

I sat. There was only one other seat in the combina-
tion living-dining room, a dinette chair with an aluminum frame and brown plastic seat and backrest. The
latter sported a long diagonal gash through which the
padding had begun to work its way loose.

"I'll have a jar of sweet tea made in a jiffy," she
said. "Just like in Carolina."

We drank lukewarm sweet tea from Mason jars. In
the background I could hear the refrigerator humming,
so I assumed Mrs. Teschel had electricity. Did she prefer
to drink her tea warm, or had she forgotten to make ice
cubes? Nobody I knew in South or North Carolina drank
their sweet tea at room temperature.

"Tell me about your son," I said. I am not an expert
at comforting bereaved persons, but I understand that

most are actually eager to talk about the departed ones. I know this sounds like self-serving rationalization, but my intentions were good for a change.

"Billy Ray"—her voice trailed—"do you mind if we talk about me?"

"Not at all, dear." I took a sip of tea.

"You see, because what happened to Billy Ray was all my fault."

"The accident?" I asked incredulously.

"Yes, in way. But that was at the end. I want to—no, I need to—start right at the beginning. Can you set for a while?"

I glanced at my watch. The hands were barely visible in the dim light. The auction would undoubtedly last for several more hours. The only one to suffer would be Dmitri.

"You go right on ahead," I said. "I have all the time in the world."

13

Leona Rose Grady came into the world with wide-open eyes that never saw the light of day. She was the first of eleven children born to Patrick Grady, a textile mill worker in Gastonia, North Carolina, and his wife Rose, an inveterate breeder. The ten subsequent children—all boys—were all healthy.

In the Grady family tasks were divided strictly along gender lines. From as far back as she could remember little Leona was expected to help her mother with household chores and care for her little brothers. Leona's blindness was never an issue, certainly never an excuse. By the time she was five, Leona could change diapers (cloth diapers with sharp pins) as well as her mother. By her seventh birthday, Leona could heat up milk without burning herself.

Although Rose Grady excelled at having babies at fourteen-month intervals, she suffered from frequent bouts of severe depression. Three weeks after her eleventh child was born, Rose drove to nearby Crowder's Mountain State Park and threw herself off the Pinnacle. An autopsy revealed that baby number twelve was on its way.

Rose's mother was already dead, so on the day of Rose's funeral, Mawmaw Grady moved in to lend a helping hand. Unfortunately Mawmaw was a heavy drinker who spent the better part of each day sitting with her hands folded in her lap, sleeping off a drunk. Little Rose, who had never been to school, spent her days cleaning up after her grandmother, changing and feeding the little ones, and cooking her father's supper. At night, more often than not, she lay awake listening to her father and his mother fighting. Church was the only thing she looked forward to. At Pentecostal Holiness Church being blind didn't matter. The music and the spirited preachers made life bearable.

Leona managed to care for her siblings, Mawmaw, and her father, who was well on his way to becoming an alcoholic himself, for three more years. On Christmas Eve, when she was fifteen, Leona met Artie Teschel at church. Leona didn't realize at the time that Artie, a native Pennsylvanian who was in town on a construction project, was twenty-eight years her senior. Not that it would have mattered.

Artie began calling on Leona, and although Mawmaw managed to put a stop to his visits, the two found time to be alone. By Valentine's Day Leona was pregnant. The couple believed themselves to be deeply in love, and on one of his sober days Leona's father agreed to sign his consent to their marriage. After leaving the justice of the peace, the two climbed into Artie's brand-new 1962 Chevy Bel Air, and headed north to Pennsylvania. They never looked back.

"You've never been home since?" I asked incredulously.

"This is my home. After I married Artie my family wouldn't have nothin' to do with me. Not my Mawmaw, not my Daddy, not one of my brothers. No, ma'am, this is my home. This is the house me and Artie moved into. This was his Mama's house. 'Course it didn't look this good then. Had wood sides. Artie and me saved a long time for them aluminum sides."

"They're very nice."

She nodded. "Artie's Mama was alive when we first moved in. That woman hated me from the get go. 'The

only thing worse than white trash, is blind white trash,'
she said. After that she wouldn't even speak to me.''

"That's awful!''

Mrs. Teschel leaned forward and I was concerned that
the dinette chair would tip over. "I don't mind telling
you, the day that woman died was the second happiest
day of my life. First was leaving Gastonia, of course.''

"You poor dear.''

She sat back. "Don't you be feeling sorry for me,
child. I've had me a good life. I had my Artie. That man
was pure heaven.''

"And you had Billy Ray.''

She frowned. "Yes. I 'spose that was really the happiest day of my life—the day Billy Ray was born. He
was a piece of Artie that no mama-in-law, no matter how
mean, could take away. But . . .'' Her voice trailed off,

"Yes?''

"Well, things don't always work out now, do they?
The Good Lord gave me Billy Ray, but I kind of just
let him slip through my fingers.''

"What do you mean?''

"There's evil in this world, you know. It's all around
us. Yes, ma'am, the devil and his angels are hard at
work.''

She paused, and I couldn't help swiveling my neck,
hoping to catch a glimpse of the old boy himself.

That woman had the sixth sense. " 'Course we can't
see it, child. There's no use looking with your eyes.
Anyway, my little boy fell into bad company—'' her
voice broke and I waited for her to continue. "It was
my fault, you see. If I'da been a better mama, he
wouldn't be out to Woodlawn now, poked in all them
bitty holes around that tree.''

It was time to step in. "Your son was killed in a car
accident, dear. You were not responsible for that.''

"Yes, ma'am, I was. Billy Ray was up to something
no good the day he died, you can count on that. Now

the Good Lord has seen fit to send him to his judgment,
and leave me with a broken heart.''

I felt terrible. Half of me wanted to give her a hug—
although I was sure she would rebuff me—the other half
wanted to reach down her throat and pull out the truth
about Billy Ray.

"I'm sorry," I said, trying desperately to walk that
fine line between pity and sympathy. "What do you
think your son was up to the day he died?"

She shrugged. "But it weren't anything good. He
went wild after his daddy died. You see, our boy was
only ten when it happened—well, that was my fault too,
on account of I married a man so much older than myself. My little boy—"

"But your husband was still a young man when he
passed," I interjected. "If you don't mind telling me,
how did he die?"

She shook her head. "Heart attack. All them Teschels
have weak hearts. You see, child, if I hadn'ta been born
blind, I coulda married a younger man. Then Billy Ray
coulda had his daddy longer."

"Yes, but then you wouldn't have had your Artie."

"My Artie! First my Artie, now my Billy."

"Are you all alone, Mrs. Teschel? I mean, do you
have anyone else up here? Some of your husband's relatives? Surely they're not all like his mother."

"Ha!" She literally spat on the floor. I was stunned.
I sipped my tea slowly. "Friends?" I asked at last.

"There's my church. They're all the friends and family I need."

"That's wonderful, dear." I wasn't sure I believed
her, but I wanted to. Frankly, I was feeling guilty for
having intruded on her life. I had no proof that Billy
Ray had ever done me any wrong, but alive or dead, he
was a source of intense pain for his mother.

"You a churchgoer?" she asked.

"Christmas and Easter. Weddings and funerals. That
kind of thing."

"You ought to go more."

I agreed. "Which church do you belong to?" I asked pleasantly. On my way back to Bedford I would drive by her church and give her surrogate family a piece of my mind. What kind of friends and family were they to leave her alone on the day she buried her son? Why was not at least the minister at the cemetery, if only to give her comfort? And why were there no casseroles waiting on the step for her return?

"The First and Only True Church of the One and Only Living God of the Tabernacle of Supreme Holiness and Healing and Keeper of the Consecrated Righteousness of the Eternal Flame of Jehovah." She said it in one breath.

"Excuse me?"

"That's the name of my church. It's up by the turnpike, before you get to Bedford. You ought to go."

I promised to think about it, if I was still in the area by Sunday. Then, with guilt nagging at the nucleus of every cell, I bade my farewell.

Sam Yoder of Yoder's Corner Market was the first Hernian to get a piece of my mind. He didn't belong to the church with thirty-three words in its name, but that was beside the point.

"You should be ashamed of yourself," I said, waggling my finger.

He looked genuinely surprised. "I beg your pardon?"

"I was in here earlier this afternoon asking about the Teschel family."

He gave me a once-over which, in my case, doesn't usually take long. "So you were. What about it?"

"What about it?" I nearly shrieked. "You said the funeral procession had just passed your store. You neglected to say that you were making fun of a little old blind lady."

Sam blinked, but it was going to take a hammer and chisel to open those lips.

I put my hands on my hips. It doesn't make me look any taller, but I feel that it gives me extra presence.

"Well?"

I was right. Sam just ignored me, and went about his tasks as a grocer as if I wasn't there. Finally, after he had waited on three customers and set up a display of Blue Lake French-style green beans, he turned to me with a sigh.

"How old are you, miss?"

"That is none of your damn business, sir."

"Well, I'd say you're about my age. Maybe a few years younger. At any rate, you're old enough to know that there are at least two sides to every story."

"What's your point?"

"Leona Teschel tell you hers?"

"She is not responsible for her son's actions. She is certainly not responsible for Billy Ray's death."

Sam gave me a pitying look and I wanted to slap him. "So, she's really been filling your head, has she?"

"Look buster," I said thrusting my chest forward in what I hoped was an aggressive move, "the poor woman has just lost her last relative—well, the last one who counts—so you can treat her with a little more respect."

Sam blinked again. "Did something happen to Tommy Lee that I don't know about?"

I felt like I was having a conversation with one of my children back when they were teenagers. Susan, in particular, was a master at non sequiturs.

"You make about as much sense as a girdle at a dessert bar," I snapped.

"Just because Billy Ray was the boy she doted on, doesn't make her suddenly childless."

I dropped my arms and deflated my chest. Not that you could tell the difference in regards to the latter.

"What are you saying? That there's another son?"

"Bingo. Her oldest. The meanest snake to slither this side of the Garden of Eden."

He couldn't possibly mean my ex-husband. "What did you say his name was?"

"Tommy Lee. I went to school with him—kindergarten through senior high. Our nickname for him was Tommy the Terrible. He made Genghis Khan seem like Miss Manners. We all hated him."

His was such a preposterous tale that I may have snorted. "Next thing I know, you'll be telling me she isn't blind."

"Oh, she's blind, all right. But handicapped people are not necessarily above the law. To put them on a pedestal is its own form of prejudice. That woman is just as mean as her son."

I stopped being a southern lady. "You're crazy."

"Did she tell you how she came to be blind?"

"She was born that way!"

"Right, like a calf is born with horns."

"I don't come from a one-horse town like Hernia. I don't know what that means."

"It's means that Leona Teschel was blinded in an automobile wreck. One that she caused. She was driving drunk."

"Come on!"

"Ask anybody. Ask my cousin, Magdalena."

"You're pathetic, dear. Dissing a blind woman who can't even drive. All right, I'll ask someone. I'll ask all her church friends."

"Her *what*? What church?"

"I don't remember the name—except that it's very long. It's up by the turnpike."

Sam's laugh was as dry as cotton. "Ah, The First and Only True Church etc. Well, you go ahead and ask them. Ask them all about Leona Teschel. They'll give you an earful."

"You're one of the m-meanest m-men I've ever m-met," I stammered. Then I slammed the door to his shop so hard the display of Blue Lake French-style green beans collapsed, sending cans rolling down the narrow aisle.

14

According to Mushroom Man, I returned to the Roach Motel just seconds after my friends picked up their keys. Peggy was busy daubing fluorescent-blue eye shadow above peepers that were already too heavily painted. The woman refurbishes her face several times a day.

"Abby, where were you?" she demanded in a peeved voice.

I let an angry Dmitri out of the closet.

"Well, when I woke up from my nap I felt much better, so I decided to take a little drive. You know, soak in the ambiance of rural Pennsylvania—by daylight, that is."

"Did you rent a car?"

"In a manner of speaking. Our motel manager let me use his. For a price, of course."

Peggy put aside the eye shadow sponge and picked up the largest mascara tube I'd ever seen. There had been ads on TV for that brand lately. A man vaguely resembling Fabio, and dressed only in a leopard skin, comes on and advertises lashes so long and thick, "Tarzan could swing through the trees on them." The claim is only slightly exaggerated. Ever since she's been wearing that brand, Peggy looks like she has dead tarantulas glued to her lids.

"Where did you go?" she asked.

"Nowhere. I mean, I just sort of meandered. How was the sale?"

I had fully expected to be back at the Roach Motel before my friends returned. Now I had to explain my actions to them, as well as apologize to Dmitri. Deflection was my only hope.

Peggy set the monstrous tube down with a thunk. "The sale was a bust."

"So, you didn't buy anything?"

"Oh, I didn't say that. Wynnell and C. J. have already agreed to rent a twelve-foot U-haul to bring the stuff back. C. J. claims she can drive one. Do you think she can?"

"C. J. could probably fly the space shuttle if she put her mind to it. But I thought you said the sale was a bust."

Peggy gave me a look of sympathy. "I was talking about men. They were all Amish, Mennonite, or whatever. They didn't look at me twice."

I bit my tongue. "So, what's on the agenda for tonight?"

"Well, there's this little place we passed on our way in this evening that looks interesting. We thought we'd give that a try. If you agree, of course."

"What's the catch?"

"None—well, the man at the front desk here said that this place hires only waiters. No waitresses."

"I see. What kind of food?" Not that it made a difference. I was famished.

"Chinese."

"Sold to the highest bidder," I said and grabbed my purse.

I fancy myself a connoisseur of Chinese restaurants, although I have been told that coming from the Carolinas I wouldn't know a good wonton from a bad kreplach, or vice versa. Still, I am savvy enough to know that your standard Chinese restaurant does not have an alpine motif, nor does it require its waiters to wear lederhosen. The Fondue Manchu was guilty on both counts.

We were seated at a table alongside a diorama of the Swiss Alps. I do believe it was considered the restaurant's best table. At any rate, I meant to sit next to Wynnell, but I dawdled, spellbound by the dramatic rendition of the Matterhorn with a cluster of chalets at its base, and got stuck sitting next to Peggy. The woman has the table manners of your average teenage boy on a hunting trip. I prayed for a strong stomach—or lockjaw for Peggy.

Hans, our waiter, made several recommendations, which we ignored. Peggy ordered moo shu pork *and* Szechuan chicken with cashews, C. J. ordered sweet and sour shrimp, I asked for Hunan beef, extra hot, and Wynnell, who has always been a baby about trying new dishes, requested two orders of fried rice. Although Hans was friendly enough, he didn't seem particularly charmed by Peggy's flirtatious behavior. To the contrary, he seemed far more interested in the table behind us, which was occupied by men. I stood up, on the pretext of adjusting my skirt, and scanned the place. Except for us, *all* the customers were men.

"You're not going to find a date here," I said to Peggy.

Peggy craned her neck for another, closer look. "Shit! Can't we go some place else?"

"Too late," Wynnell said, as she dipped a shrimp cracker into plum sauce. "We already ordered."

Peggy groaned her bitter disappointment.

"Personally, I rather like it, dear. We can have a nice peaceful dinner, without having to worry if there's broccoli hanging from our teeth, or that we're laughing too loud."

The pair of tarantulas danced. "That's easy for you to say, Abby. You're about to dump the hunkiest man south of Baltimore."

"Who says I am?"

"Oh, please, give me a break! Everybody knows you planned this trip just to tweak his nose."

"Do they now?" I tried kicking Wynnell under the table for backup, but due to the fact that I am vertically challenged, I missed.

"Yes, they do. And I, for one, am beginning to doubt that you ever intended to buy anything. In fact, I'm not even convinced you had a headache this afternoon."

I glared at Peggy. "I told you I got over my headache. What was I supposed to do? Just lie in bed all afternoon watching soap operas?"

"What did you do?" Wynnell asked. Some friend.

"She rented a car and went wandering around the back roads by herself," Peggy said.

C. J. gasped. "Never wander the back roads by yourself. My cousin Alvin did that once. Suddenly he found himself in this little town where everything looked familiar—the churches, the school, the houses, even some of the people. Then he saw this little boy who looked exactly like Alvin when he was about seven years old. Well—"

"Put a lid on it," I said crossly. "I saw that on 'Twilight Zone.' "

C. J. cast me a baleful look. "I swear, Abby, sometimes you're just no fun at all."

"I'm loads of fun, dear. I just happen to be tired and hungry." I glanced at Peggy. "I'm also tired of Twenty Questions."

"Hear, hear," said Wynnell, better late than never.

I smiled encouragingly at her.

"Well, just because I didn't stick to her like glue, Miss Redfern here gave me the third degree."

Peggy colored, although to the unpracticed eye it might have been hard to tell. "I was worried," she said. "I looked up and you and C. J. had taken off some place. I felt uncomfortable sitting there by myself."

"I went to the bathroom, for crying out loud."

C. J. shook her head. "No you didn't."

Wynnell's mouth opened, closed, and opened again. "What?"

"You didn't go to the bathroom, Wynnell. You said you were going to, but then a few minutes after you left, I decided I needed to use it myself." She turned to me. "It wasn't even a real bathroom, but an outhouse." She faced Wynnell. "You weren't there."

Wynnell scowled and the hedgerows meshed. "You were following me?"

C. J. flinched at the accusation. As our junior member she is expected to step out of line more often than the rest of us, but—her colorful stories aside—our respect is very important to her.

"I *wasn't* following you. I had a legitimate need. Besides, like I said, you weren't even there. You were behind the barn talking to a tall man with a red beard."

I raised my eyebrows, but wisely kept my mouth shut.

"Do tell, Wynnell," Peggy said. "And don't leave anything out. We want all the sordid details."

Wynnell stiffened. She was the color of boiled rice.

"I would thank the two of you to mind your own business. Y'all are as nosy as a pack of hounds. You," she said, turning to C. J., "get a life. And you, Peggy, might want to try thinking without your ovaries for a change!"

"Well!" C. J. said, mortally offended.

Peggy smiled, popped a shrimp cracker into her mouth, and commenced to chew loudly.

Hans saved the day by appearing with our dinner. He was one of those marvelously talented waiters who can stack hot dishes up the length of both arms without losing his smile or spilling as much as a drop of sauce. While he was busy placing the meal on the table, I rearranged some of little figures in the alpine diorama. The hausfrau with the watering can hit the ski slopes, and the ski-bunny with the wasp waist got to tend the min-

iature window boxes with the microscopic silk pansies.
Turn about is fair play, after all.

The food was excellent, one of the best Chinese meals
I've ever had. But I have a small stomach—at least
smaller than Peggy's, and I was finished long before the
others. Given the fact that both Wynnell and C. J. had
taken a stab at using chopsticks for the very first time,
it promised to be one of the longest suppers in the history of the Fondue Manchu. Therefore I excused myself
and found a phone in a back hallway near the rest rooms.

I don't claim to be psychic, but upon occasion I have
been known to have nagging feelings that something is
amiss, and sure enough, upon investigation I discover
that someone I love is on the brink of making a terrible
mistake. But come to think of it, since I am the mother
of two young adults, and the daughter of Mozella Wiggins—well, at any rate, the feeling was particularly
strong that evening. I hoped that it was only a reaction
to an overdose of MSG.

I didn't have a phone number for Mama, but the Episcopal Convent of the Good Hope is listed with directory
assistance for Dayton. I called them first.

"Episcopal Convent of the Good Hope, Sister Mary
Martha speaking," a cheery voice said.

"Hello Sister Mary Martha with the cheery voice," I
said. "May I please speak to one of your new recruits?
She's my mother. I don't know her convent name yet,
but her street name is Mozella Wiggins."

"Oh." There was a long silence. "Just a minute,
please."

I heard the sound of someone picking up an extension.

"Mama?" I asked excitedly.

"This is Sister Agnes," a second nun snapped. "Your
mother is unavailable."

My heart raced. "Is something wrong?"

"Wrong?" Sister Agnes barked. "Your mother's always late to chapel and she whistles on the stairs."

"Excuse me?"

"She doesn't follow the rules."

"Mama's always marched to the beat of her own drum," I said. "Anyway, how do you keep a wave upon the sand?"

"I'm afraid your mother has a problem with vanity."

"Oh, no, not the pearls!"

"What pearls? Did you know that underneath her wimple she wears curlers in her hair?"

"At least they're hidden, dear. I can't stand it when women go shopping with a head full of curlers and can't even be bothered to wear a scarf. Frankly, in Mama's case, I don't see that there's a problem."

"Oh, there's a problem, all right, but how do you solve a problem like Mozella?"

"How do you hold a moonbeam in your hand?" I wailed.

"Simply put, your mother is not an asset to the abbey."

Sister Mary Martha got back on the line. "Your mother makes me laugh," she said, and giggled.

Sister Agnes snorted. "Last night she organized a slumber party. She even started a pillow fight."

"We made smores," Sister Mary Martha said. "They were delicious."

"*Please*, let me speak to her," I begged.

"Sorry," Sister Agnes snapped. "Not until Mother Superior has decided what to do about her."

I gasped. "You're not going to punish her, are you?"

Sister Mary Martha giggled again. "Heavens no, but there is this widower in Kettering with seven children who needs a governess. Mother Superior thought your mother might like to give that job a try—just until she decides if being a nun is really what she wants. Say, does Mozella sing?"

"She can't even carry a tune on a portable radio!"

Sister Mary Martha promised to use what little influence she had to return Mama to the arms of her own loving family.

Sister Agnes was more practical. "Are you married?" she had the audacity to ask.

"No," I said warily.

"We could call it a trade—your mother for you."

I told her I was engaged to be married. "But I have this friend named Peggy Redfern," I said wickedly. "She's not even engaged, and she's ten years younger than I. You would get a lot more years of service out of her. She's out of town right now, but I could give you her home number if you wish."

The good sisters thanked me for the offer and promised to say a novena in honor of my upcoming nuptials. If I did indeed back out of marriage to Greg, I was going to owe them big time.

I called Mama's house in Rock Hill on the off chance that one of my offspring would answer the phone. Of course, if somebody did pick up, their ass was going to be grass, as my kids are fond of saying. Needless to say, I was relieved when after twenty rings, no one picked up. It's not that Mama is technologically challenged, but since Donna Reed didn't have an answering machine, why should she?

It was time to disturb the Rob-Bobs at home.

"Speak!" Bob boomed, and I nearly dropped the receiver.

Take my word for it, even though Bob is a Yankee, he has much better manners than that. Something was definitely afoot.

"Bob, this is Abby. What's wrong?"

"Nothing," he bellowed. "Nothing's the hell wrong."

"You and Rob have a fight, dear?"

"He says I'm smothering him. Do you think I am?"

"I think you give him the impression that you're jealous, and Rob doesn't do well with jealousy, dear. Anyway, you have nothing to be jealous of."

He groaned. "But he has it all. A guy would have to be a fool not to want Rob."

"Or straight," I said. "You have to start trusting him. If you don't hold him with open hands, he'll fly away for sure."

That was the same advice Mama gave me when my daughter Susan moved in with a man her first year of college. It was hard advice to follow, but I discovered that with your hands apart, it's much easier to get them around someone's neck. You can't strangle with clenched fists, after all.

"I guess you have a point," Bob said. He sounded about to cry.

"Speaking of the devil, where is Rob?"

"Didn't you hear? Of course not, it just happened."

"*What*?" It had better not be anything to do with my shop. With my kids basically on their own, and Mama requiring only intermittent care, the Den of Antiquity was what kept me going.

"Rob's down in Pineville. You see, Purnell Purvis—"

My sigh of relief blew the snow right off the Matterhorn and on to Peggy's plate. "Figures. Leave it to Rob to hobnob in a hospital. What's he appraising for that grizzly bear now, copies of the crown jewels?"

"That grizzly bear is dead," Bob said dryly. "Rob's down there seeing what he can do to help Jimbo and Skeet. The boys are taking their father's death very hard."

I felt terrible, like I had just eaten a grizzly bear, maybe even a den full of grizzly bears.

"I'm sorry," I said weakly.

Bob, bless his heart, took mercy on my humanity. "Nobody was fond of Purvis, not even Jimbo and Skeet. They were terrified of him. Rob's there helping them make arrangements and sort things out—neither of them are very bright, you know—he's there to give them comfort."

"Just the same, I shouldn't have said what I did."

"Well, you might want to watch what you say around the major."

"Oh, Lord, what's that man up to now?"

"I'm afraid our Major Calloway is fond of spreading rumors."

It was my turn to show a little mercy. "Don't let him get to you, dear. The old goat—I mean, the major—disapproves of everyone."

"The rumors weren't about me, Abby. They were about you."

"*What*?"

"He's going around telling people that he finds it a little strange that you took off for Pennsylvania the day after Purvis collapsed in front of your shop. He says that you paid Purvis a secret visit in the hospital that night. Of course that part isn't true, is it?"

I was so angry that C. J.'s relatives down in Shelby heard my expletives. At least she claims they did.

"I told him that was nonsense," Bob boomed, eager to defend himself.

"Well, you can tell him—never mind, I'll tell him myself!"

I hung up and dialed the major's house.

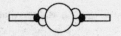

15

"You can call him back from our room," Peggy said, and took her hand off the steering wheel long enough to pat my arm.

"Ah, but I want to hear what she says," C. J. whined. "When our Abby gets started, she can really dish it out."

"Hush," Wynnell said. "Isn't anyone else's face burning with shame?"

"You mean because they kicked us out? Naw, I've been kicked out of restaurants tons of times. There's not a restaurant in Shelby that hasn't shown me the door." C. J. sounded proud.

"We weren't kicked out," I snapped. "It was time to leave. Y'all had already paid the check, for Pete's sake."

"That Hans can kick me out any time," Peggy drooled. "His hands are so strong!"

"Give it a rest, dear," I said. "You're not his type."

Peggy jerked the wheel to the left and then overcompensated to the right. Meanwhile the rest of us tried to keep up with our dinners.

"Never put anything past a Redfern," she said. "Besides, my fortune cookie said that I would soon take the big plunge. Did you get a close look at Hans's pants?"

"You have a dirty mind," I said. "The slip in my cookie just said 'Peace is a desired state of mind.' That isn't even a fortune, is it?"

"Ha," Wynnell humphed, "my fortune was in German. For all I know, it really was a curse."

C. J. bounced in the back seat with excitement. "Ooh, something like that happened to me once when I was visiting Granny Cox. I found this little slip of paper in my bowl of chili that warned me not to eat any, or I was going to get very sick."

"Did you eat any?" I asked needlessly.

"Just a few bites. I couldn't hurt Granny's feelings after all."

"And?" we chorused.

"Well, I got sick all right, but it wasn't Granny's fault. She had just got herself that new pair of seamless bifocals, and was having trouble adjusting. Of course, she ought to know better than to keep the ant bait up there on her spice shelf. If it hadn't been for that label falling into the pot, the doctor wouldn't have known what to give me for an antidote." She guffawed with pleasure. "*Ant*idote, get it?"

We groaned, as much from C. J.'s pun as Peggy's driving.

"You drive like there's no tomorrow," I said to Peggy.

She seemed to take it as a compliment and smiled.

"Speaking of which, what are we doing tomorrow?" Wynnell asked.

C. J. and Peggy didn't seem to have any ideas.

"How about you, Abby? What do you want to do?"

I grabbed a Triple A road map from a slot in the door and fanned myself. It was suddenly ten degrees hotter in the car.

"Y'all seemed to have such good luck at the auction today," I said as casually as I could. "Looks like I need to do some catching up. I thought I'd rent that old wreck from the Mushroom Man again, and hit some sales. What about y'all?"

"Oh, there aren't any sales tomorrow, Abby," Wynnell said. "Not any public auctions, if that's what you mean."

"How do you know, dear?" I asked frostily. Believe me, it is hard to sound frosty when you're forty-eight and flirting with your first hot flash. All right, so maybe it was just the Hunan beef. Southern ladies don't sweat, they merely "dew," but I was suddenly as damp as a boarding house bath mat on Saturday night.

"Red told me—" she caught herself.

"Aha!" C. J. squealed. "You see, she really was talking to a man with a red beard."

"Shut up!"

I turned and gave my best friend a gentle, disapproving look.

The hedgerows meshed, but good breeding prevailed. "All right! I'm sorry, C. J., but sometimes you go too far."

"Hey, no problem."

Wynnell, a true lady, couldn't leave it alone. "I heard about a quilt show in a town called Somerset. It's less than an hour away, but you have to go through one of the longest tunnels in America. You could go with me to that. Maybe Peggy would like to drive."

C. J., a southern lady-in-the-making, graciously accepted the invitation.

"How about it, Peggy?" Wynnell asked politely, her p's and q's clearly in order again. "We'd love to have you along."

Peggy thought driving through tunnels was a hoot. "I'm game," she said, not seeming to mind that she was an afterthought.

"Abby?"

"Thanks, but no thanks. I'm not terribly fond of tunnels."

"You didn't mind the tunnels on the way here," C. J. said.

"They were shorter," I said in a tone that defied her to argue further.

When we piled out at the Roach Motel, I was feeling like the odd woman out. Granted, I did want time to myself the following day, but at the same time, I wanted my friends to be devastated at the prospect of not sharing the day with me.

My ambivalence turned to pure irritation when the major refused to answer his phone. I must have called fifty times, and since the phones in the deluxe suite at the Roach Motel did not have a redial feature, that was a lot of lying on my back. In the meantime an oblivious Peggy chain-smoked and ate pork rinds while she watched sitcoms on the fuzzy black and white TV. I finally fell asleep with Dmitri on my chest, his paw perilously close to my mouth.

The gals got an early start, and as soon as I was alone I dialed the major's shop. It had occurred to me in the middle of the night that a career officer might prefer to bivouac in the field, so to speak, than spend a night in a house under siege. Sure enough, he picked up on the first ring.

"Major Calloway's Antique Gun Emporium," he said as cheerfully as only a Brit could at that hour of the morning.

"Don't even think about hanging up," I snarled. Rest assured that it was a ladylike snarl.

"I don't have to talk to you," he said, but didn't hang up.

"But I *do* have to talk to you."

"Make it snappy then, because I open up in a few minutes."

I glanced at Peggy's travel alarm. Pennsylvania and North Carolina are in the same time zone, and unless my roommate reset her clock, it was an hour and a half until his opening time.

"I know we've had our differences," I said pleasantly, "but I'm hoping we can at least temporarily set them aside. I mean, now that one of our own has . . ."

I allowed my voice to trail only because I was uncomfortable using the "d" word, and passed away seemed too transient. After all, folks who merely passed away might take it into their heads to pass back into the scene again.

"What?" the major demanded. "You mean murdered, don't you?"

"He *was?*"

"You tell me. You were with him when he collapsed. What did you do, slip some poison in his tea?"

"Purvis wasn't much for tea," I said. It took every ounce of willpower I had to choke back what was pushing to come through my lips. Mama has often said that honey will catch more flies than vinegar.

"You know what I mean. How could you do it, Abigail? His Auction Barn was the best thing we Charlotte dealers had going for us."

That did it. It was time to whip out the cruet of vinegar. What did I want with a fly collection anyway?

"You imbecilic blockhead! For the last time, I *didn't* do it! And if you persist in spreading rumors that I did, I'm going to sue for defamation of character. I know a lawyer with both fins and scales, and by the time he's through with you, you'll be wishing you had O. J. Simpson's bank account."

I hung up feeling much better. It was true about the lawyer. Buford wouldn't bother to spit at me if I was on fire *unless* the outcome somehow affected our children. Their good name—in this case his, as well—was sure to motivate him to come to my defense. With Timberlake the Timber Snake on my side, there was no chance of losing.

Mushroom Man tried to put a damper on my revived spirits by claiming his car was no longer available for hire. Then he did an about face and demanded double the rate he'd charged the day before. I would have argued with him—on principle, mind you—but as we were negotiating I glanced through the window and happened to notice a taxi pull up. The two men who emerged from the back seat were not on good terms with the driver, nor were they on good terms with each other. They were television journalists, judging by the mound of equipment that emerged from the trunk, but they were clearly from different networks. Things must be heating up in the Bedford Open.

I decided that Dmitri would play Watson to my Holmes that day. Leaving him locked in a closet for a few hours was one thing, but imprisoning him for the entire day was out of the question. Besides, there was a remote possibility that the Roach Motel had maid service, in which case he would be discovered, and we would both be thrown out on the street. There was nothing he could do to the Mushroom Man's car, however, that would lead to his detection. A few thoughtfully placed scratches on the upholstery might actually improve the thing.

The First and Only True Church of the One and Only Living God of the Tabernacle of Supreme Holiness and Healing and Keeper of the Consecrated Righteousness of the Eternal Flame of Jehovah is actually closer to Bedford than it is to Hernia, but the latter claims it. With a name like Hernia, what is there to lose?

I drove past the church three times before I found it, a small, white clapboard building next to a sorry-looking trailer. The ambitious name was painted on a plywood sign above the door, but the letters were necessarily small. When I was growing up in Rock Hill I had friends with play houses larger than this house of God.

There was no proper parking lot, but the bare and rutted ground under a large oak next to the highway seemed to be the preferred spot. I parked in the shade of the oak and rolled up my window, leaving a crack two inches wide.

"You be a good boy," I said to Dmitri. "Mama will be back in just a few minutes." And then, being the

good mama that I am, I opened the cellophane packet
of catnip that I'd bought at the Giant Eagle in Bedford,
along with two lemon-filled donuts, and sprinkled a
pinch of the dried leaves along the back seat. As Dmitri
rolled in ecstasy, I made my getaway.

I was surprised, but of course pleased, to find the
church door ajar. I stepped inside the small, windowless
building. There were eight short pews divided evenly
along an aisle so narrow the offering plate could be
passed back and forth without anyone having to get up.
Three bare light bulbs hung in a row above the aisle.

I glanced around, but didn't see a consecrated flame.
There wasn't even a cross of any kind. It was the
plainest church I'd ever been in. In fact, the pulpit was
a sturdy office desk set on concrete blocks.

"Welcome, sister!"

My jump qualified me for the Guinness Book of
World Records, at least in the category of women four-
foot-nine and under.

"Holy shit!" I said. Please understand that I seldom
swear, and never in a church.

"Guard your tongue, sister."

I stared at the man, who had risen like a phoenix
between the pews. He looked like an upended mop in
khaki work clothes. Beneath the full head of yellow gray
hair was a face too narrow to be contained by prison
bars. It was a grizzled face, and the part not covered by
yellow gray stubble was heavily lined. I took him to be
at least fifty, although I may have been well off the
mark. As Buford would say, the man in tan looked like
he had been rode hard and put away wet. At any rate,
he was holding a bottle of Murphy's Oil Soap in one
hand, and a wad of paper towels in the other.

Meanwhile, I could feel his eyes appraising me. I was
wearing white cotton slacks, a red-and-white-striped
tank top, and white open-toed sandals. I knew instinctively that he did not approve. Perhaps it was because it
was not yet Memorial Day.

"Is the reverend here?" I asked between gasps.

"We have no titles here. All have been ordained by the eternal flame of Jehovah and are equal in the sight of the Lord."

"Well, is there at least someone in charge?"

He dropped the paper towels and held out his hand. "That would be me. Richard Nixon."

"You're kidding, right?"

"No ma'am." His tone made it clear that Richard Nixon never kidded. "You may call me brother, if you like, but it isn't my title. We are all brothers and sisters in the Lord."

"Abigail Timberlake," I said and took his hand. My greased palm was the price of diplomacy.

He motioned me to sit. I chose the pew directly across the aisle from him. He sat turned, facing me, but I chose to face the makeshift pulpit. I felt like I was about to make confession.

"What can I do for you, Miss Timberlake?"

"I came to see you about one of your parishioners," I said.

He looked confused.

"One of your members."

"Which one?"

"Her name is Leona Teschel."

"Ah."

"Do you know her?"

"The woman is a saint."

"Is she, now?"

He waved his bean pole arms, knocking a roll of paper towels to the floor. It rolled beneath the bench in front.

"The Lord gives, but Leona Teschel is his earthly agent."

"She is?"

He waved his arms again. "This is all her doing," he said.

"I see."

"You ought to see the Sunday School rooms out back. They're real swanky."

Sunday School rooms? Had he meant the green mobile home with the dented side and the sagging steps just outside? I realized with a start that Richard Nixon was being sarcastic. "So, how do you *really* feel about Leona Teschel?"

He was on his feet in less time than it took Buford to have sex. "She's the spawn of Satan!"

"Please don't mince words."

Richard Nixon pounded the bench back with the bottle of Murphy's Oil. "This used to be a thriving little church, Miss Timberlake. Sixty-five baptized members, believe it or not."

I tried to imagine sixty-five people crammed in that little space. Maybe, if they were built like me. Or children.

"Go on," I urged gently.

"We were growing by leaps and bounds. We had plans for a larger building. We had a property picked out right in the center of town."

"Bedford?"

His face got even narrower. "Hernia, of course. Bedford is a den of iniquity."

"Please, continue."

Brother Nixon slid back into the pew. "Anyway, sister, Leona Teschel was one of our more well-to-do members—"

"Leona?"

"Sister, do you want to hear the story or not?"

"Every word, brother."

"I'm afraid it's not a very pretty story."

I leaned back against a hard, but well-polished bench. "Shoot."

16

Richard Nixon ran his free hand through the graying thatch on his head. His hair was so thick it hardly looked real.

"Even with the good offerings we were taking in, it was going to take us a while to get up that kind of money. None of us had any experience in fund-raising, you see. Then along comes Leona Teschel. You could see right away that the woman had money—drove this big fancy car and all. Then I learn that her husband was the owner of Bedford Tool and Die Company.

"Call it greed, sister, 'cause that's what it was. When Leona Teschel offered to invest our savings in her husband's company, I jumped at it. Of course the Elders had to go along with it too, but it seemed like a sure thing. You see, the Bedford Tool and Die Company was expanding, on account of an automobile plant that was planning to start up in Somerset. Leona had a newspaper clipping telling all about the start up—it was some German company, I think. The article said the plant would bring four thousand jobs to Somerset, and that the support industries, like tool and die companies, were going to profit big time.

"Well, sister, we took a vote and it was unanimous. It was like the good Lord was deciding for us. We turned over every cent we had to Leona Teschel and her husband's tool company. Eighteen percent return, they said.

We couldn't get anything like that from a bank, you know."

"Of course not."

"But the Bible warns us about greed, sister, and it warns us about the likes of the Teschels. They took our money, but the automobile plant never moved to Somerset. Bedford Tool and Die Company, which had already started their expansion, suddenly went broke. We lost it all."

It was hot in that cubbyhole of a church and he was sweating. He picked up the discarded paper towels and wiped his face. Bits of shredded paper towel clung to the stubble.

"But it wasn't just the money we lost, sister. We lost the confidence of the people. The flock. One by one they quit and joined the big churches in Hernia and Bedford."

"How many sheep did you lose?" I asked politely.

He picked a scrap of paper off his chin. "We have eleven left, sister. Not counting me."

I gave him an encouraging smile. "With you that makes twelve. That's exactly how many Jesus had."

"Jesus didn't have a mortgage, sister."

It was hard to imagine that this church did either. At least not much of one. Then again, financial burdens were relative.

"I'm sorry about what happened to your congregation, sir. But small businesses fold all the time. Surely you knew it was risky."

"Just because I'm a believer, doesn't mean I'm not stupid. You didn't see the charts and graphs. She even had blueprints of the proposed expansion. But it was all a lie, all part of a con job. There never even was a automobile company interested in Somerset. Bedford Tool and Die never planned to go through with their expansion. Word has it that Artie Teschel needed to pay off gambling debts. Although apparently our money wasn't enough, because he went bankrupt anyway."

"Couldn't you sue to get your money back?" Buford, for one, would never handle a case that small.

Richard Nixon hung his head. "We didn't see a need to sign anything. Sister Leona—Leona," he corrected himself, "was a fully baptized member in good standing. Anyway, it was our word against hers."

We sat in silence for a few minutes. He had painted a very different picture of Leona Teschel, and despite his unfortunate name, I found him easy to believe.

"Is she really blind?" I asked at last.

He nodded. "Legally blind. I think she has limited vision in one eye."

"Well, for what it's worth, she's had a hard row to hoe. I can't imagine what it would be like going through life with a handicap like that. Who knows, if I had been born blind—"

"*Born* blind?" He was sitting bolt upright. "Is that what she told you?"

I recounted Leona's biography for him. He shook his head throughout, his small mouth closing and opening in stifled protest. I was reminded of Charlie's guppies when he forgets to change the water in their bowl. When I was through, Brother Nixon took a couple of deep, gasping breaths, not unlike the guppies do just before they go belly up.

"Are you all right?" I stood, not knowing what to do. I was really going to have to learn CPR, either that or stop causing the men around me to hyperventilate.

He waved me to sit again.

"Leona Teschel was not born blind! She could see perfectly well the first time she walked through that door. The last time she walked through it too, come to think of it. No, sister, Leona Teschel brought her blindness on herself."

"She did it to herself?"

"Car accident. Leona Teschel was driving drunk as a skunk the night she plowed into Sam Yoder's car."

"The same Sam Yoder who owns the corner grocery?"

"The same. Leona ran the stop sign on Hershberger Road. Sam's daughter Rebecca was killed instantly. Leona took glass shards in both eyes and broke a rib or two. Her husband Artie wasn't so lucky—or maybe he was, depending on how you look at it. He died before the Hernia Volunteer Rescue Squad could get him to the hospital in Bedford."

I was stunned. No wonder Sam Yoder detested the woman.

"She told me her husband died of a heart attack," I said.

"He did. Indirectly. Apparently he had a weak heart, and if it hadn't been for that, he would have survived the accident. There wasn't a scratch on him."

"I see."

"Leona Teschel was convicted for vehicular manslaughter and sentenced to eight years in prison. She served eighteen months. Got out on good behavior. Ha!"

I shook my head. "There is no justice."

"Sam Yoder sued the Teschels and won. Won big time. But he turned around and donated all that money to MADD. People said he was a saint for doing that, but he should have given some of that money to us. To the church, I mean. That's where some of it came from, didn't it?"

"Perhaps he didn't know."

"I told him."

"You didn't have proof," I reminded Brother Nixon.

He stood and stretched. On tiptoes he might have been able to touch the ceiling.

"You never did tell me why you're interested in Leona Teschel," he said.

If I could have just three wishes—personal ones, mind you, not noble things like world peace and food and shelter for the homeless—they would have to be three inches added to my height, a chance to kiss Joey Anderson, my senior prom king, and the ability to lie like my children.

Susan and Charlie can spin seamless stories at the drop of a hat. It is only through luck and the occasional flash of intuition that I am able to breach their fortresses of falsehood, and then my work has only just begun. To get down to the *real* truth, I have to peel them like onions. Layer upon layer of protective outer lies must give way before the facts are exposed, by which time my children have forgotten why they are in trouble, and I am too exhausted to pursue the matter further.

I would like to have told Richard Nixon that I worked for the IRS and was investigating Leona Teschel's tax history. It would have been gratifying to tell him that she was facing a twenty-year sentence for cheating Uncle Sam. A really clever Abigail would have concocted a story in which the Department of Commerce, working in conjunction with the Bedford County Better Business Bureau, was just minutes away from arresting Leona Teschel for fraud.

"It has to do with her son, Billy Ray," I said.

He stiffened. "You a friend of Billy Ray?"

"No. I never met him."

Daddy Long Legs relaxed. "I didn't think so. You're not from around here, are you? I can tell by your accent."

"I'm from the Carolinas. I never heard of Billy Ray until a couple of days ago. For some reason, however, he died with my engagement announcement in his wallet. I find that strange, to say the least."

"Nothing surprises me about the Teschels."

"Is it true Leona has another son? One named Tommy Lee?"

His face darkened, as discernibly as if the lights in the small church had flickered, or the door had blown shut.

"Well?"

"You want to stay away from Tommy Lee," he said quietly. "The good Lord help you if you don't."

"I'm not afraid of a two-bit punk who is such a jerk he doesn't attend his own brother's interment," I said, perhaps a bit brashly.

Brother Nixon glanced at the door and then back to me. "Just the same, that man could give Beelzebub a run for his money."

"Do you know where I could find him? He isn't listed in the phone book."

The narrow shoulders approximated a shrug. "If he's dead, he's in hell. If he's alive, he's on his way there."

"I take it then that you either don't know where he is, or else you're not saying?"

Brother Nixon retrieved the roll of paper towels from the floor. With a grunt he unscrewed the cap from the bottle of Murphy's Oil Soap and resumed polishing.

When I set off to peel Leona's onion, I was already in a foul mood. It didn't improve my mood to discover that I had Murphy Oil stains on the back of my white cotton slacks. I had to either backtrack to Bedford and change at the motel, or find some place in Hernia that sold club soda, that all-time favorite when it comes to removing stains. Since Sam Yoder's Corner Market was the only place in Hernia likely to carry the product, and I was not yet ready to see him and offer my apologies, I reluctantly I headed towards town. Surely, I reasoned, I would find some place that sold club soda before I got all the way back to the Roach Motel.

I stopped at every establishment that was likely to sell club soda, but for some reason, every place was sold out.

"It's the golfers," a sixteen-year-old sales clerk told me. "They soak their balls in it."

I nodded solemnly. Buford only played tennis, but he had some pretty peculiar hygiene rituals of his own.

Just outside Bedford, however, my luck turned, and I

found a Mini-Mart that not only sold club soda, but had a special going on Mighty Mousers' Cream of Liver Pate, Dmitri's favorite brand and flavor of cat food. I suppressed a squeal of delight. In my haste to pack, I had forgotten to throw in a few cans, and my fussy feline had been turning his pug nose up at the substitutions I'd been offering him. I grabbed a shopping basket and filled it with a dozen cans of cat food, a two-liter bottle of club soda, a twelve-ounce can of root beer, a loaf of bread and a jar of extra chunky peanut butter, a can of Beanie Weanies, and a bag of plastic tableware. In case you have yet to guess, the last four items were to be my lunch.

The clerk at the Mini-Mart was the nosiest woman I'd ever met—with the possible exception of my Aunt Marilyn. She couldn't take her eyes off me. When she took the bottle of soda from me, she asked to see my driver's license.

"Very funny," I said. "Besides, the only part of me under twenty-one is the crown on my upper right molar."

"You're not from around here, are you?"

"No, ma'am." I reached for my wallet.

"You don't have a sister named Adrienne, do you?"

"No, ma'am."

"Wow," she said.

"What's the quickest way back to Hernia, dear?"

"Hernia—wow," she shook her head. "This is really weird. Who do you know in Hernia?"

"A couple of people," I snapped.

"Who?"

I plonked the correct sum on the counter and told her to can the inquisition. Then while Watson chowed down I repaired to the ladies room and tackled the oil stains on my slacks. I may as well have been giving Lady MacBeth's hands a good scrub. Finally I wised up and drank what remained of the club soda. In a couple of days the citizens of Bedford County were never going to see me again, or if they did, it would be in my shop as tourists. Then they would be the ones with the wrinkles and stains.

Having come to my senses, I stood with my fanny to the sun while I placed a call on the phone outside the Mini-Mart.

"The Finer Things Antiques," Rob said with remarkable cheerfulness.

"This is Abby, dear. It's sounds like everything's coming up roses."

"Bob's decided to go to Charleston next week on a buying trip," he whispered. "He'll be gone three days. Just imagine, three whole days without those jealous eyes following me around accusingly."

"Y'all need to see a relationship counselor," I said, somewhat sanctimoniously. Who was I to talk? Buford and I had both refused to see one; he hated the idea of paying someone by the hour just to talk, and by the time I realized we needed one, it was clear that Buford had already done the deed with titillating Tweetie.

Rob sighed. "Now you sound like Bob. Space—that's all I need. Maybe we'll both get some much needed perspective."

"Be careful. There are a lot of cute guys in Charleston, dear. Bob might get snapped up by one of them and never come back. Then how would you feel?"

"Uh—well, I mean, you don't really think that something like that could happen, do you?"

"Absolutely. Bob may be average in the looks department," I said generously, "but face it, dear, he's got that voice that could calm the Bosphorus Straits. Throw in his intelligence and charming wit—"

"Bob, witty?"

"It's a dry, sophisticated wit. Just the kind to appeal to those cultivated Charlestonians."

"Hmm."

"And creative! Who else do you know comes up with recipes like emu enchiladas?"

"Hopefully no one," Rob said and laughed.

"So, how did it go with Purvis's sons? Skeet and Jimbo doing all right?"

"Skeet says he's doing fine, now that he's got religion. Jimbo's taking it pretty hard. I think he's been drinking. Both boys want to sell the place. They have a couple of interested buyers already."

"Oh, no!"

"Oh, yes. They want to build a miniature golf course down at Myrtle Beach."

"But that's stupid. Myrtle Beach has more miniature golf courses per capita than Russia has toilets. Can't you talk them out of it?"

"So far no luck. Who knows, maybe whoever buys the Auction Barn will want to keep it that way. But frankly, Abby, rumor is that it will be turned into another strip mall—you know, a party supply store, a quick copy shop, and a Chinese takeout."

"Civilization as we know it in Charlotte has ended," I said bitterly. "Without our Monday morning auctions, what is there to live for? I may as well stay up here in Pennsylvania."

"Seriously, Abby, maybe you should. At least for a week or two."

"What? I was just being melodramatic, for Pete's sake."

"Well—and I was hoping I wouldn't have to tell you this—that damn Major Calloway has been opening his big mouth in all the wrong places."

I felt a chill go up my backside. It was either a premonition, or the club soda had begun to evaporate.

"Tell it to me straight, dear. I can take it."

"This morning, less than an hour ago in fact, an investigator from the Charlotte/Mecklenburg County police department stopped by. She asked questions about you."

"Lord have mercy," I said, and gripped the phone

box with my left hand to steady myself. "What kind of questions?"

"You know, the usual. How long had we known you. Did we hear anything suspicious that morning."

"We lied through our teeth, Abby. We told her you were a saint."

"This isn't funny!"

"You're right. Sorry. Seriously, we told her that we hadn't heard anything, that you're above suspicion, and that the major is a crackpot."

"Do you think she believed you?"

"I don't know. I sure hope so, because it gets even worse, I'm afraid."

I leaned against the phone box. "Shoot. Out with it."

"The major was right about one thing. Old Purvis did not die of natural causes. He was poisoned."

17

"What? I didn't do it!" I screamed. Fortunately there was no one else in the parking lot, although I could tell by the clerk's reaction that she heard me.

"Of course you didn't," Rob said calmly, "and she wasn't accusing you, she was just asking questions. Still, it might be better for you to lay low for a while."

It was all so hard to take in. Why would anyone want to kill Purnell? He was a crotchety miser we all loved to hate, but we all depended on him as well. Perhaps it was connected with the William Cripps. Come to think of it, Billy Ray had an ad for silver in his wallet. Maybe he was the one who sold my silver to Purvis and then . . . my mind was getting ahead of my mouth.

"Did she come right out and say that it was poison?"

"No, not in so many words. You date an investigator, Abby. You know how cagey they can be about official business."

"You're not telling me everything!" I shouted. "An investigator is not going to just drop hints about poison. Not if they're being cagey, like you said. You heard it from someone else, didn't you!"

The clerk had left her post and was staring at me through the window.

"All right, I'll tell you, but you have to swear you won't tell a living soul."

"You have my word."

"Say it like you really mean it."

"I swear on Buford's life."

"I'm not kidding, Abby. This is serious. I've broken a confidence as it is."

"I gave you my solemn promise," I said angrily.

He sighed. "Let's just say a friend of a friend did the autopsy. He said Purvis died from pulmonary edema."

"Come again?"

"Fluid in the lungs."

"Apparently he ingested a chemical called dimethyl sulfate. It's a colorless, odorless, somewhat oily liquid that is used in manufacturing dyes. Anyway, it's extremely toxic, especially if combined with alcohol. My guess is that someone slipped it into—"

"His Pernod!"

"You got it."

"But he didn't have his flask with him when he came to see me. Although I suppose he could have left it in his car."

"That's the thing. Dimethyl sulfate has a delayed reaction time. Sometimes up to twelve hours."

"Which means I couldn't have done it," I crowed. "Not since he collapsed right away."

"Unless—"

"Unless what?" I shrieked.

The nosy clerk rapped on the window and in a moment of childish weakness I stuck my tongue out at her. It is hard to be a southern lady in a Yankee parking lot, drying your buns in the sun, while someone eight hundred miles away is insinuating that you are guilty of murder.

"Unless," Rob said, his voice suddenly testy, "you paid him a visit the night before."

I slammed the phone back into its cradle and strode righteously away, my head held high. Unfortunately one of my strides brought my right foot down in the middle of an oil slick, and I hit the pavement like a ninety-eight-pound sack of potatoes. I wasn't hurt—except for my pride—but my backside now resembled a Rorschach inkblot test. My cotton slacks were the perfect blotter, and there was no point even trying to get the foul stuff off.

"The heck with it," I said, or something perhaps a little stronger than that. The way my luck was going there would be several more patterns to add before the day was through. Perhaps in some weird twist of fate, a New York art dealer, vacationing in Pennsylvania Dutch Country, would spot my mottled tush and offer me a million bucks for my britches. Let C. J. try and top that!

My fantasies sustained me, so I was practically purring when I rejoined a sated Dmitri in my rented rattletrap. The cat hair that stuck to the grease and Murphy's Oil Soap added just the right amount of texture. And believe me, the Mushroom Man's car was none the worse for the wear.

There was a sleek new car parked in Leona's driveway. It was one of those trendy dark green shades billed variously as burnt emerald, unripe eggplant, singed moss, you get the picture. My initial reaction was joy that someone—perhaps from the church—had chosen to visit the helpless old woman. Then I remembered that the helpless old woman was in fact a con woman and a convicted murderess.

I parked my jalopy in the shade of an enormous sugar maple. I unrolled the window two or three inches, but there was no need to lock it. Not that car.

"You be good for your mama," I cooed to Dmitri. "And if I'm not back in twenty minutes unroll the window some more and fetch the cops." Dmitri looked at me and then closed his eyes in contentment. He was purring loud as a lawnmower. Cream of liver pate definitely agreed with him.

I had to ring the doorbell three times before I got a response.

"Yes?"

On less than a handful of occasions in my life someone—always a complete stranger—has mistaken me for
someone else. These confused souls claim to know, or
have met, someone who looks exactly like me. I find
this a preposterous claim, since anyone who looks *exactly* like me has to be my height, and all the females
my height are in the fifth grade. I do *not* look like a
fifth-grader!

The only difference between this woman and myself
(that I could see) was that she was wearing a mint-green
terry bathrobe and a matching towel around her head,
whereas I had a test for mental stability imprinted on
my buttocks in grease.

"Uh—uh," I finally said.

My mirror image smiled. "I know, we look alike.
Well, sort of. You want to come in?"

I nodded and was ushered into the same spartan room
in which I'd sipped tea from a mason jar the day before.
This was not déjà vu, nor was I dreaming. I pinched
myself just to make sure.

"Ouch," I said. Apparently my fall at the Mini-Mart
had left me a tad bruised.

"Please, sit," she said. I sat on the same walnut
rocker. Even the needlepoint seat was the same, which
confirmed the pinch test. My dreams may have scope,
but they never have much detail.

"My name is Abigail Timberlake," I said. "But you
don't seem very surprised to see me."

"Oh, I am, all right, but you might say I was fore-
warned." She stuck out her hand. "My name is Adrienne Wheeler."

I shook it. I had the feeling that if I squeezed it too
hard, I'd be the one wincing.

"You see," she said, "my girlfriend Marsha in Bedford called and told me you were on the way."

"I beg your pardon?"

She smiled and seated herself on the dinette chair.

"Well, not to this address exactly, but to Hernia. Marsha works at the Mini-Mart."

"Oh! Your spy."

My counterpart laughed. "Marsha couldn't believe her eyes. I was just about to step into the shower when she called. She wanted me to cruise around town looking for you. I told her that was silly. But Marsha has this theory that someday my sister and I will be reunited."

A shiver ran up my spine. "Your sister?"

"My twin. We were separated shortly after birth. It was a custody thing. My dad got me, and my mom got her."

"What is your sister's name?"

She shrugged. "It was Gabrielle, but it could be anything now."

"What's your mother's name?"

"Harriet."

I breathed a sigh of relief. "My mother's name is Mozella, and I look exactly like her—only younger, of course. And the only sibling I have is a brother. His name is Toy."

"Did you say Toy? That's very interesting because I once had a poodle I named Toy. Isn't this exciting? It's just like those studies on identical twins raised apart— you know, where their spouses and kids have the same names. Sometimes they even name their pets the same thing!"

"I didn't name my brother, dear." Trust me, I would done a better job. If he had been given a normal name like Robert or David, he wouldn't be off in California parking cars and pretending to be an actor. Of course my parents didn't mean to name him Toy either, but Troy. Troy Hayes Wiggins, to be exact. But the typist at the Rock Hill records department had sliced her left index finger peeling onions and depressing the "r" key immediately after the "t" key was just too painful. When the error was discovered everyone thought it was cute, at least while he was a baby. Unfortunately my brother has never outgrown his name.

My mirror image giggled. "My birthday is February ninth, when is yours?"

"September twenty-first. Listen, dear, I know there have been cases of twins born on separate days, even separate months, but this would have been a *long* pregnancy for our mother."

She was undaunted. "What's you favorite color?"

"Green," I said. I was being flip. We were wasting time, which was the same as wasting money. Lots of nice green money.

"Oh, me too!" She leaned forward, propping her face on her hands, her elbows on her knees. She was unabashedly staring at me.

I rocked nervously. "Well, I suppose you're wondering why I'm here—"

"Blonde," she said emphatically.

"Excuse me?"

She whipped the towel off her head. Her hair was bleached a pale, straw yellow.

"You'd look better as a blonde, you know."

I saw conclusively for the first time that I would not. "It doesn't suit my skin tone, dear."

"Oh piffle! It suits me fine." She thrust an arm at me. "We have the same skin, don't we?"

"Well, I—"

"Blondes really do have more fun. You really should try it."

I promised to think about it.

"So, what can I do for you, Abigail?"

"I came to see Leona Teschel," I said quickly. That woman could change subjects faster than a cornered teenager.

"Oh, Leona. Well, she isn't here."

"But she does live here, doesn't she?"

Who knew that when I laughed my eyes crinkled? "Ha! That's a good one. Leona Teschel living here!"

I didn't like that sound of that. "Yesterday I sat on this very chair and sipped ice tea from a mason jar, dear. Leona lived here then."

"*My* mason jars? I was growing my lab culture in them!"

I swallowed hard. "What lab culture?"

"I teach biology and home economics at Hernia High. I was trying to demonstrate the importance of sterilizing jars *before* canning. I wanted my students to see how much bacteria buildup there can be on what seems to be a clean surface."

"Lord have mercy! How much is there?"

"You'd be surprised. But don't worry, Abby—may I call you that?—because most of it is harmless. The healthy person should be able to handle it. But if those jars had been filled with food and the culture permitted to grow—well, have you heard of the Ebola virus?"

"Your twin sister is twenty years younger and her name is C. J.," I snapped.

Her small face scrunched into a replica of a squeezed sponge. "What did you say?"

I made a vow to practice my emotional responses in a mirror as soon as possible. "I was just being silly, dear. But tell me, if you really are a teacher, then why aren't you at school right now?"

It was interesting to watch myself blush. "Oh well, I may as well come right out and tell you. You see, we get ten paid sick days, and the since the school year's almost over and I've used only three—well, you get the picture."

"A picture of someone playing hooky?"

Her color deepened. "You won't tell, will you?"

"Not if you tell me about Leona Teschel. You do know her, don't you?"

"Of course I know her. What's this about you being here with her yesterday?"

"I went to the cemetery for her son's interment. She

was there alone and needed a ride home. Here's where
she brought me."

"No shit?"

Being the lady that I am, I flinched at her profanity.
"This very place."

"Well, I'll be damned. She has her own key, of
course, but the nerve of her!"

"So she owns this house?"

"Yes, but she doesn't live here. She's my landlady. I
live alone—ever since my husband Buff moved out."

I jiggled my right ear with my pinkie. "Did you say
your husband's name was Buff? Was that short for Buford by any chance?"

"No. The rat's real name is Clarence. We call him
Buff because he's always working out."

I breathed a sigh of relief. The universe could barely
handle another me. It for sure couldn't take another Buf-
ford.

"Financial problems?"

She waved at the empty room. "You mean that? Nah,
he was just being greedy. The only thing he didn't want
was that old junked car out there that he was always
planning to restore. No, it was just middle-age crisis, I
guess. He traded me in for a younger model."

"No kidding! The same thing happened to me."

"Yeah, but I bet your replacement wasn't named Ca-
nary."

I nearly fell off my rocker. "Her name is Tweetie!"

We laughed so hard, I was beginning to wish that
Adrienne really was my sister.

"So tell me," I said finally, "why on earth would
Leona Teschel bring me here and pretend this is her
house? Doesn't she have a place of her own?"

"Ha, I'll say she does! She lives in the biggest house
on Elm Street. I don't remember the number offhand,
but you can't miss it. It's one of those Victorian gingerbread things—you know, really fussy. Ugh. Now I'm
sounding jealous, aren't I?"

"Green is your favorite color, dear," I said kindly.

"Yeah, well, I didn't set my sights on living in a dump like this. But Hernia teachers get paid next to nothing, and—"

It was time to interrupt. "About Leona—does she make it a habit of letting herself into your house?"

Adrienne shuddered. "I sure as hell hope not. That woman gives me the creeps. She's supposed to be blind, but I always get the sneaking suspicion that she can see me."

"Well, for some reason she wanted me to think that she lived here."

"What time was it?"

"Mid-afternoon. You might have walked in from school any minute. I guess she was taking a big risk, huh?"

"Not if she knew I was at track practice. I'm the girls' track coach, too—no, it doesn't pay any more—and we're gearing up for our final meet of the year. The track practice schedule is published in the *Hernia Gazette*."

"Hernia has a newspaper?"

"Don't tell my journalism class that. I've spent all year holding that drivel up as an example of what *not* to write and how not to write it."

"Remind me not to cross you, dear."

She sighed. "Okay, I guess that's not really a fair thing to say about a five-page bulletin of community events written by volunteers. They mean well."

It was nice to know that my alter-ego could be gracious, if pressed. I decided to press while the getting was good.

"Did you know Leona Teschel's son, Billy Ray?"

"Everyone in the community knows the Teschels. They're the meanest, drunkest—hey, she didn't send you here to get an earful, did she?"

"No ma'am."

"I mean, this place might not be much, but it's dirt

cheap. I don't know what rent is like where you come from—"

Time to cut her off at the pass again. "So, then you know his brother, Tommy Lee, don't you?"

Her face clouded. "Yeah, I know him. I was married to the son of a bitch."

18

"You're joking!"

"I wish I was. Tommy Lee was my first husband. We were married less than a year."

"What happened?"

"He hauled off and popped me, so I dumped him. Kicked him out on his bony ass. I wasn't about to wait for it to happen again."

"You go, girl."

"Well, a gal's gotta do what a gal's gotta do."

I rocked. "Did you live in this house then?"

"Yeah, it was sort of a wedding present. Unofficial, you might say. After we got divorced, Leona let me stay on."

"That was mighty generous of her, considering."

"Yeah, but I had to start paying rent. And she doesn't keep the place up, as you can see."

I wisely refrained from suggesting she scrape and paint the house herself. She seemed to read my mind.

"Buff wasn't into maintenance—except for himself, of course. That he did real well."

"Really," I said. I wasn't about to let my twin sister get away with bad grammar, not when she was a teacher, for pity sake.

"Yeah, real well. That was part of the problem you know. All the women drooled over him."

I was the only fool to drool over Buford. It was our money Tweetie drooled over, not Buford's bod.

"About Tommy Lee, dear—"

"Hey," she said, "why all the questions about the Teschels? Oh, I get it, you're Billy Ray's girlfriend from Georgia."

I blinked. "How did you know?"

"Your accent. You're not from around here. Hey, I'm sorry about Billy Ray and all. That was terrible what happened, even to someone like Billy—" She clamped a hand over mouth.

"Go on, dear, you can say it."

She shook head.

"Billy Ray and I had broken up," I said. Well, that was half true, wasn't it?

My eyes, the ones in her face, widened. "He pop you too?"

"He robbed me blind."

She nodded. "That sounds like him. But you still came all the way up here for his funeral?"

I had to think fast, something which I'm admittedly not good at. I have begged Susan and Charlie to give me dissembling lessons, but they always seem to have some excuse handy.

"I came to spit on his grave," I said, thereby shocking myself.

My other self smiled. "Lead me to his grave, sister, so I can get a piece of the action."

"I take it you didn't like my ex?"

"I told you, hon, all the Teschels are mean, rotten sons of bitches. It's in their blood."

"But Leona—"

She raked my fingers through the blond hair to fluff it while it dried. "It's like a virus. You can catch it if you hang around too long. And that woman caught it good. She's the devil with breasts, make no mistake about it. I hate her guts, and she hates mine."

"Then I don't get it. Why does she rent you this

place, and why do you put up with her as your land-lady?"

She glanced at the door and back. "Leona Teschel is my children's grandmother."

"Your children?"

"Twins. When Tommy Lee left—or should I say, when I gave him the boot—I was three months pregnant. She may be the devil with breasts, but she's got a soft spot when it comes to her descendants." Adrienne looked around the room. "Not *too* soft, of course."

"Forgive me for asking, but—"

"Oh, I know what you're thinking. It's that blood thing, isn't it?"

"Well, you did say . . ."

She glanced at the door. "Yeah, well, they really weren't Tommy Lee's kids, see? He was always accus-ing me of sleeping around, but I wasn't. Not really. Not until after he started accusing me, and then it was just that one time."

Believe me, I already knew far more about my double than I wanted to, but I just couldn't stop myself. Besides, I hadn't had a chance to watch "All My Children" since leaving Charlotte.

"How can you be so sure they're not his?"

She laughed, and I reminded myself not to crinkle my eyes. "I'm a biology teacher, remember? Tommy Lee's blood type is O negative, mine is O positive, and the girls have A-positive type blood. They're identical, you know. Anyway, it's not possible for Tommy Lee to be their father."

"Identical twins! How nice. What are their names?"

"Suzanne and Charlaine."

We established that my Charlie was the same age as Suzanne and Charlaine. The twins were just finishing up their first year at Indiana University, which, to my sur-prise was located in Indiana—not the state, but a town in Pennsylvania. Adrienne's children had a lot in com-mon with mine. All four of them were experts at begging for money, sighing, and rolling their eyes while saying "Oh, Mama, get real!" Although as Yankee children, the twins called their mother "Mom."

I wouldn't say that Adrienne and I bonded in that short period of time, but we had enough in common so that a foundation for a possible friendship was laid by the time I got up to leave. Adrienne, I'm sure, felt even closer to me, since she believed we had both been abused by Teschel men.

She accompanied me out to the car in her bathrobe, babbling about how remarkable it was that we even walked the same.

"We both put one foot forward at a time," I agreed.

"Right!"

"Otherwise we'd be hopping."

"Huh?"

"Nothing, dear."

"Anyway, Abby, I'm hoping you'll do a tremendous favor for me."

"That depends," I said sagely. Believe me, I have agreed to some horrendous sight-unseen commitments.

"Please ask your mother if she might have had another baby girl she gave away. You never know, maybe I got my birth date wrong."

Before I found myself agreeing to such a silly request, I decided to perform a little maternity test of my own. Unfortunately there was no way I knew of to prove conclusively, on the spot, that Adrienne was indeed a Wiggins, but there was an approximately fifty-fifty chance that I could prove that she wasn't.

"Do you like cats, dear?"

"I adore them."

My pulse raced. "But you don't own any cats, do you?"

She hung her fake blond head. "My second ex took them. As if the furniture wasn't enough."

"Well, I've got one in the car," I said.

Dmitri is a better judge of character than I'll ever be.

He's pure mush in the hands of a true cat-lover, indifferent to those who are indifferent to him, and outright hostile to cat-haters and those phonies who only pretend to like cats.

"Oh, goody!" she squealed, in same voice we Wiggins women use in moments of pure ecstasy.

I opened the passenger side car door. "Dmitri, dear, we have company," I called.

But my buddy was gone.

We searched the neighborhood for over an hour. We called until we were hoarse, but as any animal lover knows, cats are far too intelligent to come when called. They listen for the sound of an electric can opener or, in some cases, the rattle of tasty morsels against a paper bag.

I was on the verge of tears. "Do you have an electric can opener?"

Adrienne shook her head. "*He* took it with him."

"A bag of dry cat food?"

"That he left behind. He told me to eat it."

"Don't just stand there, dear," I croaked. "Hustle!"

She ran and got the bag and we took turns shaking that around the neighborhood. The rattling of the bag and our repetitive, and now husky, cries of "Dmitri" made us sound like a pair of twin witch doctors on "National Geographic." But it was all to no avail.

"I've had Dmitri seven years," I wailed. "I always thought he would see me through to my first grandchild—at least my first gray hair. And now he's gone! Stolen!"

"Stolen?" she rasped. "No offense, Abby, but why would anyone steal a cat?"

I glared at her.

"What I mean is, he could have squeezed through that window, couldn't he?"

I assured her that Dmitri, who weighs just over ten pounds, was too much cat to squeeze through a three-inch space. And as bright as my Watson was, he had yet to master the art of opening and closing a car door.

"Tell you what," she said, and I know she just meant to be nice, "there's really nothing else you can do. Why don't you tell me where you're staying, and if he turns up, I'll give you a call."

"You mean *when* he turns up," I said, but I was far from sure.

I had driven only a couple of blocks when I remembered that I'd forgotten to give Adrienne my room number. Perhaps a normal desk clerk would have been quite capable of transferring my call, but we were dealing with Mushroom Man. The guy looked like he lacked the energy to outrun a glacier, and manning a switchboard had to rank up there with such tiring tasks as licking envelopes and reaching for keys.

Not about to take a chance on delaying my reunion with my precious ball of orange, I turned around in the nearest driveway and headed back to Adrienne's. I couldn't have been gone more than two minutes, but when I got within a couple of houses I noticed that the dark green car was no longer in the driveway.

"Damn, but that girl must have had a hot date," I muttered.

I parked beneath the shady maple again and pondered the situation. The only thing to do now was to write a note and slip it under the door. At times I may be caught without a comb, lipstick, or tube of lotion in my purse—sometimes even without tissues—but there is always something to write on. Coupons, business cards, church bulletins, deposit slips—I could probably write a novel on the paper I carry with me. Much to my surprise and relief, I actually had a pen. "Room 12," I wrote, and just barely managed to squeeze it under the kick plate.

Just as I was reaching for the car door I heard a familiar meow.

"Dmitri?"

"Meow."

I looked up, and there was Watson regarding me calmly from a limb ten feet above my head. Boy, did I feel like an idiot. Why it had not occurred to me to scan the maple is beyond me. Dmitri is inordinately fond of high places. One of his favorite spots at home is on top of the refrigerator. His preferred spot for a snooze is on the top shelf of the linen closet, something I try to discourage ever since an overnight guest found a hair ball on her bath towel.

I may be slow on the uptake at times, but the chemical accumulations of thirty years of permanent waves have not totally obliterated my brains. I still did not have a can opener, and Adrienne had not left her bag of dry cat food, but I did have a dozen cans of Mighty Mouser's Cream of Liver Pate. An open can of that gourmet treat placed on top of the car roof brought Dmitri down from the tree in a flash of yellow.

While my buddy ate, so did I. Cold Beanie Weenies and peanut butter sandwiches washed down with warm root beer may not seem like a feast to you, but if you haven't eaten all day, it's pure ambrosia. At the end of our respective meals, it was hard to say who was purring louder, Dmitri or I.

I was beginning to feel like an old Hernia hand, and I found my way to Elm Street with no trouble. Finding Leona's Victorian gingerbread house was a piece of cake. It was by no means the only Victorian house on the street, but it was the only one that could properly be termed a mansion. Its gables and turrets were visible a block away.

"Whoa baby," I said. "That's some house! I can't wait to see the inside of this one."

Dmitri yawned. "Seen one house, seen them all," is what he meant to say.

"Don't worry little buddy, this time I'm going to lock the door."

Dmitri closed his eyes while I babbled on about Leona's magnificent manse. One of the rewards of being a pet owner was that I could talk aloud all I wanted and not feel like I had slipped over the edge. It doesn't matter that my pet hasn't said more than a dozen words back to me in seven years. If, on the other hand, I drove around talking to a bunch of bananas lying on the front seat, then well, that's what I would be—bananas.

My intent was to park under one of Hernia's ubiquitous maples again. By that time in the afternoon the temperature was well into the eighties. How was I to know that early May in Pennsylvania could be so warm? Poor Dmitri. Whoever let him out of the car at Adrienne's place probably thought of it as an act of mercy.

At any rate, Elm Street didn't have many maples; it didn't have any elms for that matter either. The trees of choice seemed to be pin oaks, which were not yet fully leafed out, and Colorado blue spruce. Since parking under a spruce is a physical impossibility unless one is a squirrel, or maybe a tortoise, I had to keep going until a suitable shady tree could be located. Finding a nice shady maple close enough to the street to cast some shade took some searching. Finally I found a handsome sugar maple three blocks past Leona's gingerbread palace.

I am not allergic to exercise, although I have been known to drive to my aerobics class which meets less than a mile from my home. Still, I felt awkward about walking alone in a strange neighborhood, even one as ostensibly safe as Hernia. Could they tell I was from out of town just by the way I walked? Could they tell I was a southerner? Was some gaunt Yankee sheriff going to swoop out of nowhere, toss me in the slammer, and force me to eat deli food?

So you see, I was quite legitimately preoccupied, and can't be blamed for not noticing one of the many garage doors open and a dark green car emerge. It wasn't until the vehicle was several houses past Leona's that I noticed it. By then it was too far away to make a positive ID of the driver. But my gut—including one can of Beanie Weenies—and half a loaf of peanut butter bread told me that I was looking at the back of Adrienne Wheeler's bleached blond head.

19

I wasn't about to make a fool of myself by running back to my borrowed rattletrap and giving chase. Besides, what business of mine was it if Adrienne chose to visit her former mother-in-law? Maybe it had something to do with the children, Charlaine and Suzanne, or whatever their names were. Quite possibly it wasn't even Adrienne in the burnt green automobile. I have been known to make mistakes before, and this time the sun was in my eyes. A white tennis cap—even gray hair—might, with the proper reflection, appear blond. So saying, I did the sensible thing and put the matter out of my mind.

The Teschel manse had a doorbell plate in the shape of a gargoyle's profile. One pushed the gargoyle's eye to ring the bell. Personally, I thought it was rather campy, although I could see how persons more architecturally correct than I might take offense. It would not have surprised me, however, if a butler named Lurch opened the door.

Unfortunately nobody answered the door. I rang that sucker a good dozen times, and I could hear the chimes quite clearly through the lead-paned door. Between rings I also heard what sounded like a door slam.

"Open up, Leona, you big liar," I shouted through the keyhole.

"Don't waste your breath."

I whirled.

The voice came from next door, where a smartly dressed woman about my own age, but of course a lot taller, stood on the property line between the two houses. I waved at her, and she waved back, and then motioned me to join her.

"My name is Betty Cole," she said, and much to my relief, did not offer to shake hands. I am not antisocial, mind you, but the custom of spreading germs as a way of introduction seems a little archaic to me. Much better the Thai custom of folding one's hands in a prayer position and bowing slightly. If everyone did that, the common cold would practically be eradicated, and productivity in the marketplace would jump dramatically. Just think what such a minor change in our social customs could do for our economy. Anyway, Betty sounded like she had a bad cold and needed to be in bed, not doing her stint as part of the neighborhood watch.

"I'm Abigail Timberlake. I was hoping to speak to Mrs. Teschel."

She made a disgusted face, and then caught herself. "Oops, you're not one of her relatives from the Carolinas, are you?"

"I am from the Carolinas, but I am most definitely *not* one of her relatives."

"That's a relief. I know I shouldn't generalize, but I was beginning to get a bad opinion of Carolinatites."

"That's Carolinians, dear. And anyway, Mrs. Teschel doesn't have any relatives back home that she's in touch with, does she?"

Betty invited me to sit on her porch, where a pair of white wicker rockers awaited. It was cool and shady on the porch and I wished I had brought Dmitri along.

"Morticia"—she nodded in the direction of Leona's house—"never has company. Except for her sons, and one of them just died. The other one lives with her."

"Do you know the family well?"

She shook her well-coiffed head. "She and I aren't speaking. I accidentally backed over her pansies the week we moved in. You would have thought I killed the family dog, the way she carried on. If I put one toe over the property line—like if I'm mowing or something— she goes ballistic. I was beginning to think that was a Carolina thing."

"I assure you that it's not."

"This wasn't what Hubert and I were expecting," she said, her voice trailing off into unmistakable sadness. "It's so hard to get used to it."

"Having nasty neighbors?"

She glanced at me and then her eyes took on a far-away look. "We're from New York, you know."

"Ah, so you must mean the cold."

"Believe me, it gets cold here too. Anyway, that's not the problem. It's the boredom of living in a small town. I don't suppose you can imagine what it is like to move from the city to a place this small."

"Not *the* city," I said, "but I have a vague idea."

"It was Hubert's idea. Things would be so cheap here we could afford to retire early. Take this house, for instance"—she gestured behind her—"do you know what we would have to pay for that back home?"

"They have Victorian gingerbread houses in New York City?"

"No, and that's exactly my point. We would have had to go to Connecticut to find something comparable, but it would have cost five times as much. *Five* times!"

I shook my head. "Maybe things are overpriced in Connecticut, dear."

"Yeah, well, at least in Connecticut they have trains that take you into the city. There is always something to do. And the shopping! Did you know that Hernia has only one teensy little grocery store? And no art galleries, no museums, and of course no concerts. Not even any movie theaters."

"Well, Pittsburgh does," I said helpfully, "and I hear it's less than two hours away."

"Ha! Two hours away on the turnpike, but Hubert and I don't drive. What kind of life is this?"

"How long have you lived here, dear?"

She frowned. "Two years, eleven months, and four days. But it seems like a lifetime."

"Where is your husband?" I asked gently.

"Inside watching TV. Some silly rerun. 'Green Acres,' I think. The screen is so snowy it's like watching a blizzard. Did you know we can't get cable here?"

"That's a fate worse than death," I said sympathetically.

"Tell me about it. I may as well be dead. It's these silly mountains, you see. They block the reception. I can't even watch 'All My Children.' "

"Lord have mercy!" She was absolutely right. Life without "AMC" is a life devoid of quality.

Betty glanced around surreptitiously. "Most of the people here are Pennsylvania Dutch—that means they're like Amish or Mennonite or something. They're real conservative."

"You don't say."

She lowered her voice. "They don't drink. *No* alcohol of any kind. Not even communion wine. You just try and throw a cocktail party."

"Bummer!"

"Hey, you're not making fun of me, are you?"

"Not a bit, dear. But Leona Teschel isn't Pennsylvania Dutch. I realize you're not speaking to the lady, but have you ever invited her to your parties?"

Betty recoiled in horror. "You've never met the woman, have you?"

I nodded vigorously. "But I have. In fact, I once thought I knew Leona quite well."

She cocked her head. "Then you'd know that she's as mean as a—uh—well—"

"A snake?"

"Yeah. And she's even meaner now that her other son moved back in."

"Tommy Lee?"

Betty shrugged. "I've never met the man, but you can see the resemblance. Especially around the eyes—well, he's not blind, but you know what I mean."

"When did this second son move back in?"

"Maybe a month ago. You should have heard them fight."

"Leona and Tommy Lee fight?"

"You better believe it, but I'm talking about the brothers. They fought like cats and dogs. Oh, they'd play some music over there, so we weren't supposed to hear it, but we did anyway."

I flashed her an accomplice's smile. "Did you hear anything interesting?"

"Say," she said, "where are my manners? You must think we Yankees haven't any. Would you like something cold to drink?"

I was as parched as toast, but I didn't want to interrupt the flow. I smiled again.

"I'm fine, thank you. So, tell me everything you heard."

"Well, I never really knew what they were fighting about, except that it had to do with business, but I could tell that one brother—the man you called Tommy Lee—thought the other brother didn't have a knack for it."

"Can you be more specific?"

She raked perfectly manicured nails through the perfectly coiffed do, thereby rending it imperfect. Then one shake of the head and it all fell back into place. Hernia might not have the amenities of the city, but it had one hell of a hairdresser.

"Careless," she said. "That's what Tommy Lee called the other one—Billy something, isn't it?"

"Billy Ray. So Billy Ray was careless."

"He didn't cover his tracks well, whatever that meant."

"Sounds intriguing." I giggled. Anything to urge her on.

"So, then Tommy Lee tells Billy Ray that he has to go back down and fix things."

"Go where?"

"I have no idea. Maybe he meant the basement. I only heard bits and pieces at a time, and that music was always so loud. I even thought of calling the police and complaining. About the music, I mean."

"But you never did, did you?"

"God!" She rolled her eyes. "You should see what passes for cops around here. Melvin Stoltzfus wouldn't last a day in the city."

It was time to steer her back on track. Folks without an agenda constantly meander in their conversations. Lord, but it drives me crazy.

"You ever hear anything really juicy?"

Betty looked as if I'd slapped her face. "How juicy do you want? Isn't that enough? I don't listen with a stethoscope, you know."

"Of course not, dear." The quickest way to redeem myself was to ask for a favor. Trust me, that ploy works every time. "Is it too late to take you up on your offer of a cold drink? My throat feels like a cotton ball dispenser."

"Do you drink beer?" she asked brightly.

"Does a squirrel eat nuts?"

"I've got Rolling Rock," she said. "That's the only good thing Hernia has over the city, if you ask me."

I wisely refrained from asking her if she felt this safe in the Big Apple. "Does the Yoder Corner Market sell beer?"

"Under the counter, so to speak. You have to ask for it a week in advance. If our real estate agent hadn't told us that, we never would have known."

"Wow!"

She got up and returned a few minutes later with two beers and a small bowl of peanuts. I scooped up as many goobers as I could in one handful so I wouldn't have to dip into the bowl again. We drank in silence for a few minutes.

Betty chuckled to herself. "A stethoscope does come in handy at keyholes. You ever try it?"

"No. Have you?"

She nodded. "One night they had the music turned up so loud, I couldn't hear a thing. I used it on the back door—it's darker there because of all the trees—anyway, with the stethoscope I could at least hear some of what they were saying."

I took a swig of Rolling Rock. "And?"

She sighed. "Same old, same old. They were just fighting about business. Something about their father leaving it to both of them, so how come one of them had to do all the dirty work."

"Dirty work?"

"I think that's what they said. The stethoscope magnifies the music too, you know."

"Do you know what kind of business?" According to Richard Nixon the Bedford Tool and Die Company had gone belly up years ago.

Betty surprised me with a belch. "Munitions, I think."

"What?" I was too early into my beer to be hearing things.

"Well, there was a lot of talk about tanks. They should be making more tanks than all that fancy other stuff. Tanks were quicker to make, and harder to trace."

I smiled warmly. I'd had enough beer to do that. The woman was off her rocker—well, metaphorically speaking. Still, a lonely, loony source is better than none.

"Are you sure? About the tanks, I mean?"

"Of that I'm positive." She waved her mostly empty bottle in the direction of Leona's and then leaned over the arm of her rocker in my direction. "Say, you don't think they're terrorists, do you?"

I shrugged. "Nothing would surprise me, dear. From

what I've heard, Leona Teschel could well be Saddam Hussein in drag.''

"No, no, not that kind of terrorists. I mean the kind that builds communes in Montana and then blows up their own people just to prove some silly point.''

I stared at her. "Did you hear something to make you think that?''

"Well, not in so many words, maybe. But just look at that house. Look at how big it is. They could have a whole cult in there right now and we wouldn't know it.''

I nodded. My beer was almost done and I have a low tolerance for alcohol.

"And with all those towers and turrets, they could hold off the FBI with sharpshooters. Who knows, maybe they're even digging escape tunnels that will lead to the mountains.''

"Cool.'' Betty's eyes glistened with newfound excitement. She no longer looked homesick.

"Of course I don't know if I'd want to live right next door. I mean, your house could be right in the line of fire. And what if they miscalculate the tunnels, and one of them exits through the floor of your basement?''

"Would you like another beer?'' Betty asked happily.

I will admit everything. One beer will give me a buzz; two beers will knock me on my butt. I had two and a half beers that afternoon.

There, I said it. Believe me, I am not proud of what I did. Even we Episcopalians will acknowledge that too much to drink is a sin—especially if, as a result, one behaves without dignity. And I, for one, knew better. If I had restricted myself to one beer back in college, I never would have ended up Mrs. Buford Timberlake. Of course, then I never would have given birth to Susan and Charlie, and might still be living with Mama. My point is that most storm clouds do indeed have silver linings, although it usually requires sobriety to see it.

The silver lining to my Rolling Rock cloud was that it loosened me up enough to impose on my hostess. That is to say, while I never drive while under the influence, I am not above conversing on the telephone, and I was suddenly in the mood to talk to Mama.

"May I please use your phone," I slurred. "I promise to return it."

Both Bettys frowned. "Long distance?" they asked in unison.

"Don't worry, darlings, I have a calling card. It won't cost you a thing."

The Bettys sighed and put down their beers. Then they led me into the cool, dark interior of the house, where a rather handsome man sat glued to the TV. The Betty on the left introduced us. I was no longer keeping track of the Betty on the right, so I don't remember what she was up to.

"What are you watching?" I asked.

"A 'Green Acres' marathon," Ed Cole said. "They're running forty-eight episodes back to back. That's like twenty-four hours of pure heaven."

Who knew that there were even that many episodes in the series? Certainly not me. Frankly, until then I had always found sitcoms that costarred pigs and Hungarian glamour gals to be a little boring.

"Have a seat," Ed said.

Since it was easier to sit than to stand, I sat on the opposite end of the couch from Ed. The Betty on the left—although perhaps there was just one Betty by now—sat between us. There was to be no hanky-panky with the handsome Mr. Cole.

I have no idea how many shows we watched, but by the time I remembered the phone call, I had become fond of the little porker. Arnold the pig was growing on me too.

Fortunately by then I was sober enough to read the numbers on my calling card—well, the easy ones at any rate. My third try got me through.

"Mama? You're home?"

"Of course not, dear. This is just a figment of your imagination."

"It is?"

Mama is no slouch. "Abigail Louise Wiggins Timberlake. You're drunk, aren't you?"

"Of course not, Mama! I'm just a teensy-weensy little bit inoculated."

"Against what. The bubonic plague?"

"I meant intoxicated—but I'm not even that. I only had two beers."

The only sound was the familiar, and oh so comforting, click of Mama's pearls against the receiver.

"Okay—and a *half*! Mama, aren't you happy to hear from me?"

"I'm as happy as a flea at a dog show," she said, but she didn't sound it.

"Don't feel bad, Mama, you'll find your niche. Besides, Sister Mary Martha thought you were a hoot."

"She did?" The hope in her voice was pitiful. It cut through me like a knife through grits.

"Have you considered taking some courses at Winthrop University? They might help take your mind off things."

"Give it a rest, Abby. I'm not upset about leaving the convent. It was no big deal. It was my choice, after all."

"It was?"

"Absolutely. Being a nun just isn't any fun these days. They wouldn't have even let me wear one of their habits to the mall. Now I ask you, Abby, what's the point of being a nun if nobody knows you are one?"

I shrugged, but apparently Mama didn't hear it.

"Well, I'll tell you—*nothing*! I may as well volunteer my time at the Rock Hill High School cafeteria. At least then I'd get to wear my smock in public."

"But are those smocks your shade of blue?" I asked gently. "Remember, you're a spring. Come to think of it, I must be a spring too. Do you still have that book with the color charts?''

Mama snorted, which is most unlike her. ''Honestly Abby, you can be so shallow at times. All this silly talk about colors, when my life has just fallen apart.''

''But you just said leaving the convent was no big deal.''

''I'm not talking about the damned convent,'' Mama snapped. ''I'm talking about me. I've been violated.''

20

I gasped. Surely I had not heard right.

"Mama, uh—were you raped?"

"What? No, I've been robbed," Mama wailed.

I was sitting in the Cole kitchen on a cute little white chair with red tulips stenciled on the backrest. There were fluffy white curtains at the window with red tulips on them as well. There were red tulips on some of the counter tiles. Goodness gracious, the cabinet pulls were red plastic tulips. Come to think of it there were red tulips everywhere. Perhaps it was the inebriation, but I found it hard to imagine anything wrong in a world dominated by red tulips.

"Did you call the police?"

"Of course, dear. I'm a senior citizen, not an idiot."

"What did the police say?"

"They said that whoever broke in seems to have used a key. Or else they were an expert at picking locks. There was no sign of forced entry."

"Aha. Are you sure you were robbed?"

"Abigail!"

"What did they take, Mama? Not the triple-speed Crock-Pot I gave you for your birthday in 1976?"

Face it, Mama doesn't own anything with which a self-respecting up-to-date robber would want to bother. No computers, no VCR, no CD player, no microwave, not even a toaster oven young enough to be carded.

Mama's only portable appliance with any street value is a black and white TV with bent rabbit ears. And forget about jewelry. Her pearls aside, except for the wedding ring Daddy gave her, Mama doesn't own a thing that won't turn green in a swimming pool.

"Crockpot?"

"Don't worry, Mama, I'm sure your insurance policy will cover it. Even if it doesn't—well, it was supposed to be a surprise for your next birthday, but I'm planning to give you a microwave oven. I know, I know, you're worried about all those dangerous rays—but they're really not, you know. Those six-legged amphibians they're finding in Minnesota have nothing to do with microwaves. They're the result of aspartame finding its way into the ground water."

"*What*?"

"You know, Mama. The artificial sweetener. I read it in the *National Deliverer*. It seems those Minnesotans drink a lot of diet colas—"

The pearls clicked furiously. "I've been robbed, Abigail, and you want to talk about deformed frogs?"

I swallowed and fingered a plastic, red tulip place mat on the kitchen table. It wasn't going to be easy talking her out of the delusion that she had been robbed. Perhaps it was her way of dealing with the loss of her convent dream, one disappointment displacing another.

"Mama, you need to make a list of everything that's missing," I said patiently.

"How can I, Abby, when there's such a mess?"

"Mess?"

"Lord child, it looks like Hurricane Hugo decided on a second coming. I couldn't find my shadow in this mess if it was pinned to me."

My heart sank. I am enough of a realist to know that my children, like many of their contemporaries, will try and get away with as much as possible. This is a sad statement about both our society in general, and my success as a mother in particular. I know there is no good excuse for this, but if Buford had backed me in the discipline department, and if our marriage hadn't gone on the skids, I might have succeeded in raising kids that made me proud.

But that was all water under the bridge now. The horse was out of the paddock and it didn't much matter who opened the gate. There was no undoing anything anyway. Besides, it might well be that a wild party or two was mild in comparison with what they could be doing. Still, to trash their grandmother's house after having been issued direct orders to stay away—that was really going beyond the pale.

"Are there beer cans lying about?" I asked, suddenly very sober and very tired.

"Excuse me!"

"Cigarette butts ground into the couch?"

"What do you think this is, Abby, a bar?"

"No, of course not. But it's possible—well, you know how kids are nowadays."

"I know," Mama snapped. "I know exactly how you are."

"*Me*? Mama, I have my own place to trash!"

"Jumping to conclusions again, aren't we dear?"

"I don't know what you're talking about, Mama." I truly didn't. The Rolling Rock buzz was practically a distant memory, but my mother wasn't making any more sense than usual.

"Susan and Charlie, right?"

"Ah, that. Well—"

"Susan told me all about it, dear. She didn't leave a thing out. At least that couple used the guest bedroom and not mine."

"She told you *that*?"

"Shame on you, Abby, for even thinking that your children would turn right around and disobey a direct order from you. You should have more faith in your kids."

"Yes, ma'am." There was no point arguing. "Mama, was it vandals? Did they break things?"

"Mercifully no—well, at least not much. They mostly just scattered things. Abby, my entire house looks just like your room when you were a teenager."

"Mama!"

"Except that now there is no awful smell. I don't keep dirty clothes wadded up in the closet."

"That's not fair—" I caught myself. "Mama, it sounds like the intruder was looking for something specific. You've got to try and think of what that might be."

I swear I could feel the breeze generated by Mama's sigh. "I told you, Abby—oh, my God—wait right there!"

What else was I to do? I mean, besides pull my hair and stamp my feet? Thank God for those red tulips. They were the only thing that kept me from going out of my head with worry. By the time Mama got back on the phone I had determined that the wallpaper border in the kitchen contained 142 red tulips and *one* yellow tulip.

"Abby, it's missing!"

"What a relief!"

"Abigail Louise—"

"What a relief that you're all right. So, what's missing?"

Click. Click. Click.

"Mama! Out with it."

"Well, you were never supposed to know, Abby. I didn't want to hurt your feelings."

"But it's okay to drive me crazy instead!" I screamed.

Betty stuck her head in the door but I waved her away.

"Remember I gave you that English tea service, dear?"

"It rings a faint bell."

"You see, I bought a present for your brother Troy as well. Only, I forgot to mail it before I left."

"So what's so bad about that? It doesn't hurt my feelings if you give your son presents. And you didn't tell Toy about my gift, did you?"

"No."

"So what he doesn't know won't hurt him, right? Just take the insurance check when it comes and buy him another gift."

In the ensuing silence I counted eighteen red tulips on the dish towel wedged in the handle of the refrigerator door. No yellow tulips.

"I don't know where to find a replacement," Mama said softly.

"Try the yellow pages. Mama, there are oodles of pro shops in the area. How hard is it to find a putter?"

"I didn't buy Toy a putter! I bought him a silver tea set."

"*What*?"

"I don't care what you say, Abby, your brother is going to settle down and get married some day. And when he does, he deserves to have nice things just like you."

"What kind of silver tea set? It's not like mine, is it?"

"Not that it's your business, Abby, but how else do you think I was able to afford two English tea sets? By buying two identical ones, of course! You'd be proud of me if you knew what kind of deal I got."

"I'd be stunned," I said. I already was.

"Abby, promise me you won't say a word about this to your brother."

"My lips are sealed." Toy and I haven't had a real conversation since I told him I thought his Hollywood girlfriend, whose name is Bambi, bought her curves in a doctor's office.

"Are you enjoying your tea set, dear? Of course you're not. You're off in Pennsylvania having yourself a nice little vacation. By the way, when will you be home?"

"That's hard to say, Mama. I'm having a ball. Maybe in couple of days. Look, do me a big favor and stay at my house until I get back."

"Whatever for?"

"Or stay with one of your friends. Louise is in town, isn't she?"

"I'm not a baby, Abby. I was almost a nun."

"Mama, what if you had been home when the burglar broke in? What if you had surprised him, and he or she had a gun? What if the burglar wasn't really after the silver, but just happened to find it? What if it was you they wanted?"

"Okay, I get the point. I'll stay over at your place. But I'll bring my own towels. No offense, dear, but you really should use softener in the rinse cycle. Those little anti-static sheets you throw in the dryer with them isn't enough. And did you ever turn your guest mattress like I suggested?"

"Not to worry, Mama. I went out and bought an automatic mattress turner. That thing should be spinning as we speak."

"There's no need to be sarcastic, dear."

"Whatever you do, don't change the wallpaper in the bathroom. I'm very fond of beige and ecru seashells on an aqua background." To be honest, I hated that paper. It was in there when I bought the house, and I just hadn't had time to do anything about it. Now, not only was I going to feel better with Mama staying at my house, but I was guaranteed to have a brand-new bathroom when I got back. Trust me, whatever she chose for a replacement would be a welcome change.

"Well, Abby, is that all you have to say? This call is costing you a pretty penny."

"It's my penny, Mama. And it isn't all I have to say. I want to ask you a very important question."

"Shoot, dear." What a clever woman, trotting out her slang to disarm me.

"Do I have a twin sister?"

"Abby, have you been smoking pot again?"

"*What*?"

"Oh come off it, Abby. I found that joint under your mattress when you were in college."

I slapped my free ear to make sure it was working. It was.

"What did you say?"

"That reefer. Isn't that the other word for it?"

I haven't been so shocked and embarrassed since that time my bikini top came off on the water slide at the church picnic.

"Mama!"

"Are you stoned again, or not?"

"It was just that one joint," I wailed, "and I didn't even inhale!"

"Then what's all this nonsense about having a twin?"

I told her about Adrienne.

"If you saw the woman, you'd know what I mean. Except for that horrible hair of hers, we're like two peas in a pod. You would tell me if it was true, wouldn't you?

Mama didn't just laugh, she howled. A church-going lady who still wears crinolines and can't be parted from her pearls has no business braying like a banshee.

"Are you quite done?" I demanded after about five minutes, when the howls had subsided to mere whimpers punctuated by gusts of giggles.

"Almost," Mama gasped.

"Mama, I'm hanging up if you don't stop this minute. This call is costing me a pretty penny, remember? You said so yourself."

The giggle gusts grew to be gales.

I did what I'd threatened to do and hung up.

Without asking the Coles' permission, I dialed The Finer Things. There was no answer, not even the answering machine. I dialed the Rob-Bobs at home. Ditto. In desperation, I called the major.

"Hullo. Major Calloway's Antique Gun Emporium here," he said in his clipped British accent.

"Hang up on me, buster, and I'm calling the cops."

There was a startled gasp. "I don't know what you're talking about."

"You seem to be jumping the gun, Major. I haven't said much of anything yet."

"Well, whatever it is, I don't know anything about it. I certainly didn't do it."

"Didn't do what?"

"You can't trick an old fox like me, Abby. I've been there and done that, as you young folks say."

"Thanks, but flattery won't get you anywhere with me today. Look. Major, I'm not out to harass you. All I want is your cooperation."

"Cooperation is what made Britannia great," he said cagily.

"Good, then maybe this will be a piece of cake for you." Who was I kidding? Syria would elect a Jewish prime minister before the major's right hand cooperated with his left. It was a wonder the man could even tie his shoes.

"But I'm not going to confess to anything I didn't do."

"No one is asking you to. Besides, who says there is anything to confess to?"

"Cut the crap, Abby, and state your point."

"Why Major Calloway, how vulgar of you. Okay, here's the deal. I need you to get a message to Rob Goldman—or even Bob, for that matter—he doesn't seem to be at the shop or at home. Tell him that my mother's house was broken into and—listen, Major, what I'm about to say is strictly confidential."

I heard an indignant huff. "We of the Bombay Chargers are the soul of discretion. In fact, we had our own remedy for wagging tongues—we cut them off."

I nearly severed my tongue with my teeth. It was all I could do to keep from reminding him that his discretion had all but made me a murder suspect.

"Just remember your own remedy, dear. Now, I want you to tell Rob that someone stole a silver tea service from my mother's house. Tell him that I have reason to believe it was another William Cripps reproduction."

"I beg your pardon?"

"A copy like the one I bought at auction. Tell him that."

"You don't say!" The miserable man sounded gleeful.

"Can you find him and tell him that?"

"Abigail, I fail to see how this little bit of unfortunate news is urgent. Why don't you tell him yourself when you get back?"

"Because they need to start spreading the word. Whoever stole my mother's silver tea set might try to sell it to Charlotte dealers. They might even try to sell it to Skeet and Jimbo. They're a little slow on the uptake, you know."

"Ha!" The major had a laugh that could set dogs barking. "Those two lads are as dumb as posts, as you Americans are so fond of saying."

"Which is exactly why Rob needs to warn them. Unless, of course, you'd like to do it yourself."

"Ha!"

"And another thing, it wouldn't surprise me if whoever stole Mama's tea set had something to do with Purvis's death. I don't know what it is yet, but I have a gut feeling it's all tied together."

"You don't say! Is this your roundabout way of confessing?"

I slammed the phone in its cradle. I huffed and I puffed, but I did not blow the Coles' house down. It was only by counting red tulips again that I calmed down enough to join the world.

The Coles were still in the living room watching the "Green Acres" marathon. Much to my surprise, Betty Cole seemed mesmerized by the porcine program they were watching. Thanks to me the woman had finally found a worthwhile hobby.

"Is this the episode where Arnold orders pepperoni pizza for everyone in Hooterville?" I asked. "Have they gotten to the part where he eats a slice and then realizes he's just become a cannibal?"

"Yes," Ed grunted, "but it was sausage pizza, not pepperoni."

"Shhh," Betty said.

I tiptoed towards the door. "Thanks for letting me use the phone," I whispered, "but I have one quick question before I go."

"Make it snappy," Betty snapped.

"Why is there just one yellow tulip on your kitchen border?"

"That's not a tulip, that's mustard," Ed growled.

I closed the door silently behind me.

Thank goodness Dmitri was right where I left him. In fact, he was the picture of contentment—stretched out under the rearview window, catching a stray ray of the afternoon sun—but the second that wily cat heard my footsteps on the pavement he assumed an attitude. You would have thought I'd stuffed him in a bag along with eight other cats and sent him to St. Ives.

"Cut it out," I ordered.

Dmitri hissed at me, which is the cat equivalent of me cussing.

"Okay then, no more Mighty Mouser Cream of Liver Pate."

Watson looked at me balefully, but hushed his hiss.

"I have one more person to see, sweetie, and then Mama will take you back to that lovely motel."

Meow.

"That's right, dear. If anyone can shed some light on the subject, I bet she can."

21

Magdalena Yoder was not happy when I showed up at PennDutch Inn unannounced. "Do you know what time it is?" she demanded.

We were standing on the wide front porch. A southern woman would have invited me to come in and sit a spell, take the load off my feet.

I glanced at my watch. "It's six-nineteen—give or take a few minutes."

"Exactly. It's supper time."

"This will only take a minute."

"Can't you come back tomorrow, dear?"

Dear? The woman hardly knew me.

"This is urgent."

"So is supper. Sly wants his pie."

"Stallone?"

She rolled her eyes. "Who else?"

"I suppose Pitt wants his grits."

"Actually he prefers oatmeal. With cinnamon and brown sugar."

The door behind her opened and a stout woman in Amish garb muttered something in Pennsylvania Dutch. I recognized the woman as Magdalena's cousin, Freni.

"Tell Cher I'll be right there," Magdalena said irritably.

More muttered Dutch.

"King can sing if he wants to. I just don't want him telling those gruesome stories at the table."

The door slammed.

"Celebrities," I said, "you can't live with them, and you can't live without them."

"*You* deal with celebrities?"

"They drop by my shop all the time. You know, Fonda on his Honda, Dolly on her trolley, Chase in his Chevy."

The beady eyes flashed. "It's a Harley, not a Honda, and you're a hoax. You don't know any of these people. You're just a celebrity-watcher, and we have a name for that around here."

"Is it 'curious'?"

"Trespasser." Magdalena turned to go inside.

"Okay, so I misrepresented myself. I'm sorry."

She stopped, but didn't turn around.

"I'm here investigating a murder."

Magdalena whirled and I nearly fell backwards off the porch I was so surprised. "That case is officially closed," she snarled.

"Excuse me?"

"You meant"—she swallowed and wiped the palms of her hands on a crisp white apron—"tell me what you meant, dear."

"May I sit?" I pointed to the row of Adirondack rockers.

Magdalena nodded and picked the closest chair for herself.

I sat two chairs to her right. "Well, my name really is Abigail Timberlake, and I really am an antique dealer, but I'm not here to buy antiques."

She waved a hand impatiently. "You told me all that before. Your visit has something to do with Billy Ray. And like I told you before, I don't remember going to school with him. Now what's this about a murder?"

"Forget school," I said, willing my dander down, "but you know far more about the Teschels than you let on. Seems like everyone has a strong opinion where they're concerned.''

"I'm a Mennonite. It's against my beliefs to bad-mouth people.''

I'm sure my eyes were flashing every bit as much as hers. "I don't want gossip, I want facts. I believe that the Teschels are responsible for the murder of a friend of mine.''

"Oh, I'm so sorry.''

She sounded so sincere I felt guilty for fudging. "Well, not a friend exactly. More like a colleague.''

"Here in Hernia?''

"Pineville, North Carolina. Just south of Charlotte. Purnell Purvis was his name. He owned an antique auction barn and—well, it's really hard to explain. But Purnell was poisoned and I think a Teschel did it.''

"What do the police think?''

"To be honest?''

"The whole truth and nothing but the truth. The second you stop being honest with me, I scoot on back inside. Supper might be almost over, but afterwards Ringo wants to play bingo. Not for money, of course. We Mennonites don't do that.''

"Well, the whole truth is that some idiot—''

"Ah, ah, ah, let's watch our language, dear.''

"Sorry. A fellow dealer who calls himself a major has been insinuating that *I* poisoned poor Purnell. He got that idea because Purnell was in my shop talking to me just minutes before he collapsed out front on the sidewalk.''

"I see. So you're up here trying to clear your name, is that it?''

"Yes, but—''

"Been there, done that.''

"Excuse me?''

"Isn't that what you English say when you want to convey the fact that you've been in a similar situation?''

"I guess so,'' I said guardedly.

"Well, I've been in your shoes." She glanced at mine, which were about half the size of hers. "So to speak."

"You have?"

"As a matter of fact, on more than one occasion. Hernia is not as dull as it seems. Anyway, I know just how frustrating it can be. So, how do you think I can help you? Be specific, dear."

"I don't know," I wailed. "I can't prove any of my suspicions."

Magdalena stood up. "I don't have time—"

"Okay, okay! I think the Teschel family is in the reproduction business."

Magdalena sat down. "Ach, they're selling black market babies?"

"What? No! I mean they're reproducing silver English tea services. Very good ones. Good enough to fool the experts."

"Is there money in this?"

"A whole lot." Perhaps it was time to be as truthful as Magdalena wanted me to be. "I paid twenty thousand dollars for one of those tea services."

Magdalena rolled her eyes.

"All right then, it was eighteen thousand, five hundred, but when you throw in taxes and buyer's fee, it comes to just under twenty thousand—well, if you round it up."

"That much for a teapot?"

"Sugar and creamer too, of course."

"You English and your ways," she mumbled.

I let it pass. "Like I said, I have no proof. I saw Leona's house today—a great big old thing. They could easily have a workshop in there."

Magdalena shook her head. "I don't know anything about silver-making, but I've watched the Amish shoe horses plenty of times. You need heat to bend metal."

No duh. "I'm sure Leona has a stove," I said.

"More heat than that, I think. But you may be on to

something. Those Teschel boys were always topnotch artists.''

''I thought you never went to school with them!''

The beady eyes fixed on me indignantly. ''I didn't. You remember that railway viaduct between here and Bedford.''

I confessed that I didn't.

''Well, anyway, for several years there it was a bulletin board of the Teschel boys' filthy imaginations. Sam Yoder's store got hit a couple of times too. Mayor Tudweiler—he was mayor then—tried to get the boys to channel their talent into something decent. Like a mural about the Amish.''

''No go, huh?''

''The Amish wouldn't have it—they shun publicity. The Teschel boys' drawings got even filthier after that. At any rate, they may have painted disgusting things, but they did it very well.''

''That's more than you can say about a lot of contemporary artists,'' I said, hanging my head. I am not a prude, nor do I believe in censorship, but a lot of artwork I'd seen lately seemed created for one purpose only, and that was to shock. Perhaps somewhere there was an artist whose intent it was to instill other emotions, possibly delight.

''The world has gone to hell in a hand basket,'' I said. ''Oops—pardon my French.''

''Amen,'' Magdalena said quietly.

''But if what you said is true—about the heat, I mean—they would have to have some kind of studio or something.''

''Or a factory.''

''Right.''

''Like the Bedford Tool and Die Company.''

I looked up. ''Yeah, right. Unfortunately the Bedford Tool and Die company is defunct.''

Magdalena scratched her nose. ''That's news to me.''

I smiled from the catbird's seat. I actually knew more about the town than Magdalena.

"The business went bankrupt after that automobile plant backed out of building that Somerset plant."

"Leona Teschel never filed Chapter Eleven."

"She didn't? But the reverend—I mean, Richard Nixon said—"

"Ach, the man is a simpleton."

"Your language, dear," I chided her gently.

"Well, it's a fact. Richard couldn't stack two stones if they were numbered."

"He said Leona swindled his congregation out of a great deal of money."

"That's partly true. But I have it from a good source that the bulk of that money was *invested* in Atlantic City."

"Real estate?"

"Ach," said Magdalena throwing up her hands, "I'm beginning to think you're not so bright yourself."

"Just call me Little Richard."

"Shhh, he'll hear you." She nodded in the direction of the dining room.

My eyes widened to saucer size. "*The* Little Richard is in there?"

"He's a wonderful guest. Always brings me flowers."

I ached to crash Magdalena's supper table, but good manners and the urge to end my sleuthing compelled me to focus.

"You mean to say that Richard Nixon gambled away most of his church's funds?"

"Yah, I'm sorry to say it, but he did. And what a shame too—they had such a nice little congregation going up by the turnpike. Anyway, the man is a dreamer. He thought he could get a quicker return on the church's money in the casinos. I heard he lost every penny—even his bus fare. He hitchhiked and walked back. It took him eight days."

"Wow. Now tell me, what do you mean Leona never filed Chapter Eleven?"

"That was just a rumor. Maybe started by Richard himself."

"But your cousin Sam sued Leona in the wrongful death of his daughter, didn't he? Or is that just a rumor too?"

"Ach, but that man can talk. Yah, Sam did sue, but he lost. Apparently it wasn't such a cut and dried case."

"Oh?"

She stared at me, the blue eyes with their black pupils boring into my soul. "That's family business," she said.

"I understand. I have two teenagers myself."

"Marijuana," she whispered. "That's what they said it was. Sam's daughter Rebecca was, uh—"

"High?"

"Yah, high. She didn't have a license either. Sam had to tread softly." She wagged a long bony finger at me. "This is family business, you understand?"

"Yes, ma'am. But at least Leona spent eighteen months in jail, right?"

"Right. For tax evasion. It had nothing to do with the accident."

"I see."

"You shouldn't believe everything you hear."

If I resented her snide paternalism, at least I didn't show it. Instead I managed a self-deprecating smile that was worthy of Mona Lisa.

"At least the Teschels managed to pay their debts and still hang on to their business, right?"

"Yah."

"But I looked in the phone book. There isn't a Bedford Tool and Die Company listed."

"That's because the name has been changed. It's now the Southern Pennsylvania Metalworks Company. I understand they've expanded operations. In addition to tool-making, they now make wrought-iron products. But you shouldn't have any trouble finding it. Just go back to Bedford and take Business 220 south. Just before its junction with regular 220 look to your left. It's just a hop, skip, and a jump from your motel.''

I shook my head. "I can't believe it. I just can't believe it."

"Ach, don't get me wrong! The wrought-iron bed I bought from them was for *my* room, of course. My guests expect Amish furniture."

"I mean I can't believe what a fool I was. Taking Richard Nixon at his word just because he's a church elder. If I was—forgive me—your height, I'd go back there and wring his scrawny neck."

"You mean his considerable neck, don't you?"

"What? The man looks like beanpole on a diet."

"Pinched, narrow face? Hair like a mop head?"

"That's him."

It was Magdalena's turn to shake her head. "That *isn't* him. Richard Nixon is built like a pot-bellied stove. That was Tommy Lee Teschel you spoke to."

22

I nearly fell off my rocker. "Get out of town!"

Magdalena gave me a quizzical look.

"That's just an expression, dear," I said kindly. "It's just that I can believe it. I was really played for a sucker. But I don't get it, why would Tommy Lee pretend to be Richard Nixon?"

Magdalena sniffed. I hope it was a cold coming on, and not her opinion of my intelligence.

"He got you to believe that his company was defunct, didn't he?"

"Yes, but he said terrible things about Leona Teschel. His own mother!"

"Didn't you know?"

"Know what?" I'd seen Eddie Murphy's movie *The Nutty Professor*, but there was no way I was going to believe that the woman I met as Leona was Tommy Lee as well.

"Tommy Lee and his mother hate each other's guts. To my knowledge they haven't spoken to each other in years."

"You don't say!"

"You see," Magdalena glanced around, perhaps expecting Sly to be done with his pie, "Rebecca Yoder was Tommy Lee's girl."

I gasped.

"That's right. Tommy Lee took it just as hard as Sam.

I don't think he'd hesitate to make his mother come across as wicked as Jezebel.''

"Tommy Lee Teschel and Sam Yoder's daughter. It's hard to imagine.''

Magdalena shrugged. "The truth is Rebecca was always a little wild. She wasn't a Mennonite you know. Sam married a Methodist and converted. Three hundred years of tradition went right down the drain.''

I gave her my heartfelt sympathy. "Tell me,'' I added, "how did Billy Ray fit into the equation. Whose side was he on?''

"Near as I can guess, he played it right down the middle. He worked with his brother in the family business, and he still managed to live at home with his mother. The Bible warns us about that, you know?''

"Living with one's mother?''

"Ach, against serving two masters.''

"Well, now he's dead, and I understand Tommy Lee moved in with his mother.''

"Yah. How do you know this?''

"I spoke to their neighbor. A very lonely woman from New York.''

"Ach, there are so many of them now. Urban refugees they call themselves. Hernia used to be such a quiet, God-fearing place where everyone knew everyone else.''

"You still seem to keep track of people, dear, and Betty Cole is no slouch in that department either. And speaking of knowing folks, what can you tell me about Adrienne Wheeler, Tommy Lee's ex-wife?''

"Ach, what a beautiful woman!''

I beamed. "How kind of you.''

She leaned forwarded and studied me. "You know, you bear a faint resemblance to Adrienne. If you fixed yourself up a little you could be very pretty.''

"Thanks,'' I said dryly. "So, you know her well?''

"I've known Adrienne since we were girls. We didn't move in the same circles, of course.''

"You didn't?" I wondered how many circles a town the size of Hernia had.

"The Wheelers—that's her maiden name—are Baptists. Still, it broke her heart when she married Tommy Lee—which of course she wouldn't have done, if Rebecca Yoder hadn't died in that terrible accident."

"What kind of person is Adrienne? Do you trust her?"

"Ach, she's the salt of the earth. I don't believe in divorce, you know, but Adrienne Wheeler is—well—she would be the sister I've always wanted."

"You have a sister—Susannah."

Magdalena colored. "Just the same. Adrienne is smart and hardworking. And if you ask me, she's just as pretty as any movie star." She nodded to the gathering inside, which was growing rowdier by the minute.

"But Adrienne has bleached hair," I wailed.

I might have had a chance to prove that I was just as smart, if not as pretty, as my twin sister, but a horrible discordant noise inside drove Magdalena to her feet.

"Mercy me," I said, "it sounds like a cat fell down your chimney." I prayed that it wasn't Dmitri.

"It's that heavy medals again."

A heavy pulsating base clarified her statement. "You mean the rock music—heavy metal."

"Yah, that's the stuff. I told him no more heavy medals!" Magdalena shouted over the din. "It puts the cows off milking."

"Who?" I shouted back. "Surely not Little Richard!"

"Pat!" she cried and stormed back inside.

I never saw her again.

The fact that I had to turn on my headlight—my rented wreck had only one—should have tipped me off to the time. At that northern latitude the sun in May goes to bed well after decent folks have had their supper.

Therefore I have no choice but to admit that I was a thoughtless, inconsiderate friend.

Wynnell, C. J., and Peggy were pissed. Pardon my French. I really do disapprove of that vulgar term, but it best fits the scene I walked into when I returned to Room #9 at the Roach Motel. I didn't expect a welcoming committee, but neither did I envision a pack of howling banshees, eager for blood. I dropped Dmitri, who disappeared, tail inflated, beneath the nearest bed.

For the next several minutes the women ranted and raved half-heard complaints, while I hung my head and muttered half-heard apologies. At last they calmed down enough so that we could begin a conversation of sorts.

"Abigail Louise!" Wynnell hissed, sounding for all the world like Mama when I have sorely missed the mark. "How could you do this to me?"

"Do what, dear?" I asked calmly.

"Stick me with *them* for a day!"

The cacophony resumed, and I had to wave my hands like an umpire to bring the volume down a few decibels.

"She has a lot of nerve," C. J. said, tugging at my arm. It was clear to me that her intention was to steer me into the bathroom for a private audience. Not being quite the fool folks generally think I am, I resisted.

"Ladies, please—"

"But Abby, the quilt auction was supposed to be a group event, wasn't it?"

"I already explained my absence, dear," I said with utmost patience.

"No, I mean the three of us." She nodded at Wynnell and Peggy. "We were supposed to go to the quilt auction, together, right?"

"So?"

"So Wynnell and Peggy didn't even go. They dumped me off there by myself. You might not be aware of this Abby, but I'm still a vulnerable young girl."

"You're twenty-four years old, for crying out loud," Wynnell muttered. "Quit acting like a baby."

I glared at her and Peggy. Neither of them had the decency to flinch.

"Well?" I demanded.

Peggy shrugged, but said nothing.

Wynnell sighed. "Okay, so I got sidetracked. We passed a museum of miniatures on the way to the auction and I made Peggy drop me off. Oh, Abby, you should have seen what they had in their collection! I could have spent days there."

"I didn't know you were fond of miniatures, dear."

"Well, I used to be fond of you," Wynnell humphed, and picked up my hairbrush. I prayed that she would resist the temptation to use it.

"And you, Peggy," I said sternly, "what did you do?"

"Men!" C. J. and Wynnell chorused.

Peggy barely blushed. "The men at the auction were all Amish. I may as well have been in church. So, I decided to have a cup of coffee at the service center on the turnpike."

"Pick anyone up?" I asked, not unkindly. After all, with Greg on the verge of exiting my picture, I could use some trolling tips.

C. J. and Wynnell cheered. This time Peggy had the decency to turn a respectable rose.

"Well, actually—hey, this is really none of y'all's business."

"It is if you have to wait an hour outside a museum after it closes," Wynnell snarled.

"You're just jealous," Peggy hissed.

The hedgerows met in a scowl that would have frightened a scarecrow. "*I* have a husband, Peggy. I don't need to throw myself at the first thing—"

"Ladies, pleeease," I begged. I turned to C. J. "Did you buy any quilts?" I asked brightly.

She nodded. "Three. A Dresden Plate and a Star of Bethlehem. But the third one is really strange."

"Oh?" Much better to encourage C. J.'s inane fantasies than allow a full-blown cat fight in a ten-by-twelve motel room. Especially when the only real cat present was too scared to show itself.

"The third quilt," C. J. said loudly, "is a very simple patchwork, but when you look at it closely you can see that there is a secret message embroidered along the hem."

"You don't say!"

"Oh, yes. Of course I can't read it because it's in Amish, but I can guess at what it says."

"You can?" Perhaps I had committed a tactical error.

"It probably says, 'Help, I'm being held captive by the Amish.' "

"I'm sure it does, dear."

C. J. grabbed my arm. "You don't believe me, do you?"

"Well—"

"Because a similar thing happened to me when I was ten."

I pulled loose from her grip. "You bought an Amish quilt with a secret message?"

"It was the first day of summer vacation, and to celebrate I bought a box of Crunch'N'Snack. You know that caramel corn with the little prize inside?"

At this point I was more intrigued than annoyed. "Do tell," I said dangerously.

C. J. beamed, but the pair of two-legged cats moaned. Apparently they'd heard the story before.

"Like I said, I was eating a box of Crunch'N'Snack, but instead of a toy, I found a little rolled-up message stuffed in a tiny plastic tube. It looked like a piece of aquarium hose. Anyway, I had to use a magnifying glass to read it, and it said, 'Help, I'm being held captive in a Crunch'N'Snack factory.' "

"Get out of town!"

"I'm not kidding. But my mama thought it was a prank I was trying to pull on her. She pretty near beat the tar out of me."

"Bless your heart." Just between you and me, I was speaking to C. J.'s dead mother.

"But that wasn't all, Abby. A couple of months later—I know, because school was back in session by then—I bought another box, and it too had a note in it. I even showed it to my friend Tina on the playground the next day. It said, 'I'm still being held captive at the Crunch'N'Snack factory. Why didn't you get help?' "

"Why didn't you see a shrink?" Peggy grunted. "Lord knows all that Crunch'N'Snack went to your head."

C. J.'s chin shot up and forward and she held up a poorly executed fist—a girl's fist, Toy called them when I was growing up. You know the kind, with the thumb *inside* the clenched fingers.

"Eat this," C. J. said.

I gently pushed C. J.'s fist down. "Well," I said, "what a lovely little story."

"It's not just a story, Abby, and I'm not through."

I gulped, but wisely said nothing.

"In fact, I haven't even gotten to the good part. You see, a month after that, there was this story on the front page of the *Shelby Gazette* about a dead body they found in a secret warehouse of the Crunch'N'Snack factory. It was a woman, and she was chained to the wall. She was wearing some kind of work smock, and in her pocket they found a notebook, a pencil, and about two feet of plastic tubing, just like the kind they use on aquariums." She glanced at Wynnell and Peggy triumphantly. "So now you know the rest of the story."

"Lord have mercy," I said, and then struggled to suppress a yawn.

Wynnell was not nearly as gracious. She gave us all a chance to study her uvula.

"Y'all have to excuse me," she said, "I'm beat and I want to hit the sack. It's going to be a long day tomorrow."

I cocked my ears—well, metaphorically speaking, although in high school I dated a boy who really was capable of doing just that.

"You have big plans for tomorrow?" I asked sweetly.

Wynnell yawned again, setting off a chain reaction. "We all do. We're going home."

"Excuse me?"

"H-O-M-E," Peggy said. "What part didn't you get?"

I felt like slapping her.

"Where the heart is," C. J. said, and somehow managed to sound wistful.

I didn't stamp my foot, but I'm sure they could tell I was plenty peeved. Mama says my mouth puckers when I get highly emotional.

"Did y'all just forget to consult me, or was this intentional?"

The hedgerows rose and fell. "Good grief, Abby, you said we were coming up here for a couple of days. Well, it's been a couple of days. Besides, we've already rented the U-haul to take back our loot."

"Et tu, Brutus?"

"Well, somebody has to drive it, Abby. All we could get is a truck with a manual transmission and C. J. doesn't know how to drive one."

C. J. nodded vigorously. "I do so know how to drive one. I just said I'm more comfortable with an automatic."

"Close enough," Wynnell snapped.

"Ah, come on, give me a chance!"

I waved at them to shush. "So, that's it then? I bring y'all along on *my* trip, and y'all decide when it's over?"

"It was *my* car," Peggy said, "and it still is. We can leave any damn time we want."

I slapped my thigh instead of Peggy's face. There was no point in arguing further. I was outvoted by my so-called friends.

*   *   *

With apologies to Dmitri, there is more than one way to skin a cat. There was still an opportunity for me to get a look at the Southern Pennsylvania Metalworks Company, and not involve the ladies. The Mushroom Man lived within walking distance of the motel and had agreed to let me keep the car keys overnight. Not only had I planned to use the vehicle the next morning, but I had in fact paid dearly for the privilege to come and go with it at will. In retrospect, if would have been far cheaper to buy a used car. That, I could at least leave behind as an act of mercy to whomever followed in my footsteps.

Fortunately, it is very easy to tell when Peggy is asleep. When she is fully under, her mouth hangs open wide enough to swallow a tennis ball, and she drools like a mastiff. It was simply a matter of lying quietly, and allowing my eyes to adjust to the dim light created by the street lamp outside. Finally, when Peggy was in danger of drowning, I pushed Dmitri gently off my stomach, and slipped out of bed. It took me about ten minutes to dress, even though I had cleverly made the clothes I planned to wear accessible by announcing to Peggy at bedtime that I was setting out my traveling clothes for the following day.

My chief impediment to a quick and quiet getaway was that ten-pound ball of purring fur. While I was pulling on a sweatshirt, Dmitri rubbed against my bare leg and meowed. I immediately scratched his cheek, which set him to purring. The second I stopped scratching, however, the monster meowed again.

"Stop that!" I whispered.

But Watson would not be stifled. I dressed with one hand, while scratching with the other, and finally managed to get my blue jeans on, albeit backwards. Of course I took them off and put them on right, but in the course of things, I accidentally stepped on my loved one's tail. The poor dear emitted a screech that broke the sound barrier. I felt sure my goose was cooked, but luck was with me, and Peggy continued to bubble and burble like an unwatched pot. Believe me, my nerves were shot by the time I was ready to hit the night.

There remained the problem of what to do with the frustrating feline. After all, I just couldn't leave him. If he stood by the door and meowed piteously or, worse yet, jumped up on Peggy, my absence would surely be noticed. But I didn't want to take him with me either. If he escaped—or was otherwise "liberated" from the car—I would have a heck of a time trying to find him, even with a can of Mighty Mouser's as bait. During the evening clouds had rolled in, and the night sky was as dark as Buford's heart.

"Damn you, Dmitri," I mouthed.

My precious bundle of potential allergies purred.

They say lightning never strikes twice in the same place, but I have had three or four brilliant thoughts in my lifetime. I had one just then. Without further ado I scooped up Dmitri and slipped undetected from the room.

23

Peggy's Lincoln Town Car was going to make the perfect holding pen for my wandering Watson. Of course I didn't have a key, but it was no secret that Peggy kept a spare inside a little magnetic box affixed to the inside of her front bumper. I found it with no trouble and was ensconcing Dmitri comfortably in the back seat when cerebral lightning struck for the second time that night.

As long as I was going to use Peggy's car, why not actually borrow it? Why not make *myself* comfortable in the front seat, and leave my feline friend in the Mushroom Man's rattletrap? It would certainly make my getaway and return quieter, and besides, what did a cat care about leather seats and a CD player? So, borrow Peggy's car, I did, but I certainly didn't steal it.

I had no trouble finding the Southern Pennsylvania Metalworks Company. It was right where Magdalena said it would be, at the junction of Route 220 and Business 220, outside the Bedford city limits. There were a few other businesses along that stretch of road—a brickyard, a used car lot, an automobile repair shop, a recycling plant—but except for the occasional security light, they were dark, and looked deserted. SPMC was no exception.

The two-story brick building was set surprisingly close to the road, separated from it by only a narrow parking lot, barely five spaces wide. Clearly the zoning restrictions in Bedford were more lax than those back home in Charlotte. Two massive oaks anchored this asphalt strip, and despite—or perhaps, because of—the presence of a security light above the building's main entrance, the extremities of the parking lot were dark and sinister.

I may borrow cars when the opportunity presents itself, but I do not have a criminal mind. Nonetheless, I thought to turn off the headlights (thank goodness Peggy's model did not come equipped with running lights) before turning into the parking lot. The space marked "Reserved for CEO" was unfortunately within the influence of the security light, so I parked in an unmarked spot deep within the shadows.

It is safe to say that Business Route 220 is not a hotbed of activity at midnight. Since leaving the city limits a mile or so back I hadn't seen one moving car. When I stepped outside of Peggy's car the only sound I heard were the distant "barumps" of bullfrogs that inhabited the weed-choked drainage ditch on the opposite side of the road. No doubt they were rejoicing over impending rain, and I couldn't say that I blamed them. The second I emerged from the air-conditioned cavern of the Lincoln, I was drenched with sweat. *Okay*, as everyone knows, good southern girls don't sweat, we merely dew, but I was on Yankee soil after all, and if this was dew, then the Mississippi River could be blotted up with one heavy-duty paper towel.

I cursed myself for having foolishly planned to wear my heaviest clothes on the return trip to Charlotte, and just to be fair, I cursed Peggy for plotting to turn us all into Popsicles. Then without wasting another breath I set out on foot to reconnoiter the premises.

Theoretically at least, I'd watched enough James Bond movies to know how to break and enter. In real life I have a hard time opening the cellophane bags inside cereal boxes, and I can never, ever pull that protective foil seal off a jar of Jif peanut butter without mutilating it first with a knife and a pair of pliers. Face it, as a Bond beauty, I was a bust.

For one thing, I could barely peer over the windowsills, which incidentally were covered with a soft but pungent layer of bird droppings. The panes themselves were so filthy that, even if all the lights had been left on inside, I wouldn't have been able to see anything smaller than an elephant. James can, of course, open doors with a credit card, whereas I can't even insert mine into the ATM without having it spit back at me half the time.

I pride myself on my tenacity, but I am ashamed to say that just then I was feeling about as tenacious as a Carolina snowflake in April. The windows may as well have been nailed shut, and after a few feeble attempts to open the door with my house keys, my American Express card, and an eyebrow tweezers, I plumb gave up. A sensible Abigail would be back at the Roach Motel catching her quota of ''z's.'' Come to think of it, a truly sensible— make that a wise—Abigail would be safely tucked in her own bed in Charlotte, or just possibly, down in Key West fishing for grouper with you-know-who.

As Mama always says, you have to let go of the old, before you can grasp the new, and it wasn't until I'd let go of my plan to break into the Southern Pennsylvania Metalworks Company that I noticed the smaller building behind it, all but hidden by a massive maple. A cracked, weed-riddled sidewalk led directly from the former to the latter—or at least appeared to. There were no security lights in that area of the property, and I stubbed both big toes before I'd walked a dozen paces.

''Damn you, Abby,'' I said—talking to oneself is, after all the highest form of intelligence—''next time bring a flashlight.''

Abby agreed that she had been remiss, and we proceeded carefully together.

It wasn't until I got close enough to where even *I*

could have hit the smaller building with a stone, that I realized it was surrounded by a chain-link fence. It was soon apparent that the gate was secured with enough locks to tucker Houdini, and you can bet I abandoned any notion of climbing the fence when I espied the nasty coil of razor wire strung along the top.

"Good things come in small packages," Mama used to say in her attempt to build my self-esteem, but until the day I see a four-foot, nine-inch fashion model, I will never be truly convinced. But that dark (and about to be stormy) night in the mountains of southern Pennsylvania, I became a temporary believer.

Just as I was about to give up for the second time, the night's first flash of real lightning illuminated a hole in the fence. Technically speaking it wasn't even a proper hole, but an area along the bottom of the fence where someone, perhaps the installer, had removed the bottom three rows of links to accommodate the roots of a tree. If I lay flat on my back, and turned my face to the side, I could just manage to squeeze under the fence—well, I might have, had I truly been as flat-chested as Buford always claimed. Having come that far, however, I was not about to let two molehills become a mountain, so I did the only practical thing and removed my bra. Gravity did its work and I made it through in one piece, although thank heavens I was wearing a sweatshirt and jeans.

If you ask me, only an idiot would erect such a formidable barricade around an unlocked building. Need I say more about the Teschels's mental prowess? And I think it was safe to conclude that Leona Teschel had not been the last of her clan to leave the building. It wasn't the front door that was unlocked, you see, but a side door. As everyone knows, a woman would have checked all the doors at least three times each, and sniffed for gas leaks, even if there wasn't a stove on the premises.

It was even darker than Buford's heart inside the building so I had no choice but to turn on a light. Fortunately my fingers found the switch before encountering any wildlife. The overhead bulb was probably no more than sixty watts, but for a few seconds it felt like I was looking into the sun. Then as my eyes began to adjust I found myself staring at a scene from an Indiana Jones movie. There were roaches everywhere—more roaches, I'd wager, than there were paying guests at the Clinton White House.

Of course I screamed. I assure you, however, that it was a controlled scream; of short duration, perfectly on key, and it originated in my diaphragm. In all modesty, it was more like the first note of an aria than a shriek. At any rate, the roaches seemed to be even less happy than I, and they scrambled for cover.

The source of the infestation was immediately obvious. The Teschels might live in a Victorian gingerbread house in the finest part of Hernia, but they were slobs. Hungry slobs. I had never seen such an array of empty fast-food containers. Who knew that Bedford had two Chinese restaurants? Wok Like A Man certainly wasn't listed in the phone book, although judging by the mounds of detritus around me, the restaurant in question may well have closed its doors year ago.

Distracted by bugs and garbage, it took me longer than it should have to see that I had hit pay dirt. The furnace, the anvils, the tools, sheets of beaten silver, even photographs of museum-quality pieces—it was all there. Two long wooden benches covered with the accouterments of forgery. The only thing missing was a finished reproduction. I would have given anything, including an inch of my height, to have a Polaroid camera with me.

"Well, well, well," I said to myself, and to an exceptionally large and surprisingly bold roach who was peeking over the edge of a pizza box.

The scabrous brute waved his antennae in obvious agreement.

"Abigail, you are something else," I said, basking in

the moment. "Not only are you one red-hot mama, but you're an ace detective. If Greg Washburn had an ounce of sense he'd be worshipping at your temple of love, instead of fishing in Florida. But you know what? You really don't need him, dear. You could have any red-blooded American male with a pulse you please."

Although not red-blooded, and lacking a pulse, the roach seemed to agree. The randy fellow hoisted himself over the edge of the box and came barreling at me. I jumped back from the workbench, but just in case he was capable of flight, I reached for a large cardboard box on the floor near me, which I planned to hold up as a shield. The damn thing had something in it.

Something heavy.

Something that felt like it might be metal.

I forgot the amorous roach and peeked inside. Wrapped in a single sheet of tissue paper was the most exquisite eighteenth-century epergne I'd ever seen. All right, so it was the first eighteenth-century epergne I'd seen outside of a museum, but at the risk of being rude, how many epergnes can you remember seeing, eighteenth century or otherwise?

"Epergne," I purred. The word was French in origin and the first "e" was long. The "g" and final "e" were silent.

Epergnes are essentially elaborate, tiered centerpieces. A gold or silver frame holds a central basket, or vase, around which are suspended smaller versions of the same. They are invariably ornate, often with delicate scrollwork or piercing.

The epergne I beheld was pierced silver in the rococo style. If I had to bet the farm, I'd guess it was a copy of a late eighteenth-century English piece. Beyond that, I would be just as accurate in guessing tomorrow's soccer score for the Sri Lanka team in the Asia Cup.

I struggled with the morality of taking the epergne with me. As evidence, you understand. Just in case Tommy Lee showed and cleaned out the place while I

was contacting the authorities. It was one of my shorter
moral struggles.

Edward Marlon was your typical Yankee sheriff. He
was on the short side, slender, and had a washboard
stomach. He had a full head of curly blond hair that
made me want to run my fingers through it. His brown
eyes shone with intelligence, and he had all his teeth.
Unfortunately the man had a strong Yankee accent, and
the astonishing ability to speak faster than the human
ear could hear.

"I didn't quite catch that," I said, for the umpteenth
time. "Would you please repeat what you just said?"

To his credit, the sheriff made an obvious, and seem-
ingly painful attempt to put brakes on his words.
"Isaidthatwassomestormwehadthere."

"I understood that!" I cried joyfully. Believe me, un-
derstanding Sheriff Marlon was as close to being bilin-
gual as I was ever going to get. "Now please, say
something else."

The sheriff frowned. "Howaboutletsgetdowntobusi-
ness?"

"All right. Like I said on the phone, I want to report
a crime. In fact, several crimes."

He extracted a notepad and pen from his shirt pocket.
His movements were uncannily familiar. Except for his
height, hair, and eye color, he might have been Greg.

"Howaboutwestartatthebeginningthen.Letmehave-
yourfullnameandaddressfortherecord."

I complied. If only that fly on the wall was Miss Wil-
liams, my high school Spanish teacher who claimed I
didn't have an ear for languages. Boy, was she ever
wrong! But I will spare you the trouble of having to
read Sheriff Marlon's words as I heard them. It isn't
natural to talk even as fast as your average Yankee,
much less faster than the speed of light. My Aunt Marilyn in Atlanta is convinced that fifty words or more a
minute is likely to produce cancer of the vocal cords.

While I won't go that far, I do think that if the good
Lord had intended for us to rattle away like machine
guns, he wouldn't have created so many vowels.

Of course the sheriff had no trouble keeping up with
me. "Now, just what are these crimes you want to report?"

"The big one is murder," I said.

Sheriff Marlon cocked his handsome head.

"Oh no, not me," I hastened to assure him. "I didn't
commit these crimes. I'm just reporting them."

This dual-speed conversation was not being held in
the sheriff's office, as you might have imagined, but at
Imogene's House of Pancakes, where Imogene herself
served pancakes, as well as other breakfast treats. It was
four o'clock in the morning and we were the only customers in the place. Our corner booth was the cleanest
table in the joint, which wasn't saying much. A good
archeologist could, by carefully slicing through the res-
idue, catalogue every meal ever served on that Formica
platform.

"You saw someone commit a murder?" the sheriff
asked.

"Yes—well, not exactly. But I saw Purnell Purvis
collapse after he'd been poisoned. It happened on the
sidewalk right outside my shop, the Den of Antiquity."

"Where was this?"

"Charlotte, North Carolina," I said proudly. "The
Queen City."

"Let me get this straight. You want to report a murder
that happened in another state?"

"Well, the murderer lives here."

"Was the murder reported in Charlotte?"

"Of course," I said indignantly.

"Then I fail to understand. What does this have to do
with you?"

It was time to think fast. Unfortunately I had a better
chance of programming my VCR correctly. If it hadn't

been for Imogene's sudden appearance I might have incriminated myself.

"You'nz ready to order?"

Short, blond, and handsome turned to me. "Well?"

I had yet to consult the menu, a single laminated pink sheet of paper. Judging by the grease on the thing, Imogene was a good cook.

"I'll have two eggs—sunnyside up, bacon—not too crisp, grits—"

"We don't have any of that."

"I see. Do you have cornbread?"

"We serve breakfast," Imogene said through pursed lips.

"Biscuits?"

She grunted.

"The usual," Sheriff Marlon said.

"It'll be out in a minute." Imogene beamed at the sheriff and then, as if by magic, disappeared.

"What's the usual?" I asked.

"Blueberry pancakes. Now where were we?"

He raked tanned fingers through the blond curls. I almost moaned aloud.

"We were talking about Tommy Lee Teschel," I managed to say solemnly.

"Ah, so he's the killer."

"You know him?"

"Unfortunately just about everyone knows Tommy Lee. So far he's managed to keep himself out of serious trouble, but I guess you could say we were all kind of waiting for the shoe to drop."

"So you'll arrest him?"

"Is there a warrant for his arrest in South Carolina?"

"North Carolina, and no, there isn't any warrant. You see—well, they don't have all the information. They don't have the proof."

The brown eyes regarded me frankly. "You do?"

"You can say that again. It's right out there in my car."

24

No one should set an eighteenth-century epergne atop a sticky table in an all-night pancake house. I was at least guilty of poor taste.

Sheriff Marlon whistled in appreciation. "Where did you get this?"

"I got me one just like that," said Imogene, appearing out of nowhere.

"I bet you do," I said.

"Got it at Walmart over in Somerset," she said, plunking down our platters of gristle and grease.

"You don't say."

She pointed to my sapphire ring. "I got me one of them too."

"You lucky woman."

"Only I wear mine on the right hand. When I ain't working, of course." She pointed again. "That mean you're married?"

I almost didn't answer. But the sheriff's ears had perked up, so I couldn't leave the question hanging.

"I'm not married. This was a gift from an elderly friend for whom I once did a favor."

When she dematerialized, I continued. "I found this epergne in a little building out behind the Southern Pennsylvania Metalworks Company. Tommy Lee has a secret workshop there where he makes reproductions of silver masterpieces. He sells these things as originals in

Georgia and the Carolinas. Who knows, maybe he sells them here too.''

He poured half a bottle of boysenberry syrup over his short stack. "Tommy Lee gave you a tour?"

I attempted a bite of bacon. It was so crisp it shattered into a million pieces. I moistened a finger and dabbed up a few of the closer shards.

"Of course he didn't give me a tour. I arranged that on my own."

To my surprise, he shook his handsome head. "Let me get this straight. You're confessing that you broke and entered—''

"I didn't break and enter," I snapped. "I squeezed under the fence. The door just happened to be un-locked."

"Okay, so we've got trespassing and illegal entry." He pointed to the dish. "And theft."

"*What*?"

He nodded at the dish. "Does that belong to Tommy Lee?"

"Yes, but it isn't like you think."

"Then tell me how it is," he said, and took an enor-mous bite of pancake.

I spilled the beans. Figuratively, but it wouldn't have mattered had it been literally. There was already almost as much syrup on the sheriff's tie as there was on his plate.

"That's some story," he said as he mashed the last few crumbs between the tines of his fork.

"Every word of it's true. So, when are you going to arrest Tommy Lee?"

He smiled. "I'm afraid it isn't that simple."

"Well, then get a search warrant. You'll find a work-shop back there, just like I said."

"To get a search warrant I have to convince a judge that there is *probable cause*. No offense, Miss Timber-lake, but all I have is your story."

"And this!" I rattled the epergne.

"Which you came by illegally, if I may remind you."

I was about to bust a gut with frustration. "But you can't just let a hardened criminal continue on his merry way. Who knows who he'll kill next."

"I didn't say I wouldn't begin an investigation," he said quietly.

I breathed a huge sigh of relief. That was at least a start.

"Okay, you don't know me from Adam, and suddenly I show up with this crazy story. I can appreciate that. But I am a highly respected member of the Charlotte business community."

He nodded. "I don't suppose you'd mind, then, if I checked out your story?"

"Why should I mind? Of course you won't be able to speak to Investigator Washburn. He's off in Florida fishing for grouper."

"I'm sure his colleagues could fill me in."

"And just for the record, I don't know anything about dimethyl sulfate. In fact, I'm not even sure about pulmonary edema."

The brown eyes widened. "What?"

Imogene's miraculous appearance saved me yet again.

"Phone," she said, not even looking at me.

The sheriff picked up the epergne. "Mind if I take this with me?"

"Help yourself," I said, trying to sound casual. As if I would just take off with the piece like some common thief!

While Sheriff Marlon took the call, I tried to eat. The biscuit was so sweet I spit it out into my hand. I was beginning to think Wynnell was right. We southerners might like our sweet tea, but northerners take the cake when it comes to sugar consumption. No doubt the Yankees would have lost the war, had Sherman not had a dentist traveling with him.

My eggs were indeed sunnyside up, but they were as raw as the day the hen laid them. Although they lolled about on a bed of grease, I doubt if they'd even had a chance to warm up to room temperature.

Sheriff Marlon returned sans epergne.

"Where is it?" I demanded. My ire is capable of cooking an egg in a minute flat.

"I put it my car for safekeeping," he said, and had the audacity to wink. "You told me to help myself."

"I didn't think you were going to keep it."

"It's evidence, isn't it? Surely you weren't planning to keep it, were you?"

I shook my head sadly.

He smiled broadly. "How's your breakfast?"

I glanced around for the skulking Imogene. She was nowhere to be seen.

"Fine."

"Good, because I can't cook nearly as well as Imogene."

"I beg your pardon?" If you ask me, the guy was moving a little fast, even by Yankee standards.

"Bedford County Jail does not pretend to have haute cuisine."

"What?" It's a good thing I have short hair, because it was standing on end. I stood up to keep it company.

Sheriff Marlon remained seated. "Is that your Lincoln Town Car parked just outside?"

"Well—uh, I—it sort of is."

"I see." He took a sip of tepid coffee. "Well, we just got a call reporting it stolen."

"I can explain!"

The big brown eyes regarded me calmly. He didn't seem about to slap cuffs on me, despite his tough talk. I sat down.

"The car belongs to a friend of mine—Peggy Redfern. I was only borrowing it."

"Did you have her permission?"

"No, but I'm sure she wouldn't have minded. She was asleep already, you see. Besides, Peggy borrows things from me all the time."

"She minded enough to report it missing."

I muttered something unkind under my breath. Believe me, it was justified. The woman couldn't help but notice that I was missing along with the car. Even Peggy can add two and two.

"I didn't quite catch that," the sheriff said. I think there was a twinkle in his eye.

I held out my hands, palms up. "Book me."

He laughed, displaying perfect white teeth. Considering the amount of sugar in his diet, teeth that perfect had to be caps, which meant that either Pennsylvania sheriffs were paid a lot more than their Carolina counterparts, or the Marlons had family money. Either way, being arrested could have a silver lining.

"Relax," he said. "I've sent my deputy out to pick up your friend. They'll be joining us here in a few minutes. Maybe then we can settle things a little less dramatically. By the way, how do you like the Motor Coach Motel?"

"You mean the Roach Motel? Although, come to think of it I haven't seen a single roach there. But the Southern Pennsylvania Metalworks Company, on the other hand—"

"So you like it?"

"Well, it probably beats sleeping in a drainpipe somewhere—but just barely. Confidentially, the manager looks like he crawled out of drainpipe. Talk about weird!"

"Robert's my brother."

"Oops! Sorry!"

I never knew until then that it is possible to be so embarrassed that one can actually feel faint. I clutched at the sticky table edge for support.

"I hear he rented his car to you."

"That was very kind of him."

"It used to be mine."

"Well, I just love it."

"It's a piece of junk," he said, brown eyes twinkling. "And you're right, Robert is weird."

By then I didn't care if Sheriff Edward Marlon carted me off to jail in shackles. In fact, I was beginning to wish he would.

Peggy was delighted to get her car back. There was no doubt about that. And I honestly don't think it had even occurred to her that I might be the thief.

"Well, where did you think I was?" I demanded. "Out walking the streets?"

Peggy shrugged. "Face it, Abby, you're a strange bird. You could have been anywhere, up to anything. I just didn't have you pegged as a car thief."

"I didn't steal it."

"Of course I won't press charges or anything, because you are a friend. Just make sure that next time do me a favor and ask first. All this worry and lack of sleep tends to be hard on a girl's complexion." She smiled coyly at the sheriff.

"My Aunt Tina Marie was a streetwalker," C. J. said, shaking her head. "Ooh, Abby, I would get out of that business if I were you."

"I'm not in that business!" I hissed.

"That's what my Aunt Tina Marie always said, but we knew better. You don't make that much money playing church bingo. Anyway, she was—"

"Give it a rest, dear," I said through clenched teeth.

"Why, Abby, what ever happened to freedom of speech?"

I waggled my eyebrows in the sheriff's direction.

C. J. giggled. "Ooh, I see. Well, did you know that rice is the most popular breakfast food in the world? Of course, in much of Asia it's served as gruel made with fish stock. I had some once. It tasted like the bottom of an aquarium."

Wynnell pushed her plate away. "Please," she

begged, "can't we talk about something else? Anything—except food."

I reached across the table and patted her arm affectionately. The poor woman was as green as the sheen on her ham.

Since the entire troop had shown up to accuse me of car theft, the sheriff and I had been forced to abandon our cozy booth for two tables pushed together in the middle of the room. Why the latecomers had even bothered to order was beyond me. They could have gotten a better meal just by chipping away at the table with their forks.

"Speaking of food," Peggy said, "this is, without a doubt, one of the best meals I've ever eaten. Don't y'all agree?" The poor woman was serious.

As if sensing that her reputation as a cook was at stake if we answered, Imogene materialized, a platter of sausage links in hand.

"On the house," she grunted.

Sheriff Marlon glanced at his watch. "Thanks, Imogene, but I've got to run."

"So soon?" Peggy looked up from her plate to the man, to the platter, and back to her plate. Sausage or sheriff, it was a hard choice.

Imogene plunked the platter directly in front of Peggy, thereby making the decision a whole lot easier. "We still on for tonight, Edward?"

"You bet."

Imogene smiled broadly and disappeared in a cloud of grease.

Sheriff Marlon stood up. "Miss Timberlake, may I speak to you?"

"Sure."

C. J. nudged me. "I think he means alone."

I stood up as well.

"Hey, it was *my* car she stole," Peggy said, but reached for the serving tongs. There was no need to worry about her interference, not until the platter had been licked clean.

After everybody finished breakfast, the gals and I drove back to the Roach Motel with the windows wide open. The rain had washed the heat out of the air, and it was the kind of morning I'd order everyday if I could.

"So, Abby, where were you all night?" C. J. asked with the special tactlessness of the very young.

They say the best defense is a good offense, and despite my good southern upbringing, I can certainly be offensive if the need arises.

"I couldn't sleep," I snapped, "so I went for a spin. What's it to you?"

I know what you're thinking. You're thinking that I should have leveled with the gals at that point. Perhaps they had a right to know about Tommy Lee's counterfeit antique operation. But I was too tired to rehash it all.

C. J. gasped at my rudeness. "Ex*cuse* me for living!"

Peggy was not so easily put off. "It was my car, damn it. I have a right to know where you took it."

I released a long, low sigh. It gave me time to think up a good lie. Thank God my kids had at least taught me that.

"Okay, you got me. I drove into Pittsburgh, if you must know."

"Oh, really?" Peggy said brightly. "An old boyfriend perhaps? Someone you went to college with?"

"I knew it," Wynnell mumbled, "I just knew it. It's because of the problems you're having with Greg, isn't it?"

"Guilty on both counts."

"So that's where you've been sneaking off to," C. J. squealed. "An old boyfriend in Pittsburgh! Oh Abby. Tell us all the dirty details."

I sighed again. "There's really not much to tell. Turns out Tommy is a priest now. A Catholic priest. We just talked."

"Ooh, Abby! Dating a priest!"

"But two trips to Pittsburgh in one day?" As the only other mother in the car, Wynnell had reason to be skeptical.

I turned and smiled the hedgerows back into submission. "He had an emergency today. Last rites or something. We didn't get a chance to talk. So we met at an all-night bowling alley."

"I see." Clearly she didn't.

"The youth group was there with him. It was just a good-bye, damn it. You know—closure." I swear, I was starting to choke up at the sad scene playing in my mind.

"I dated a priest once," Peggy said wistfully.

"Wow, two trips to Pittsburgh just to talk to a married priest," C. J. said. I suppose the admiration in her voice should have made me feel guilty.

Peggy glanced down at her gas tank gage. Sometimes she's slow to get the point.

"You drove my Lincoln to Pittsburgh, Abby?"

"I remembered to fill it," I said quickly. There was no need to worry about the odometer. The woman thinks those little numbers are some kind of bonus points she'll get when she trades in the car.

C. J. leaned forward. "I bet it was just like in *Casablanca*."

"Excuse me?"

"You and the priest saying good-bye. Ingrid Bergman and Humphrey Bogart. Only it was a bowling alley, instead of a foggy airport."

"Sure," I said. After all, it was one of her nicer fantasies.

"But don't worry, Abby, you won't be alone for long. For some strange reason, men seem to be attracted to you. Take that hunky sheriff, for instance. He had the hots for you."

"He did not!"

"Ooh, but he did. What did he want to see you alone about? Was he asking you on a date?"

"C. J.!" Wynnell said sharply. She tapped me on the shoulder. "What *did* he want?"

"It was about Dmitri," I lied. My, how it was getting easy to fib.

C. J. leaned forward and patted my shoulder. "I'm so sorry."

I turned in my seat. "Why, dear?"

"Believe me, Abby, I know how hard it is to lose a cat."

"But Dmitri—"

"When Puddlejumper died, I cried for hours. You won't believe the amount of salt I lost. The doctor said it was the worst case of sodium deficiency he had ever heard about."

"Give me a break," Wynnell moaned.

"No, really. Of course that was before my Aunt Lottie Mae got a job peeling onions on an Israeli kibbutz near the Dead Sea. They grow these especially strong onions there, and as soon as she started peeling the first onion, Aunt Lottie Mae began to cry."

"What's so unusual about that?"

"Nothing. But you see, Aunt Lottie Mae couldn't stop. They say she cried her weight in salt in just three days."

"Gracious," said Wynnell, who really has a soft heart, "did she see a doctor?"

"The kibbutz didn't have a doctor, so they sent her to one in a small town halfway between Sodom and Gomorrah."

"And?"

"Nobody knows. She was never seen or heard from again."

"You're nuts," Peggy said. She turned to me. "So, Abby, was that all the cute sheriff had to say? Just something about your cat being dead?"

"Dmitri is not dead!" I nearly screamed. "Sheriff Marlon simply wanted me to know that the Mushroom

Man has agreed not to hassle me for what Dmitri did to his car last night.''

"What did Dmitri do?"

"Let's just say you can be glad that I drove your car, and left Dmitri in the other."

Peggy was not amused. "I'd sue you, Abby. I don't care if you are my friend."

"Yeah well, Mushroom Man wanted to do the same, but his brother talked him out of it."

Peggy gasped. "The Mushroom Man and that hunky sheriff are brothers?"

"Lord have mercy," Wynnell cried. No doubt she'd been entertaining fantasies that Sheriff Marlon, whom she clearly liked, was a transplanted southerner.

I nodded. "It's true. Hard to believe, isn't it?"

"Well, I think our motel manager is cute," C. J. said, just to be contrary. She was obviously miffed that we had taken her Aunt Lottie Mae's story with a grain of salt.

"You think he's *cute?*"

"Not everyone has the same taste, Abby. Besides, he's kind of sweet. Last time I was in the office he gave me a complimentary newspaper."

"That was the *Pennysaver*," Wynnell humphed. "He gave us each one."

"So? Y'all are always after me to meet some nice young man, aren't you? Well, maybe I have."

"Good, then you get to go in and pay the bill when we check out. Maybe he'll give us a discount."

C. J. turned sodium white. "But I'm the youngest. I'm barely more than a kid. Y'all are always reminding me of that."

"Which means you should listen to your elders," Wynnell said, and tapped the back of my seat so I would know she was in on the joke.

Peggy may be irritating, but she's no slouch. "Let me do your makeup first. We might not have to pay anything."

In a rare moment of solidarity, Peggy, Wynnell, and I began to tease C. J. mercilessly. Who knows how far we may have taken it—possibly even driven the poor girl to tears—had we not had to stop for a red light.

Almost immediately the driver of the car beside us began to honk furiously.

"What the hell?" Peggy growled. "These Yankee drivers . . ." Her voice trailed off and she stiffened.

"Holy Moly!" Wynnell cried. "That's you, Abigail!"

"Jeepers!" C. J. gasped.

Peggy shook her head. "Damn if it doesn't look like you."

I pinched myself just to be sure it wasn't. I said "ouch," but my double didn't.

"It isn't me," I announced.

"Of course not," C. J. said. "That woman's a gorgeous blonde."

I pinched C. J.

25

drienne Wheeler followed us back to the Roach Motel. All the way there my friends marveled at our resemblance.

"Except that she's blond," C. J. said for the umpteenth time, patting her own dishwater blond hair. "And men prefer blondes, you know."

"Says who?" Peggy was a redhead—probably a natural redhead at one time, although only her hairdresser knew for sure, along with several dozen men.

C. J. ignored Peggy. "See how you could look, Abby?"

I tried to pinch her again, but she had wisely scooted out of reach of my short arms.

"It's definitely a bottle job," Wynnell said loyally. "Besides, our Abby could be blond if she wanted to, but she'd rather rely on her personality, than on peroxide."

That wasn't strictly true. Once—in college, when I undoubtedly had less personality—I gave the old bottle a try. Unfortunately, my hair did not take to the chemicals well and turned a sickly shade of green. No hairdresser dared touch such damaged tresses, so for six months I walked around looking like I had a dead plant on top of my head.

In the motel parking lot the comparisons continued.

"Y'all are even the same height," Wynnell said, after

she'd made us stand back to back, and balanced her
pocketbook on our heads.

"Two baby peas in a pod," Peggy said, although I'm
sure she meant it kindly.

"Well, they're not exactly alike," C. J. said, and
snickered.

I turned and glared at her. "I know, dear. She's blond,
and I'm not."

"Yes, but that's not what I meant."

"Then do tell," I said through gritted teeth.

"Well, since you put it that way, Abby. Miss Wheeler
here is blessed in the bosom department and you—
well—your Wonder Bra is still wondering."

Peggy and Wynnell had to restrain me. Well, if the
truth be known, I let them think they were restraining
me. Wynnell couldn't open a pickle jar if you unscrewed
the lid for her, and Peggy never grabs anything tightly,
lest she damage her perfect nails.

"Just let me get my baby pea hands on you," I
shrieked.

C. J. was hopping from one foot to another, like a
boxer with a bad sense of timing. "Oh yeah, what would
you do then? Reach up and punch me in the stomach?"

"Ladies!" Wynnell said sharply. "We are not
alone."

Adrienne Wheeler smiled gamely. She was a high
school teacher after all.

"I'd like to speak to Abby, alone," she said.

As might be expected, there was a good deal of grum-
bling, particularly from our junior member. I righteously
pointed out that if we were to leave that day still, someone had to rent and load the U-haul, and it wasn't going
to be me. I had yet to buy a single thing in Pennsylvania
that wasn't digestible—if you don't count my breakfast.

"I'm normally much better behaved," I said when we
were alone, "but I didn't get a wink of sleep last night."

"Tell me about it."

"You too?" Not that I cared what blondie did with

her time. No doubt she'd been partying all night and was going to call in sick again today.

She motioned in the direction of her car. "Do you mind if we sit down?"

"Actually, I do." How stupid did she think I was?

"Fine, we'll stand. Look, Abby—"

"You can call me Ms. Timberlake. I saw you drive away from Leona's house yesterday afternoon. All that crap about Leona Teschel being the devil with breasts, the virtual mother-in-law from hell, and there you were, consorting with the enemy."

She laughed, and take it from me, our laughs do not sound alike. Had there been a healthy male donkey within five miles, one of us would have been in trouble.

"So that's it! You won't get in my car, because you're afraid of me?"

"Bingo, sister. Although I prefer to call it careful."

"I should have known. Magdalena tried to warn me."

I recoiled in shock. After a few false starts I managed to sputter a couple of coherent words.

"Magdalena? Me? Magdalena talked to *you* about *me*?"

"She was concerned about you, Abby."

"I can take care of myself just fine, thank you!"

"Oh, I know. You are a very resourceful woman. I suspected that Tommy Lee was up to some kind of shady business, but I never would have guessed it was stealing silver."

"*What*?"

"It's funny, because I've driven by Southern Pennsylvania Metalworks Company many times—even stopped in a few times to harangue Tommy Lee—but I never really noticed that little building out back before. Or if I did, I didn't think much about it. Not until you crawled under the fence."

"You followed me?" I shrieked, sending a flock of starlings in a nearby tree into orbit.

"It was Magdalena's idea. She was afraid Tommy

Lee might catch on to you. She sent me over as a—''

"Spy!"

"Lookout. I mean, what would you have done if Tommy Lee had caught you in that little building where he hides his stolen goods?"

"They're not stolen, they're counterfeited, dear. He makes those things right there."

"You're kidding? Tommy Lee made that silver thing you found in the box?"

"That's my guess."

"Damn! When we were married that man couldn't change a light bulb without written instructions."

"So, you were playing watchdog for me, were you?" She nodded.

"I didn't see a car."

"I had to park at the bowling alley and jog all the way. It's a good thing I'm a track coach and run with my girls now and then. But when you started to leave, I really had to scramble. Tore this on that damn fence." She fingered an L-shaped rip on her denim blouse, just above her waistline.

Aha! So it wasn't just her bosoms that were bigger.

"Perhaps you need to lose a few pounds, dear," I suggested kindly.

"I weigh ninety-six pounds dripping wet. How about you?"

She had me beat by two measly pounds. Big deal.

"You still haven't told me what you were doing at Leona's house, Adrienne. At least you haven't tried to deny it."

"I was paying my rent, that's what! Our conversation about the old bag being my landlady reminded me that it was almost two weeks overdue."

"Do you expect me to believe that! Ha!" Confidentially, that male donkey was going to have a hard time choosing between the two of us after that laugh.

Adrienne dug in the pocket of her jeans and extracted a slip of paper. "This is my rent receipt! Signed and dated yesterday by Leona Teschel herself.''

"What does that prove?"

She thrust the paper in my face. "These are the same jeans I wore yesterday when I helped you look for your stupid cat. Do you think I normally carry a freshly dated receipt with me on the off chance I need to placate some anal-retentive skeptic?"

My good southern manners prevented me from slapping her face—well, those and the fact it would have been too much like slapping myself.

"I'm just trying to be careful," I whined.

"Well, it isn't me you need to be afraid of. You really going home today?"

"As soon as the girls get back with the U-haul."

"Good. You'll be a lot safer down there."

"Don't be so sure. Someone back home was poisoned a few days ago. I'd bet my bottom dollar that the Teschels were behind it."

She paled. "Trash. Just like I told you. They're all trash."

"I suppose you saw me speak to the sheriff?"

"Corner booth until your friends joined you."

"Wow, you're good!"

"What did the sheriff say?"

"He said he'd try to get a warrant to search the Southern Pennsylvania Metalworks Company." I paused dramatically. "*And* he asked me out on a date," I said.

"Lucky," she said, and gave me a sisterly tap on the shoulder.

"Of course since I'm leaving today, he's all yours. If you wise up and dye your hair back to the way God intended, the sheriff might not even notice the difference."

She inhaled deeply. "Nah. These puppies would give me away."

I tapped her back—perhaps a bit too hard—and thanked her for her concern.

"Keep in touch," I said warmly.

"Say hello to Mama," she said, and smiled.

I said hello to Mama sooner than I would have liked. I had stretched out across the bed, with a happily purring Dmitri on my chest, when the phone rang. The sudden jangle startled my bundle of purrs, who pushed off with his back feet and left scratch marks on my sternum.

"What?" I said, perhaps a bit testily.

In my defense, I was in pain. Besides, C. J. had already settled our bill with Mushroom Man who, as it turned out, was named Brando. Brando Marlon.

It had not been a pleasant experience. Mr. Marlon had added all sorts of frivolous charges to our bill. Whoever heard of a motel charging for those little soap bars? Or toilet paper for that matter? Peggy's makeup job on C. J. hadn't done a bit of good, and when she returned to the meager bosoms of her friends, the poor girl was in tears.

Mr. Marlon gasped at my greeting, but said nothing.

"Look, you little weasel," I growled. "We paid your damn bill, and checkout time isn't until eleven. What more do you want? A pound of flesh?"

"Why Abigail Louise, how you talk!"

"Mama?"

"And after all I've done for you. I gave you the best years of my life and—"

"Endured thirty-six hours of excruciating labor—"

"Forty-two."

"What?"

"Forty-two hours," Mama said. "I didn't want you to feel guilty, Abby, so I always knocked off six hours when I told the story. The worst six hours, if you really must know."

"Mama, I'm sorry. I didn't know it was you. I thought you were the motel owner."

"Never mind that, dear, just tell me why it is I'm always the last one to know."

I racked my brain for things I might have neglected

to tell her. There were a few things I would purposefully *never* tell her, but she had about as much chance of finding those things out herself, as I did playing in the NBA.

"Mama, I don't have the slightest idea what you mean—unless it's about Greg. FYI, we haven't officially broken up. We're just taking a careful look at our relationship."

"Well, you'd be a fool to drop Greg, Missy, but that's not what I'm talking about. I want to know why you didn't tell me Susan's getting married."

I dropped the receiver, which slid off the bed, and in the process of retrieving it, I kicked the night stand, toppling a K-mart specialty lamp. The base of the lamp survived intact, but the muslin shade was dented. I did my best to reshape it before picking up the phone. Crises with Susan were inevitable, but another encounter with Brando Marlon was to be avoided if at all possible.

"Abby, are you still there?" Mama sounded like she was talking to me through a can tied to a string.

"I'm back, Mama. I just dropped the phone. Now what's this about Susan getting married?"

"That's what she said. Tomorrow morning at eight o'clock. At Glencairn Gardens."

"Over my dead body," I grunted.

"Then you better hurry home, dear."

"I'm coming home today, Mama. Wynnell and C. J. are going to be driving a U-haul back, so they may stop overnight halfway. Wynnell's nervous about driving through the mountains and C. J. isn't nervous enough, and she doesn't even know how to drive a standard shift. I'd offer to drive, but those trucks are kind of big, and besides, I didn't buy a single thing. But Lord, I hear that Wynnell did. And Peggy. Acres of quilts and some good Amish furniture too. I don't think C. J. was quite as lucky, but she told me about a nice—"

"Cut the chit-chat, dear. This call is costing me a pretty penny."

"You mean *me*. It's costing *me* a pretty penny."

"I don't think so dear, unless you've started paying my bills."

I thought about that for as long as it takes a pint of ice cream to start sweating on a warm summer day.

"Mama, are you back at your house in Rock Hill?"

"Of course, dear. Where else would I be, Timbuktu?"

"My house, Mama! You were going to stay at my house until the police arrested Purvis's killer. Remember?"

"Oh, they already did that," Mama said, and hung up.

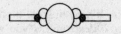

26

I immediately dialed back.

"Motor Coach Motel. How may I help you?"

"Mr. Mushroom? I mean, Mr. Marlon?"

"Oh, it's you, Mrs. Timberlake. What do you want?"

"Me? How did you get on the line?"

"You'nz have paid your bill, haven't you?"

"Yes."

"So that means you're officially checked out. When that happens, all outgoing calls are routed through this switchboard."

"But I'm still in the room, damn it!"

"Through my generosity, I might add. If that scrawny dishwater blonde hadn't put up such a good fight, I wouldn't be letting you keep the room until she gets back. A bill paid, is an exit laid. That's my policy."

"I need to make a call," I said, biting off each word, "and if you don't get me an outside line, I'm telling your big brother."

"Who?"

"Edward Marlon, Bedford County Sheriff, that's who."

He hung up. However, when I dialed Mama's number again, it rang straight through.

"Mama!" I screamed. "Who did they arrest for Purvis's murder?"

"Lord have mercy, Abby, God gave me only one set of eardrums."

"Then you'll be out your only set, if you don't hurry up and tell me."

The pearls whirled. "Oh, all right, but you should read what your namesake says about phone manners in today's column."

"Mama!"

"Major Calloway. Doesn't that just beat everything?"

"Frank Calloway? *Our* Major Frank Calloway, of Major Calloway's Antique Military Emporium?"

"I think you're the one who needs a new set of eardrums, dear."

"But Mama, Frank's all bark, and no bite. Did he confess?"

"No, but he will. The police found his fingerprints all over my house, and then they searched his house and found that tea set I bought for Toy."

"I suppose they got a search warrant," I said bitterly.

"Of course, dear. This isn't Iraq."

"Well, that solves half a mystery," I said.

"And you're halfway making sense," Mama said. I love her dearly, but that woman has more cheek than the real Marlon Brando.

I told Mama to get as much information as possible out of Susan, and under no circumstances should she allow her granddaughter to be married unless I was there. I fully planned to be there, but life, like a road through the mountains, has a way of taking some unexpected sharp turns.

I took a sip of the coffee Peggy brought back. It was stone cold, and we had barely cleared the city limits of Pittsburgh.

"Can't you drive any faster?" I wailed.

"Lordy, Abby, I'm going ten miles over the speed limit as it is, and we just passed a smoky a mile or so back."

"That was a city police car, not a smoky. And for your information, my mama drives faster than you."

Peggy's eyes narrowed. "I have yet to get a speeding ticket, and I'm not going to get one above the Line."

"Damn it, Peggy, I'll pay the fine!"

"Getting stopped isn't going to get you home any faster. And if they throw us in jail—well, we just may get back in time to watch your grandchildren graduate from college."

I started to argue, but when I saw the firm tilt of her chin, I settled for sulking. Sometime, not long after that, the sulking turned to slouching, and the slouching to slumber. Forget the images of sleeping babies—mine never did—and think cat. Think Dmitri, who can spend an entire day curled up on my bed, and then has the temerity to stretch and yawn a few times before settling down for the night.

When I awoke it was dark, and the car had stopped moving. For some strange reason I was sprawled on my back across the rear seat. I tried to sit up, but an invisible sledgehammer slammed into my forehead, right between the eyes, knocking me flat on my back again.

I groaned.

"So, Sleeping Beauty finally awakens," Peggy said. "Well, it's about time."

The woman must have borrowed the can on a string from Mama. She sounded a lot further away than the front seat. I managed to prop myself up on my elbows for a few seconds, just long enough to glance out the window. It was indeed night. There were more stars sprinkled across the sky than were dandruff flakes on my black velvet dress the last time I wore it.

"Are we home already?"

"No, but don't worry your cute little head, Abby. This is as far as you're going."

"What?" I tried sitting again, but the pain in my head was unbearable. I lay still and closed my eyes. "Peggy, I don't feel very well."

"Well now, that's too bad."

Perhaps it was my imagination, but Peggy didn't sound the least bit sympathetic.

"I said I don't feel very well. My head's killing me."

"That's to be expected."

"What happened? Were we in an accident?"

To my astonishment, Peggy laughed, her voice suddenly clear. "The accident has yet to happen."

I lay quietly for what seemed like an eternity. Perhaps it was all a bad dream and I really would awake in my own driveway back in Charlotte. If so, there was nothing to do but wait the nightmare out.

But it wasn't a dream, and I wasn't asleep. Peggy had lit a cigarette, and I could smell the smoke. Dreams— well, my dreams at any rate—seldom, if ever, include smells. Still, it didn't compute.

I licked my lips, which felt like emery boards. "You don't smoke."

"Wrong. I haven't smoked for twenty years, but I do now. I want you to know, Abby, that this accident is going to hurt me as much as it's going to hurt you."

"What accident? I don't understand. And how do you know it's going to happen?"

"Because this accident has to happen. There's no way to avoid it."

"Are we stuck on a railroad track? Because if we are, the best thing to do is just abandon the car. I know it's new, and you're very fond of it, but insurance will cover it." It was strange, but talking actually seemed to ease the pain. Or maybe it was time.

"We're not stuck on any damn railroad track. But this is a good place for an accident, don't you think so, Abby?"

"Where are we?"

"Why, New River Gorge, of course. Sit up, Abby, and see for yourself."

This time I was able to sit. I took it in stages, like a baby. In fact, I seemed to take as long as a baby learning to sit, but I was grateful that at least my head no longer pounded. It merely throbbed.

"All I see is the dark," I said. Someone had brushed the dandruff off my black velvet dress.

"It's going to rain, Abby. That makes it just about perfect, don't you think?"

"I don't know. Perfect for what?"

Peggy took a final drag on her cigarette and mashed it into the ashtray. Then I heard her open and close the glove box.

"Your death, Abby. That's what we're talking about. And just so you know, I've got a double-action automatic pistol pointed at you."

In retrospect I think I can honestly say that my blood did not run cold. Perhaps I was too shocked to be properly scared. I don't think I even perspired unduly. Maybe a little dampness in those areas most vulnerable, and a light sheen to my forehead, but otherwise, I was the picture of calmness.

"Why am I going to die? Is someone going to kill me?"

Peggy chuckled. Under other circumstances it would have sounded utterly benign. She might as well have been reacting to a joke I'd told.

"That's the beauty of it, Abby. You still don't have a clue, do you? So you see, when I kill you—and it *is* going to be me—no one will be the wiser. Because if you don't have a clue, then no one else does."

"Then clue me in, dear."

"I thought you'd never ask! Well, well, where to begin . . ."

"The beginning?"

"Gracious no, that will take too long. How about with my late dear cousin, Billy Ray Teschel?"

"Your *cousin*?"

"Tommy Lee too, of course. Which—"

I gasped. "Leona Teschel is your *aunt*?"

"By marriage of course. Abby, Abby, Abby . . . how

long have we been friends? Five, six years?''

''Since I bought my shop. Four years.''

''And in all that time, you never once asked if I'd ever been married.''

''I figured you'd tell me, if you wanted me to know.''

''Why weren't you more curious, Abby? Didn't you think I was a good enough friend?''

''Of course, but—''

''Don't interrupt me, Abby. I'm about to tell you a story. You see, Abby, we Teschels have always been a talented bunch. I may not be especially artistic, but I have other talents. Hidden talents, let's say.''

While she paused to light another cigarette, I bit my tongue.

''Tommy Lee, of course, is the artist in the family. He's really good, don't you think?''

I said nothing.

''That was a direct question, Abby. You're supposed to answer those.''

I remembered the double-action automatic pistol. ''The epergne is exquisite. And so is my tea set. I suppose he made that too.''

''With his own two talented hands. I, however, was the brains behind the whole thing. I did the market research—learned what would sell where, and supplied Tommy Lee with photos he could copy from.

''Now, Billy Ray. He was supposed to be our salesman because, lord knows, I couldn't sell that kind of upscale merchandise. Not in my shop. You know the kind of stuff I carry.''

''Second-hand junk,'' I muttered.

''What was that?'' she snapped. ''What did you say, Abby?''

''I said you have a lot of spunk.''

''Yes, I guess I do. It took nerve running that kind of operation. Sometimes you had to make difficult decisions. Letting Billy Ray go was one of the hardest.''

''You fired him?''

She didn't seem to mind the question. In fact, her laugh could have cut through a concrete block.

"We didn't exactly fire him. His car tore up before it could burst into flames. Real life isn't always like the movies."

"You killed your own cousin?"

"Shut up! I didn't give you permission to speak." She took another drag on the noxious weed. "Anyway, Tommy Lee did the actual deed. He messed with Billy Ray's brakes. But hey, we had to do it. That screwup was about to pull us all under.

"I mean, I told Billy Ray to sell one of the tea sets in Atlanta, one in Dallas, and one in Chicago. But that damn fool was lazy and dumped two in Atlanta, and one in Charlotte. If he'd stopped to think, he would have realized that Atlanta and Charlotte have a lot of cross traffic in the antique market."

I momentarily forgot the peril to my life and limb. "Why not hawk one of them in New York?" I asked.

"Never, ever sell a major con piece in the Big Apple," she said, sounding like Mama giving me advice on how to date. "Appraisers there see too many real pieces. They're far too savvy."

"L.A.?"

"Ha. The idiots out there would never pay what those pieces are worth. Even the con pieces. The pioneers left their culture behind at the Mississippi River, if you ask me."

Who knew that our own little Peggy could be such a regional snob? I wanted to slap her silly for chauvinism. But only after tweaking her nose, by informing her that the same person bought both the tea sets "dumped" in Atlanta. I wisely kept my mug shut, however. There was no point in dragging Mama deeper into the mess.

She took another toke. "It's a real shame about you, though. I always kind of liked you. Sure, you're something of a know-it-all, and you can be abrasive at times. But what the heck, who's perfect? If only that idiot Billy

Ray hadn't got it into his head that you were the one who needed to go. And carrying that engagement announcement in his wallet—I never would have sent him that, if I had known his true intent. I just told him to get the silver back somehow. Not to kill you."

"How thoughtful of you, dear." I stuck my tongue out, but of course she couldn't see it.

"Ha!" she barked. "Just be glad you never met the man. I swear, Aunt Leona must have had an affair. I don't see how my Uncle Artie could have spawned such a nincompoop."

"Well—"

"At first he actually thought the picture I sent him was a joke. He thought it was Tommy Lee and Adrienne's engagement announcement, only with the names changed."

"You think Tommy Lee looks like my Greg?"

"In your dreams. My cousin is much handsomer. Anyway, there you have it. It just kept getting out of hand. Lord knows I didn't want to do away with Purvis! Where are we going to get our merchandise now? Those sons of his don't know diddly-squat about the business!"

"Why should I care?" I wailed. "I'm going to die, remember?"

"That's right," she said, matter-of-factly, "and we better get started. I need to check into a nice motel and catch some 'z's.' I had to sit all day in some damn state park waiting for dark so this overlook would empty. Then I had to wait for you to wake up. I wasn't about to kill you without an explanation."

"How very thoughtful, dear."

"That's sarcasm, isn't it? And I thought I owed you an explanation because we were friends. Fine then, if that's the way you want it. I won't bother to tell you about Dmitri."

"Dmitri!" What kind of a mother was I, to have forgotten all about him?

"On second thought, you *deserve* to know. Well, Abby, I threw your precious cat over the edge."

"What edge?"

"The overlook, silly. That bag of fleas fell like a rock. How far is it down to the river? Four hundred feet? Maybe five hundred." She chortled maniacally.

"You bitch!" I screamed, and lunged at her.

It was a stupid mistake, one she easily took advantage of by whacking me on the head with the pistol. When my mental dandruff cleared, she was all business.

"Move," she grunted. "Get out of the car. I've got the safety off and I'm itching to shoot."

I did as I was told. My legs were understandably wobbly, like those of a newborn colt, but with some gentle nuzzling from the muzzle of the gun, they became strong in no time.

"Now give me your ring!"

"What ring?"

"That ostentatious sapphire that's worth a king's ransom."

"I don't have it on me."

I heard the safety click. "Don't you lie to me, you little snot. I can see that thing glinting, even in the dark."

I practically ripped the ring off my finger.

"Now hand it over."

A larger and braver woman would have tackled Peggy then. A more knowledgeable woman would have chopped that gun right out of her hand. Oh, if I had only listened to Mama and taken martial arts courses when I was in college.

"Aaaah," Peggy sighed, when I dropped the ring in her hand. "Aaaah." It was practically orgasmic.

I took a quick step back. "It's cursed, you know. The previous owner was murdered. I'd be careful—"

"Shut up!"

I did as bid.

"Now turn and march!"

I envisioned myself prancing along to a John Souza tune. The best I could do was shuffle. Even had I been the picture of health, the going would have been slow. We were headed down narrow, winding wooden stairs on a treacherously steep, wooded slope. Clouds had completely covered the sky by then, and the overhead tree cover contributed to the inky blackness. I literally could not see my feet. The stairs were not built for folks of my height, and I did a lot of stumbling. Had it not been for the wooden hand rail to guide me, I would have stumbled off the stairs, into the woods, and possibly rolled down the slope. Unless a tree stopped me. It was worth giving a try.

Except that the bitch could read my mind.

"Don't even think about ducking out on me," she rasped. "I'll shoot at whatever I hear."

I clung to the railing and stumbled on. As we neared the gorge, the trees thinned and the wall of trees on the opposing side of the gorge assumed a faint gray shape. At last I stood on the final platform, with nowhere else to go but down the abyss. My mind raced. There didn't seem to be anything I could do. Death by bullet, or death by bashing, what would a more sensible gal choose?

Bashing. Definitely bashing. Who knows, I might land in a tree just beneath the rim, and be merely scratched and bruised. Or if I jumped far enough, I might miss the rocks altogether and land in the New River. Every now and then, don't folks survive jumping from the Golden Gate Bridge? How high was that? At least I was a good swimmer. Thank Buford and the Fort Mill water park for that.

I took a tentative step towards the edge and all hell broke loose. Well, it certainly sounded like the demons from hell, although it was only Dmitri. I have been accused of exaggerating this part of the story, so from now on, I'll tell you exactly what happened, with no embellishments of any kind.

To the best of my knowledge—it was still too dark

to see properly—I had inadvertently stepped on my cat's tail. Either my ten pounds of joy had somehow managed not to go over the cliff, or had survived the fall, and crawled back up. My best guess is both, that he landed in a treetop just over the edge. At any rate, Dmitri's pained yowl caused Peggy to drop the gun. When I heard the thunk of metal on the platform I lunged instinctively at Peggy, who apparently lunged at the gun.

We missed each other, but I was luckier. I banged my nose and chin on the bottom step. Peggy Teschel Redfern, however, went sailing over the edge of the Red River Gorge and except for one long, and rather satisfying scream, was never seen or heard from again.

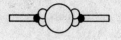

27

"**M**ore tea?" Mama asked.
      "I would," C. J. said and held out her cup.
"*Please*," I whispered.
"Please what?"

I groaned. Well, it was Mama's fault. It was her idea to throw a tea party and serve the beverage out of a genuine imitation William Cripps teapot.

In her inimitable style, Mama had insisted we use the set she gave me before her departure to the convent. She was saving Toy's set, she said. Someday, she insisted, the boy Toy would get married.

As for the third set, the Kefferts had agreed to take it off my hands for what I paid for it. A good deal of publicity had been generated by Peggy's plunge to oblivion—you might even say the case broke wide open. At any rate, Tommy Lee's faux pieces were considered so good, that they commanded almost as much as the originals. Almost.

They were certainly good enough to make Major Calloway lust in his heart to the point of becoming a felon. Even though I had persuaded Mama not to press charges, the law was not quite as sympathetic. The old goat was on probation and required to perform more hours of community service than Mother Theresa. His shop, Major Calloway's Antique Emporium, was up for sale. We in Charlotte may suffer fools, but we do not buy from them.

"I don't get it," C. J. said, as she reached for the last of Mama's crumpets, "why was Tommy Lee living at home, if he and his mother hated each other so much? My cousin Dorothy—"

"Because," I said quickly, "they didn't trust each other. They each wanted to keep an eye on the other, and living in the same house was the best way to do that."

"I forget," Wynnell said, "did Tommy Lee confess first, or was that after his mother turned him in?"

I snorted. "After. And that was only to plea bargain."

Mama's pouring hand froze. "His mama turned him in to the police?"

"He killed her favorite son, Billy Ray."

Mama's free hand patted her pearls, seeking comfort. "Still, a mama turning in her own flesh and blood!"

"Wouldn't you turn me in if I killed somebody?"

My dear, sweet mother looked absolutely stricken. "Bite your tongue, Abigail Louise. I wouldn't turn you in for all the cotton in Dixie."

"Not even if I—you know—bumped off Toy?"

"Not even then." Mama's lips formed a thin, hard line.

"Don't you be getting any ideas now, Abby," Wynnell said.

"Geez, that Peggy was really something," C. J. said, shaking her head in wonder. "Imagine just knowing how to give someone a pulmonary enema."

Wynnell and I howled. Even Mama laughed. In fact, she had to set the teapot down she was shaking so hard.

"That was pulmonary edema," I finally gasped.

"Whatever!" C. J. said, hotly offended.

"And she didn't know exactly what effect the dimethyl sulfate would have. She just knew it could be fatal if consumed. Peggy used to work for a textile plant in Gastonia. She'd seen the warning labels on the drums.''

"But that was a long time ago, wasn't it? How did she get her hands on the stuff when she decided to kill Purvis?''

"Who knows?" I glanced at Mama, who seemed to be safely looking elsewhere. "She probably slept with someone who still works there," I mouthed.

"I heard that!" Mama had turned around and was giving me a compulsory frown, although the corners of her mouth were turned up.

I couldn't help but smile back.

"But your coffee," C. J. persisted. "Didn't she put something in that?''

"Just a couple of sleeping pills. But you have to remember, I hadn't slept a wink the night before.''

"I knew there had to be a good reason I never liked the woman," C. J. said loyally.

Wynnell cleared her throat. "Come, come. You liked her just fine, and you know it. What you don't like is being shnookered.''

"That's 'snookered,' " I said, not unkindly.

"And then there's the sapphire—oops!" C. J. clamped a hand over her mouth.

It was too late. I let out a wail that was heard in Alaska and caused two dog teams to veer off the Iditarod Trail.

"It wasn't insured," Mama whispered.

"At least Dmitri is okay," Wynnell said, and the eyes below the hedgerows glowered at the youngest of us present.

I dabbed my eyes with the corner of a linen napkin. "Yes, thank God for that. The vet said he didn't have a scratch on him. Which means that Peggy probably did. I doubt if she even got close to the edge with him. She probably just dropped him, thinking he'd run away.''

Mama wasn't about to sit and watch helplessly as one of her company napkins turned black with mascara.

"Well," she said, "unless the next question is a matter of life or death, I suggest we nail this subject closed and talk about something else."

"Men!" C. J. squealed.

"Argh."

"Now, Abby," Mama said sternly, "remember what I keep telling you. There are other fish in the sea."

"She's talking about Greg," I said to my friends. "My mother doesn't realize that I'm over the jerk. Fishing for grouper, indeed! He was fishing for groupies."

Of course I wasn't really over Greg. I would probably never be entirely over the man. But I had moved out of the shocked stage and was well into anger. Who knew, maybe I could harness some of that steam and write a bestseller. *Short Women Who Date Tall Handsome Creeps.*

Mama's eyes flashed. "What kind of a father would he have made to Charlie and Susan?"

"Speaking of Susan," C. J. said, "wasn't she supposed to get married? That's all you could talk about when you first came home. I never did hear how that turned out."

"Ah, that." I looked pointedly at Mama.

My dominant gene source blushed. "Well, we all make mistakes, don't we?"

"What she means is, she jumped to conclusions. Susan was getting married in a movie the drama department was filming at Glencairn Gardens. I heard she made a lovely bride, but thank God it wasn't for real."

"Amen," Mama said.

"I'll drink to that!" Wynnell took a sip of her tea.

"Speaking of weddings," I said, "I wonder how the Rob-Bobs are doing."

"Ooh," C. J. sighed. "Hawaii, can you imagine that?"

"I didn't think they'd ever get back together," Wynnell said, "but I'm glad. I can't wait until they return. Just the other day I needed their expert advice—"

"Expert!" I practically shouted. "I nearly bought the farm—make that a gorge—because of Rob's expert advice."

The doorbell rang and Mama bustled off to answer it. She was back in the space of a sneeze with a Cheshire cat grin on her face.

"It's a man," she whispered. "For you, Abby. He says he has a date with you."

"Me?"

"He said his name is Edward Marlon. Ha, Marlon! That's a kind of fish, isn't? You see, Abby, I told you there would be other fish!"

"Sheriff Marlon?" C. J. trilled. "The hunk from Pennsylvania?"

I jumped to my feet. "It's not what y'all think—okay, so maybe it is. Eddy and I have been on the phone a lot and, well, there you have it. But I really didn't expect him to just show up at Mama's door."

"But he did ask you for a date, remember?"

"Lordy," Wynnell groaned. "Our little Abby is dating a Yankee."

I fled straight into Edward Marlon's arms.